AS IN EDEN

R. M. Lamming was born and grew up in the Isle of Man. She is the author of two previous novels and lives in London.

R. M. LAMMING

As In Eden

faber and faber

First published in 2005
by Faber and Faber Limited
3 Queen Square London WC1N 3AU
This paperback edition published in 2006

Typeset by Faber and Faber Limited
Printed in England by Mackays of Chatham plc,
Chatham, Kent

A CIP record for this book
is available from the British Library

ISBN 978-0-571-22643-6
ISBN 0-571-22643-4

2 4 6 8 10 9 7 5 3 1

To Ma,
with love and gratitude.

For nothing is so real as that which is spiritual.
Christopher Smart, circa 1761

EVE

We fled. The bright, calm green of *There* and sun-lit rippling of the River, the fruit scents, the scents of lilies and gentle, enclosing shades – they were collapsing round us. They were folding into Unlight, and nameless things.

We have taken time to find names. I will use names. You children are familiar with them. So I will use them.

We fled from horror and a voiceless howling in us. We ran with bowed backs and our heads low while beneath our feet the grass shrivelled. And the faster we ran, the faster *There* came after us to hold us, the more it sprang up round us to keep us *There*, in what was bright and green and beautiful, and yet wherever we went it was collapsing, twisting into tangles and sharpnesses, pushing us on –

The first time I slipped and my hand came down to steady myself, it fell against a thorn bush. I didn't cry out, we were beyond cries. I recoiled from this new thing, this flesh-hurt, but inside I also said yes. My flesh said yes. Throbbing and stinging, its red sap oozing, it knew that what it felt was part of what was done, and I knew it was, and I ran on. Only later did we feel amazement, the man and I, at how much pain our bodies give us –

But none of that is strange to you, my children. You know pain –

And yet I think you are still amazed by it.

We fled. We bore this pain with us, seeking escape, only escape – until a new horror dawned: what escape? What end is there to us? We are from the Great One that has no ending. And so our running and our horror and the bright green collapsing –

The thought opened in us – They would be for ever. There would be no ending.

Oh my children.

Oh my children.

I have no names for the depths of Mercy. They are deeper than the skies.

Time came.

As we stumbled and thrashed, running everywhere, nowhere, a brilliance filled the darkness behind us: suddenly there *was* a *Behind us*. It shone where we had been, and in that Light lay all the green and loveliness of *There*. Before us lay wilderness.

We stopped running. We clung to each other, and cowered in the dust. *There* lay at our backs. Now we crouched among thorn trees and stones. The smell of dust was in our nostrils, we ached with trembling –

The red sap – the blood – dried on my hand.

Time had come, and none of this would last for ever.

So we clung to each other until we were weak and fell into the first sleep of our new understanding. It was full of stillness and something I have seen since in many infants.

It was full of being here.

We woke up cold. A harsh wind was blowing. We were high in the hills. We sat huddled on a rocky shelf and stared across the desert, its pinks and greys and the sun rising and the dust scuffing, and still we hadn't spoken. Since we'd begun to run we hadn't spoken, but as we sat there, the man gripped my arm. He wouldn't look at me. He said nothing. He stared out across the wasteland, and I was quiet, turning in my mind how it was I, not the man, who in the centre of *There* had had the Thought. It was to me, not him, that the Thought had come, swiftly and smoothly like a serpent slipping through the branches. I had pulled down a fruit from a tree, and as I'd sucked in the sweet juice, I had understood that everything around me, and everything I was, need not be as they were unless I chose that it be so. I had understood that there was also an Opposite.

And I had told him.

Now he sat shivering with the cold, his eyes on a desert.

I must take care of him, I thought. And I said in myself, *Hear me, Great One. Help me.*

But still we didn't speak. We were chilled to the bone, there on the ledge.

Time passed.

Then I got to my feet. I was first. He didn't stop me. He stood up when I did, and he began to climb down to the plain. I followed. Once we were there, 'Water,' I said, 'food.' He looked about, and pointed the way he felt we should go. I let him lead me. Who was I to lead us? I had had the Thought.

Our feet bled. The stones were sharp. Never since have I known such sharp stones, nor such bitter cold. Adam walked in front. Our loss walked with us. Everywhere was Loss – but we no longer ran headlong: a calm lay on us.

And when the cat came, snarling and bounding, I felt sure that it came for me. I stood still and waited. It came springing towards us from a distance behind and away to our side. The creature's teeth were bared. Over its snout the skin crinkled back. It was a new thing, like yet unlike the gentle creatures *There*, who came nuzzling and breathing on our hands where we no longer were. And I thought, *This beast can pulp me like a fruit.* Then I thought, *Adam has only to go on walking and let this beast crush me. When that's happened, perhaps he'll find himself back There –*

But at the same time, I stooped and snatched up a stone. I crouched and waited for the cat with that sharp weight in my fist; and Adam turned. He had heard the snarls; he had sensed my movement. He turned and saw the cat. At first he stared, and then he came running back. He did as I'd done: he snatched up

3

a stone. Then he ran past me, on towards the cat, hurling his stone and snatching up another. When the beast leapt, Adam fell beneath its weight, as if in play. Not a cry from him. Only from the cat came snarlings, and from the stones, the sound that stones make when they're rolled upon and shifted in their dust.

Cat and man wrestled.

You understand this, children. Daily you take your lives and throw them at this: hunter and hunted – and which is which? You sing songs and tell tales about it. But that first time, I watched unbelieving. I couldn't move. A sickness squeezed me.

Don't leave me here, I said silently to Adam. *Don't leave me alone here.*

They tumbled in dust and blood. The cat's claws slashed Adam's back. I saw Adam's hand, scarlet, forcing up the beast's head, and then losing its grip.

At last I moved.

I remember little. Only the fury, the whipping tail, the talons, the beast's stench, and the pain as its great shoulder rolled on where I clung, striking at its throat – if I did strike –

Our first kill. Somehow it happened.

The cat lay shuddering on the stones. Its water stank. We crawled away as far as we could, in case it sprang up. We hid behind a rock and lay there, shaking and weeping.

First tears.

Later, I licked Adam's wounds, and the gash on my leg. I rubbed my hands across the claw pits in his back, and held his head on my knees while he moaned of thirst, always of thirst –

Until a reasoning came.

The cat had known where to drink. The way it had come might lead us to where it had drunk.

We said this reasoning and I stood up, but Adam only sprawled and watched. So then I threw a stone that hit him on his belly. He grunted with surprise. I threw another, and at that he got up and lunged at me, raising his fist, but as he stood there swaying, most of his strength left him, so that his hand came down heavily across my back, steadying him.

We half carried each other. The sun sank, a red eye slipping into its lid, flooding our way with blood-light that carried darkness in it and the fear of cats –

And yet in that slipping of the sun, and the stars' coming, and the silent darkness opening over us, and the moon's shining a thin arc, we smelled the sweetness of water; and soon we drank.

Adam thought faster afterwards. I would have sat by the waterhole, thanking the Great One, but he dragged me from it.

'Cats,' he said.

So we hid between boulders. We didn't sleep. I would have licked Adam's sores, but he pushed me off. His face had changed. The child curves had gone from it. Not that I could name such things. Not then. He watched all night, his eyes moving. *Great One*, I said, *keep us safe*. Then I would have slept, but Adam sat tensed, his eyes moving, always moving, watching the shadows beyond our hiding place, so I stayed awake and watched with him, and we shivered with the cold –

Until at last dawn came. Our second in Loss.

The first, we had hardly noticed; but this second day-break, seeping scarlet then yellowing, deepening with where we were, still where we were –

Not *There*

We feared it.

We huddled and moaned. We hid our faces on our knees. We tried to burrow out of where we were, back through our heads into *There*, but strange insects came and ran across our bodies, stinging our cuts, so that, in the end, to be rid of them, we crawled out from among the boulders, stood up in the sun –

And on that second morning, we felt warmth. We stood receiving it; the bitter green of a bush that grew close to our

5

boulders gleamed, and the sight of it was strengthening. So we crept again to the water-hole, and finding no beasts, we drank deeply and quickly.

Then Adam touched my arm. Crouched by the water, he was squinting at the sky, and he pointed at dark shapes circling high up, at a distance from us, where we'd left the cat.

'They see our food,' he said.

So that day, we learned to drive off vultures, and we ate from the carcass they would have stolen from us. Our first meat.

We learned fire later –

But first we learned the fire in the pits of us, so that lying together, and pushing to be closer, Adam deeper in me, the struggling became a blaze that we couldn't name.

You have your own names for it, children.

To us at the start, that blaze was a searching for *There*, and yet not for *There*, for a place in the newness of what we'd become that was more than Here but made sense of Here, a search releasing in us tremors of forgetting that were almost remembering, as if in that blaze our bodies had been brushed by the wing of some trapped bird that flew between what we'd become and what was lost.

What was lost, we called Eden.

And one night, pulling from me in his sweat, and lying back against the rock, Adam asked me, 'What will happen when the fruit drops? When the young comes? Will you still be with me?'

'I don't know,' I told him.

He looked helpless. My breasts were heavy, and they ached. I held them as often as I could. It comforted me. They seemed to understand more than I did. My belly had grown as round as the moon just before it turns again towards thinness.

'I don't know what will happen,' I told him.

He wept.

*

6

The child came. To face its coming, we had found a crack in the base of a cliff, not so large as the caves we found later, but it seemed enough at first. It saved us on three sides from our fear of cats, so that we needed only to watch in one direction, and with the rest of our strength, we could fight greater fears.

One night Adam whispered: 'This thing might rip you apart and climb out stamping in your blood. How can we know what's been made in you?'

'In Eden,' I said, 'when the young dropped from their mothers, all was good. You and I both saw it.'

'That was in Eden.' He watched me with terror in his face. He laid his hands on my belly.

'You must take care of it,' I said, 'if it destroys me.'

'If it destroys you,' said Adam, 'I'll smash its head on a rock.'

But I saw he didn't hear what he said, and then my pain started, and I screamed.

Adam howled and fled. I see him still in my mind, running from the mouth of the cave, out into the moonlight. I called after him, but only once. It was worse to call and have him not come back: my own fear stopped me – fear and astonishment not because Adam fled but at the spasms and stretchings of my body, the anguish of it, the power of all it did whether I understood or not, as though the Great One spoke directly to it, and I seemed carried on that power no matter how much I screamed, and I did scream, the water gushing down my legs.

Later, Adam crept to the cave mouth. He squatted there with the moon behind him. The child was happening. I crouched braced against the rock wall and shuddered it down. The flesh I am shuddered it out of me. And Adam crept back. His hands received it.

So Cain was born, the child of our fear.

Time passed, and after him another came. Abel came.

Abel was born in the twilight coolness, not far from a river bank. We had found a place there among the rocks, a hollowing in the mountain side. It was greener country than where Cain was born. And this time we were not afraid. Adam stayed with me. Between the clenches of labour, I rested on cat skins and goat skins that he'd laid down for me, and the child came easily. He cried in the hands of Adam with such a strong, clear voice, that Adam smiled.

'My son,' he said.

But our child Cain crouched soundlessly by me, gripping my fingers in his fist, and he looked from the blood that straggled out of me to the new life that Adam held, and his grip tightened.

'We'll call this new life Abel,' I told him, 'just as we call you Cain.'

He said nothing.

We learned fire later – the fire of lightning in the dry grass and bushes. We learned to pluck a branch from the flames and carry it with us, and feed it to other branches, so that sometimes our night was warm and free from fear; and on those nights, especially on those nights, we told our sons where we'd come from. We spoke of Eden and the Great One. Adam would say things we couldn't mention in the day, his face glowing in the brightness from the fire, and our sons squatted beside us, feeding the flames with branches we'd gathered, listening and working to eke the fire out through the night.

'We knew no pain in Eden, and no cold. The cats lapped water from our hands. The Great One walked among the tall trees. We heard the Great One's voice in the centre of what we are, and we were filled with joy – until the Thought came.'

Only once he said: 'Until your mother's Thought came,' and then he lowered his eyes, snapping a bone he held. It was the wing bone from a bird we'd eaten, and he looked at me across the fire, then lowered his eyes again.

Cain punched me in the side. 'What does he mean?' he hissed. 'Was it *your* thought? Why did you have it?'

I didn't answer.

'I want Eden!' said Cain, and he sprang up and kicked me. 'I want Eden!'

I said nothing. Neither did Adam. But when I saw that Cain would kick me a second time, I turned and struck him. Then he whimpered and crawled close and laid his head on my lap. But Abel was quiet. He squatted by his father and fed the fire, and as always when we spoke of Eden, his eyes were bright.

'Tell us more,' he said at last. 'Tell us more about the cats, and how they drank water from your hands.'

Our sons grew. Abel taught us laughter – reminded us of laughter. We had forgotten it. He laughed at the play of sunlight and shadow, and patterns in the water, or at an insect as it ran across his fingers, or the shy ways of many creatures, and the stubbornness of things – the wet clay forming bowls that bellied and flattened, the mats we wove that drifted open –

And one day, he brought some creatures to our cave. They followed him there, three wild-eyed sheep, which Adam and Cain would have killed, but Abel ran his hand through the wool on the back of one of them, and said to his father, 'Let them live for now. We can drink the she-one's milk, and when they've made another young one, we can kill an old one if we must, when we have nothing else to eat, and we'll still have the number that we have now.'

Adam was pleased. So after that, Abel searched for more sheep.

Cain also taught us. He made weapons and other sharp things. He took sticks and sharpened them, and thrust them into the ground at the opening of the caves we lived in. Then a time came when he said to Adam, 'If you leave this place because you think there's no more food, I'm not coming.'

'Then you'll grow hungry and weak, and then you'll die,' said Adam. 'I see it when I hunt. What is weak quickly dies.'

But Cain said, 'I'll force this earth to feed me. You'll see.'

And we watched him, dragging the points of his sticks through the earth, and scattering berries and grass seeds he'd gathered.

'What good will that do?' I asked him.

'You'll see,' he said. 'If you stay.'

He fenced his work and watched over it. He hurled stones at the birds that came with their sharp beaks to pluck the seeds out of their hiding places. He dragged water from the river in skins and pots. He killed a cat. And once he clubbed two of Abel's sheep, broke their backs in his anger, because they'd found a way into these fields he'd made and eaten the green shoots.

Abel skinned those beasts in silence. He had learned how to bring fire out of wood and grasses without the need for light-ning from the sky. It was a learning he'd stumbled on in play – that was the way of Abel – and he loved this fire, we all did, but Abel especially, because so often in the firelight we'd spoken of Eden.

One of the sheep that Cain had slaughtered Abel burned on a fire. Adam and I saw the smoke and found him burning it. He did this in a secret place.

'Let it go to the Great One,' he told us.

The sight of so much food whitening into ashes angered Adam. He hit Abel on the chest and roared at him, and I thought my son would strike back, so I said, 'Better we starve than that we keep from the Great One what Abel wants to give.'

At that Adam looked afraid and, crouching down, he scooped up a handful of dust and sprinkled it over his head.

We gorged ourselves on the other sheep. It was sweet and wholesome. Our bellies swelled with so much meat, and as we rested in the shade afterwards, Adam smiled at Abel.

'My son,' he said, 'you've done well. You've done well.'

Abel smiled back. But as for Cain, he stared into the distance.

Abel sang. The sounds came from his throat, and his father and I understood them. There were no words, only sounds, and sometimes as I wove the reeds, or skinned the kill, I tried to let those sounds come from my own throat, but they wouldn't come. Only tears came. Sometimes round the fire at night, Adam and I would both sing with Abel. It could be done then, and a strength in the sounds we made would bring us to our feet, stamping and flinging our hands to the stars; but Cain didn't sing. He would take up his spear.

'The cats will have the sheep,' he said, 'but that's not for me to think about. I have the fields to watch.' And he would leave us.

I went after him once through the cat-stinking shadows. I followed him with fear thumping in my chest, until he turned and stared at me.

'What do you want?' he asked.

'I'll come with you,' I said.

'Go back,' he said, turning away again, but I followed him all the same, down to his fields. I watched the night out with him. He made a small fire. It smouldered. He didn't understand fire as Abel did. We crouched over it and didn't speak.

Great One, I thought, *protect us.*

Cain gripped his spear, and sometimes rocked on his heels and closed his eyes, and his mouth worked with things he was thinking, but I didn't ask what they were. At dawn he said, 'What I've planted has grown ripe. It can be eaten soon.'

'You've done well, my son,' I said.

He looked at me with fierce eyes. Then he lowered his head, and scraped the shaft of his spear in the dust.

'You've done well,' I told him, and maybe he would have spoken then, but glancing up, across my shoulder he saw Adam coming from the cave, and all he said was, 'My father.'

When he reached us, Adam's voice trembled. His hand squeezed my arm. 'Your place is at my fire,' he said. 'You'll spend no more nights out in the open.'

'I was here with our son,' I said. 'I was not alone.'

'Your place is at my fire,' said Adam again, and then he would have spoken to Cain, but Cain had turned his back, and was already walking away, so Adam didn't speak.

Later that day, when the heat was past its height, I sat at the mouth of the cave with Adam at my side, and in the distance below us, we could see Cain working in his fields, cutting and tying in bundles what he'd grown, and further away, we could see Abel with his flock of sheep. The sky was softening towards coolness. The grasses in Cain's fields glowed with a yellowness richer than the earth's, and where Abel was guarding his sheep, the land was green from the river.

Adam's scent was in my nostrils, his warm skin.

'The flock's growing,' he said. 'Abel needs more green land.'

'I know,' I said.

'Both our sons have done well,' said Adam.

I closed my eyes when he said that, and something that was hard in me, and as dull and as unseen as a stone, split open like a bud after the rains have reached it. And when I looked around me again, I saw tall trees, the sunlight glinting on their leaves; I smelled a perfume of lilies, and we sat on gentle grass, and in the distance where Abel was, with his sheep, shone the River, and nearby, just beyond the trees, Cain worked, gathering his grain, and everything was drenched in a sweetness I remembered –

'What is it?' said Adam. He hit me on the shoulder. 'What is it? Speak to me!' he said.

And I saw the dust again. I looked into his frightened face. I looked out from the cave mouth and saw the rocks, the barrenness that pushed against Cain's fields, and how narrow the band of green was, where Abel's sheep fed –

'What are you smiling at?' said Adam. He punched me again. 'What's wrong with you?'

I didn't tell him. I felt faint with the sweetness fading in me, and with what I couldn't say, hadn't the words to say. I took his hand, and would have held it, but he plucked it back. His eyes were full of tears. He pushed me from him.

He knows, I thought.

'I have to see to the snares,' he said, and left me.

Inside myself I sang for the rest of that day. I was full of laughter. I took meat and cheese to Abel, and he showed me a lizard he'd trapped, and how it watched us sideways, and the swiftness of its tongue. He set it free afterwards, and in his eyes I saw my own laughter.

Then towards dusk I went to Cain. I ran my hands through the yellow corn. I helped him bind the last stacks, and when I said, 'If you had a woman, and two sons, this grain could feed all of them as well as us!' he raised his head from his work and laughed. It was not like Abel's laughter. Cain laughed with pride and a fierce pleasure. But there was a gladness in the sound that made me laugh back, almost as if we often stood in his fields, laughing.

Then he said, 'I'll give the Great One a part of this grain. Go back to my father. I'll build the fire before I sleep, and we'll burn the grain in the morning.'

'That will be well done,' I told him. 'Then the Great One will have received gifts from both our sons.'

'My best two sheaves,' said Cain.

After that I left him. I went quickly to the cave where Adam waited, and that night as we ate, I said to Adam, 'Cain will make a gift to the Great One tomorrow.'

Adam nodded. He ate and drank. At last he said, 'You're happy.'

It was a word we used only of how we'd felt *There* in Eden, so when he used it sitting by the fire, in the dust, meaning today, here in this place, you're happy, again I thought, *He knows*.

13

We watched the stars sharpen.

Then Adam spoke of greener country. He thought we might find it if we walked further from the mountains.

'But there'll be no caves,' I said.

'I'll make us one,' he told me, 'better than this.'

I laughed and so did he. His face was full of hope. He pushed me down on my back and thrust into me. I spread my hands on his head. We didn't understand what you understand, my children. I didn't understand the whiteness in his hair, but we thought it a message from the Great One, and I liked my hands on his head or in the hair of his chest, because my own hair was also whitening. Often I pulled strands of it to where I could see it, in front of my eyes, and stared at it. I was glad that his hair had this same whiteness.

At dawn, Cain stood over us.

'Now I'll burn the grain,' he said.

We went with him. Near where he'd grown the corn, he had made a great heap of branches from the thorn trees and bushes by the river, and on it he had laid two bundles of his grain, the thickest bundles, and they gleamed in the early sunlight.

Cain took dry grass and squatted to rub fire-sticks.

'Abel should be here,' I said. 'He could have brought the sheep nearer, and been here.'

'There's no need,' said Cain, rubbing the sticks. So we waited while he did that.

'We could have brought fire with us from the cave,' said Adam. 'Our night fire was still alight –'

'Fresh flame is best,' I said.

Soon the fire-sticks smouldered. A spark leapt out into the grass, and Cain fed the burning grass with more grass until a flame rose, and when he'd set alight some twigs that crackled and spat in his hand, he sprang to his feet and shouted, 'Great

One, do you hear me? Look what I'm giving you! Take my best! I offer you my best!' and he lit his gift-fire.

It burned well at first. The dry sticks flared brightly, but before the fire could rise into the grain, a smoke began to twist through its brightness, dark and cloudy, and in that smoke the flames flickered and began to shrink.

Cain moved burning sticks about. He snatched some from the fire and flung them up onto the grain but they slid off the tight bundles. Others he held to the higher branches of the great heap, but all that came was smoke.

'You've gathered from the wrong trees,' said Adam. 'These branches have sap in them.'

And you've built your fire too high, my son, I thought, but I didn't speak. Cain's face was angry. He grabbed hold of a branch that was burning and flung it with a long, slow swing, so that it crashed against the grain and lay there, balanced on the sheaves, and I said to myself, *Now they'll burn!* But the branch slipped and fell down the other side of the heap, and only a black mark showed on the bundles, and as that happened, the dry sticks beneath the damp ones shifted in their burning and collapsed into ash, bringing the heap lower, and a great smoke rose.

It was then that Abel appeared. I didn't know why he'd come. He came to where I stood with Adam.

'What's Cain doing?' he asked.

'He's giving his sheep to the Great One,' I answered. 'The bundles of grain are his sheep.'

Abel's eyes narrowed at the smoke, and his nose crinkled.

'He's made a bad fire,' he said. 'I saw him down by the river in the night, gathering wood. He came twice. The second time, I saw him pulling up bushes and I called to him, but he didn't answer. He dragged the bushes away, and I've brought my sheep closer, and come.'

'Why?' I asked him.

'He was strange,' said Abel. 'Why pull up bushes in the night?'

Then he went to his brother. Cain held a thick branch, and he was poking at the blackened base of his fire, trying to spread what was left of the flame. Abel smiled, and said something to him. Cain stared. Abel went on speaking. Then Cain raised his stick and waved it, shouting, 'Go away! Did I ask for your help? Go away!' and he ran at Abel, brandishing the stick, and Abel jumped aside, and the look on his face was one I'd seen often on Abel, when he saw something new that he was ready to laugh at, like the swift tongue of the lizard and its eyes. He laughed. Then he came back to where I stood with Adam.

'He won't listen,' he said. 'He doesn't want help. I'll go back to my sheep.'

'And I'll go,' said Adam. 'Why wait here in the heat of the morning, while Cain rebuilds his fire? Let him offer his grain in the evening, or tomorrow, or without me.'

'Stay,' I said to Adam, but Cain, who'd stood watching as we talked, shouted, 'Go! Go! All of you! I don't need you here!'

So Adam and Abel left, but I squatted in the dust, and waited.

The fire no longer burned. He pulled his grain bundles from the heap, and kicked at the mound of branches. Then he came and spoke to me.

'I have to gather more wood,' he said. 'There's nothing for you to stay here for!'

'Gather wood if you must,' I answered, 'if you think the grain won't burn without it. I'll wait.'

At dusk the bundles burned. They turned dark and smouldered. The flames licked them, but they didn't blaze. They went slowly. Adam wasn't there. He had found goat tracks and we needed meat. He hunted late into the twilight and came home long after the moon had risen.

But I saw Cain burn his corn. He didn't shout again to the Great One but burned it silently. I saw him kicking at the ashes.

'Now we can eat the rest with good feelings,' I told him. 'Our bellies can be full and we'll be strong because of it.'

He didn't answer.

He brought most of the rest of the grain to us, but for many days after that, he kept away from the cave. He made a place for himself down by his fields. He gathered stones and piled them up in a curve and spread a cat skin across them, and on the cat skin he spread thorn branches. At night his fire flickered, and we saw it and knew that he was there. I took him meat and corn baked with water into a hard paste.

'Your grain's stored in our cave,' I told him, 'so why sit here alone? Why don't you sleep where we sleep, and hunt in the days with your father?'

'I have these fields to protect,' he said. 'I have to make the land ready to plant the grain I've kept back, and so make more grain.'

'Will the cats harm these barren fields?' I asked. 'Will the lizards? Or the sheep? There are no green shoots now to be trampled or eaten.'

He didn't speak. He only made a movement with his shoulders, as though to shake my words off.

'Your father wants to leave this place,' I told him. 'We must find greener country. You can have better fields there, and Abel's sheep will grow fatter in a greener place.'

Then he looked at me with hard eyes and answered, 'Abel's sheep can go where you want. Abel can go. But my fields are here. I've told you before. I won't go with you.' And he pointed at my belly. 'That one can go,' he said.

'You are my son,' I said. 'Come with us.'

But he said again, 'My fields are here.'

Abel came often to our cave. He brought his sheep along the river bank, and came to us, and ate often at our fire. He laid his hands on my belly and laughed.

'You'll come with us,' Adam said to him, 'and find a better place for the sheep.'

'I'll stay near you,' said Abel. He reached out and ran his fingers through my hair. The whiteness in it made his face watchful, and once he asked us, 'How many days is it since you left Eden? Do you know?'

Adam and I stared at each other.

'I know the number of my sheep,' said Abel. 'Have you a way to tell me the number of the days?'

At last Adam pointed at the great line where the earth meets the sky, the long line that moves ahead of us as we walk.

'Like that,' he said.

And that day, I said to Abel, 'Talk to your brother. When we leave here, he must come with us.'

But Abel looked dark. 'He can come and find me if he wants to talk,' he said. 'He already knows my thoughts.'

'Talk to him again,' I said.

My belly grew rounder. Then one morning when I woke, Adam told me, 'We'll wait until the new one comes. This is a safe place for him to come to. And you'll walk faster when he's not inside you.'

I was glad. I touched Adam's face, and smiled. He was crouching at my side. The smell of grain stacks was strong behind him. He liked my touch and smiled back. I wanted to ask then if he knew, if by the mouth of the cave, he'd ever seen the tall trees and smelled the lilies, but instead I told him, 'The Great One will show us where to go.'

'The Great One,' said Adam. Then I got to my feet, and we didn't speak again, except that, as he took up his spear, Adam said, 'Abel will say there's a time for his sheep also to have new ones.'

'You must speak of these things together. You must talk,' I answered.

After that he left me. I stood outside the cave, and saw him go down between the boulders to the fields, and along the bank of the river to where the sheep grazed. Cain wasn't in the fields. And I couldn't see Abel.

I stretched out a goat skin to be cleaned. I took a sharp stone to scrape it with, but I didn't use the stone. I sat and held the skin on my lap. I felt weak. *Great One*, I thought, but no other thoughts came.

I was waiting.

The sun rose. I didn't move. Its heat pounded on my neck. I watched insects glistening in the goat hair. And after that, I stared ahead, down the slope, and watched Cain scrambling up towards me. He came swiftly like a beast, clawing at the rocks.

I didn't shout or stand to greet him. I was too weak.

He shone with sweat. Soon he stood tensed in front of me, and on his brow I saw a deep gash. He was panting. In one hand he clutched a pointed stone, sharper at the edge than any I'd seen; and as I looked at him, I remembered the cat, the first cat, on the first day out of Eden, and how I'd thought, *It can pulp me like a fruit.*

I waited for him to speak.

'I'm leaving here,' he said. 'You won't see me again.'

He gave a strange smile, and ran a finger down his cut and sucked the blood. I wanted to ask, *What have you done?* Instead I picked up the stone that lay by me, the scraping stone. He saw that, and his smile deepened.

'The Great One doesn't want me here,' he said. 'I'm going.'

'You're hurt,' I said.

Cain's smile stretched. It showed his teeth, and a sickness spread in me. The child in my belly lay stone-still.

'What has the Great One told you?' I asked. 'You said you wouldn't leave your fields. Do you know the voice of the Great One?'

'I do now,' said Cain, 'but I won't hear it again.' And he turned away. He raised his hand with his stone in it, and turned from me. He began to scramble down the slope, and as he went, my strength came to me, so that I leapt to my feet and ran after him. I grabbed his arm. He wouldn't stop, and I fell and slithered after him, holding him –

'What have you done?' I shouted. 'Why are you going?'

He pushed me, but I kept my grip. So then he struck me, one blow across the face, and still I held him. But at his second blow I was stunned, and the grip was lost. He peered down at me.

'Keep the new one safe,' he said. 'I've killed your other son.'

Then he ran. I watched him scrambling down to his fields and away from them, and away from the river, and as he went, he raised his hands and ran with them clutching his head.

I lay where he'd left me. Adam found me there when he came back. He came early. It hadn't felt as it should, he said, the hunting. Pain thundered through me. I couldn't walk. I told him what Cain had said, and I pointed at a circling of birds in the distance, by the river.

'Find him,' I said. 'Find Abel.'

But Adam's face was unlistening. His eyes raged. He lifted up his spear and let out a roar. Then he began to run, shouting for Cain. I couldn't stop him. I watched him leaping down the slope and running and I heard him roaring and saw him fling his spear into Cain's fields, as though into his son's heart.

I spread my hands on my belly. The new life in there moved: it was not dead. I felt it kick, and I said to myself, *This may be all that's left.*

So then I crawled to the cave, and I lay at its mouth and waited for Adam to come to me with the blood of Cain on his spear, and I watched the birds that circled in the distance by the river, and I thought of Abel lying there, and pains trembled through my belly, and I wept for all of us. I clutched dust in my hands, and sent my anger after Cain, hurling it at his back, and I sent my anger after Adam who was running to kill Cain, and I sent my anger to where the birds circled, anger with the birds and anger with Abel because he'd been killed. And I let my anger fall on the one inside me, because it wasn't Cain and it wasn't Abel, and it was coming and would need me.

But my fiercest anger I flung at the Great One.

What have you done? I said. *What have you done to us?*

No one answered. I looked out on the earth and the rocks. Cain's fields were already dust-coloured. The sheep had wandered from the river.

Give me now, I said, *tall trees and the scent of lilies.*

None came. Only pains, and the reddening of the sun's going down, and the bright, thorn-sharp light of stars.

I closed my eyes.

I'm dying, I thought. *I'll be like the earth. I'll rot into the earth.*

But the new life in me kicked strongly, and my eyes opened again. So I lay waiting for what would happen, staring at the night.

Adam came at dawn. He crouched by me and gave me water.

'I've hidden our son,' he said, 'in the earth. I've hidden what was Abel.' Then he said, 'I didn't find Cain. I saw his foot marks, but the Great One told me not to follow.'

'The Great One spoke to you?' I asked.

'I knew I mustn't follow,' said Adam. 'So I found our other son.' His tears fell. Then he said, 'You did this. All of it. It's because of you, everything. Without you, I'd be still in Eden.'

He wiped my face.

The new one was coming. Adam stayed and watched. He pulled our new son out of me and bit the stem that linked him to me. He licked the blood from the new one's head and held him as if he thought he might do to him what he'd said once he might do when Cain came, and dash the new one's head on a rock.

'Give him a name,' I said. 'This is a new son from the Great One, because we've lost Abel.'

Adam didn't answer.

'We'll call him Seth,' I said.

'Seth!' said Adam, and then he laid our new son between my breasts. 'Be stronger than Cain,' he said, 'and wiser than Abel.'

'Let him be what he is,' I said. The new one wailed against my skin, and in the sound I heard the sound of Abel and of Cain, and my grief tightened in me, but it also sweetened.

Some of you are his children, my children. Seth's children.

We took Seth and found a greener country. We planted grain there as Cain had shown us, and we kept sheep there as Abel had shown us. We took his flock with us from their scattering by the shallow river, and they grew fat and made young ones in the greener country. Our backs ached with work. Seth grew strong. He laughed often, but not as quickly as Abel. Sometimes he was silent and sharpened stones or made spears, and once when I watched him, I said, 'Your brother Cain made good weapons, but your father uses them more skilfully.'

'What is brother?' he asked. 'What is Cain?'

So that night, when Adam was with us, after we'd eaten, I said, 'Tell Seth about his brothers.'

I thought Adam might kill me. A stillness fell on him. He looked at me, and made a deep sound in his throat. I groped beside me for a stone. But then Adam turned to Seth and, pointing at me, he said, 'You came out of her. Out of her belly. Cain came out before you. And there was another. His name was Abel. Cain killed Abel and ran away.'

'Why?' asked Seth.

We didn't answer. But Seth leaned forward in the firelight and went on speaking. 'Are there more? Are there others like us? Where's this Cain now?'

'We don't know where he is,' we told him.

'There are no others like us,' said Adam.

'How do you know?' asked Seth. 'Cain may have found others.'

Adam stared. Then he turned to me, as if it wasn't Seth who'd spoken but I, and he shouted, 'Were there others in Eden? How can there be others?'

'What's Eden?' asked Seth.

'It's where the Great One is,' I told him, and at that Adam sprang to his feet and kicked dust into the fire and went out into the night.

'Not today,' I said to Seth, 'but another time, I'll tell about the Great One.'

Seth smiled. 'What was Abel like?' he asked. 'Wasn't he as strong as Cain?'

'Be quiet,' I told him.

'The Great One will make me strong,' he said.

'What do you know of the Great One?' I asked. Then I flicked ash over his feet, so that he laughed as Abel used to laugh, and I saw Abel in his face.

Later, when he was almost fully grown, I told Seth of Eden. Alone without Adam. There were more of us by then. There was a brother for Seth, strong and swift-footed. He had gone with his father to bind corn, and only Seth's sister lay beside me, naked and whining. She was not yet two moons old.

I spoke of Eden.

'The Thought was mine,' I said, 'that drove us out of it.'

Seth watched me skin a hare that he'd killed. He watched the skin pull off, and he grunted and looked out across the fields. Then he looked at his sister.

'This is a good place,' he said, 'but I need someone for this.' He held the part between his legs. 'There must be others,' he said.

'In Eden –' I began.

'This is a good place,' said Seth again, 'but I need someone.'

'Go and look for them,' I told him.

*

He left us. We would have gone with him, but our strength was less than his, and there were the children. Also Adam said, as Cain had once said, 'My fields are here.'

It seemed quiet afterwards. We lay together in the nights for longer than we'd done through many seasons, and we were silent together in a new way, as though all that had been done and everything we'd seen might somehow bring the Great One to us saying, '*Enough*.'

Adam's arms had grown thin. His hair was white, and his belly soft. My own hair had turned white, and my breasts had become as you see them, my children, straining for the earth.

'We're old,' I told Adam, 'like the sheep that sicken and die. We've become like them.'

We were lying together, and he pushed into me.

'We must make another child,' he said.

'Are you afraid?' I asked.

Adam laughed. 'I face death every time I hunt,' he boasted. 'Why ask me now?'

'It's different,' I said, 'this being old.'

He lay still after that, and wouldn't let his seed pour into me. He lay breathing on me. His nails bit into my shoulders, and he said, 'I want to see Eden.'

'The Great One may take us back,' I said, 'when we die.'

But Adam was sleeping.

Often in those days I almost told him what I'd seen at the mouth of our cave once, long before – the tall trees and the shining of the great River, and how I'd smelled the flowers of Eden – but when I tried to speak of it, I thought, *It will anger him, if he hasn't seen these things*, and when I tried to put that thought aside and make ready to speak, a flicker in his eye seemed to warn me, as though he said to me, '*We know things we don't know how to talk about. Where are the words?*'

So I didn't tell.

Only one evening, when Adam was pleased because I'd laid

his hand on my belly and told him that the Great One was sending another life, I came close to it.

'I'll kill a sheep to thank the Great One,' he said, 'because this life is coming although we're old.'

I sat close to him. Our swift son was bringing in our sheep from the pasture. Our daughter sang as she played with stones in the house. A breeze cooled us. Adam smiled at me. Then he laid his hand between my legs, so that I laughed and told him, 'You're old, but even so you're young, as you were in Eden.'

'I know,' he said.

Later that summer, Seth came back, bringing his woman.

And now you've heard our story, my children. Tell it later to those who come from you. And when you speak of Eden and how we fled from it, remember what I've also told and almost said. That's enough. You must see it for yourselves.

LOT'S WIFE

This one came back for me. His face is beautiful, but as he holds me by the hand, I don't stare round at him. I'm not that kind of woman. And besides, 'Look ahead,' he told me, 'Lot's wife.' He laughed. 'Do it this time.'

I asked him, Am I dead?

'Where I come from,' he answered, 'no one asks such questions.'

Then he began to lead me – where we're going. He doesn't tell me where that is.

'A new path,' he said.

Will I see my husband again? I've asked. And my daughters?

'Trust me,' he said, 'trust me.'

He's very calm. He feels safe to be with. His eyes are green. They're the colour of fresh shoots after a rainfall.

When Lot came home with him, this man and his companion, these green eyes frightened me. So foreign. From somewhere so distant, I told myself, no one could even name the place. As if we didn't have enough of foreigners. Lot himself was nervous. He brought the two men in, and he was fussing and smiling.

'Do you know who they are,' he whispered, 'these two men? Cook your best for them, woman!'

And then almost at once the shouting started. 'Bring them out! Bring those two men out! We want some fun with those beauties!'

All that wild nonsense – far worse than usual, more than any evening when the brutes came shouting for our daughters. And then the stones began, thrown against the shutters, and some great kicks thudded against the door so that we all stared at it.

'Bring them out! Bring out those travellers! We want to show them a trick or two!'

Lot went pale.

'You see what you've done,' I said, 'bringing home strangers. Bringing trouble here –'

Then came a blow on the door that took my breath from me.

'I'll go out to them,' said Lot. He turned to the strangers. 'It's often like this,' he said. 'These city dwellers have never accepted us here. But I'll go out and reason with them.'

What can you do with such a man? How do you argue with a husband who thinks that people's hearts will change if you live quietly in their cesspit with them?

'We should never have come to this place,' I said.

He wasn't listening. He'd taken the pin from the bolt. He was opening the door.

He half went out –

Jeers and drunken hoots greeted him.

'Neighbours,' he said, 'have your joke. But would you violate the laws of hospitality?'

They shouted back obscenities.

'Friends –' he said.

But they yelled at him, 'Bring those travellers out or we'll go in and take them! We've a right to know them better! We mean to know them very well before this night's over!' And then they laughed, and shouted more unspeakable things –

'Lot –' I said. I went close to him and started plucking at his coat. I could see across his shoulder the grinning of their faces, watching him and hating how he stood there. 'Lot,' I said, 'come back inside –'

They heard my voice and surged forward. He blocked their way.

'Take my daughters if you must,' he said, 'but not my guests. I'll bring out my daughters –'

Someone moved me aside. It was done swiftly. My arms gripped, I was almost lifted from the ground: was it by this one with the green eyes, or his companion? I don't know. And they pulled Lot back into the house. They took hold of him, dragging him back across the threshold and slamming the door. Then they took the pin that he held clenched in his fist and secured the bolt, while outside the mob howled. A pot smashed against the shutters –

Our daughters crouched low in a corner, their hands over their heads. Lot couldn't look at them. He couldn't look at me. He'd offered them. He'd offered our daughters, just as a true-born city-dweller would have done.

'They'll lose interest in a while,' said one of the travellers. 'You'll see. They'll go soon.' It wasn't this one who leads me now. It was the brown-eyed one who spoke, eyes as brown as mine, as anyone's, but not like ours. 'They won't get in,' he said.

I pinched Lot's arm. 'How could you?' I whispered. 'Our own daughters?'

Then at last he looked at me, and said, 'Can't you understand what these men are? These guests of ours?'

'It seems I understand nothing,' I told him.

And everything went quiet. It was as sudden as that. The mob left. We heard them calling to each other streets away, suddenly they were streets away, laughing and banging on shutters.

As for the rest – but I'd meant what I'd said: I understood nothing. Months of begging Lot to take us out of that city and hearing how he couldn't – this reason, that reason – and all those who'd followed him there scattered on the plain, then two strangers come, and all at once we're stuffing things in sacks, planning to be gone before sunrise.

'You may depend on it,' said this one, the green-eyed, 'here on the plain, something terrible will happen tomorrow. But not to you, Lot, nor your family. We'll lead you to safety.'

'How do you know?' I asked. 'Are you spies? Which king's invading us this time?' And turning to Lot, I said, 'You see how slack you've been! You've let our people wander off in all directions, and now we're alone here, in this foul city, with another war coming –'

He hushed me, shaking his head and flapping his hand, as though to rid himself of a fly's buzzing. 'Just do as you're told, woman,' he said. He was suddenly hunched and shaking like a sick beggar, and he was staring at the traveller. 'Just collect together whatever's needed –'

'I don't see how they know what's going to happen,' I told him. 'Let them explain to me –'

But Lot groaned; and this green-eyed one smiled, and said, 'We know, because it's in our nature to know. Think of it, if you like, as an interpreting of signs. As to what will happen, keep your mind on getting away from here. That's simplest and best.'

And his smile was so grave that I found myself believing him.

'Something terrible?' I said.

'It's true,' he said.

And what does Lot do? What does my husband do? Our daughters start wailing for their worthless betrothed – drunks, the pair of them, I said so from the start, though Lot would have it that they weren't as bad as most and might be influenced for the better – What does he do? That husband of mine who'd offered his daughters to the mob, and started to shake at a few words from a traveller, he goes out into the night, hunting through the drinking houses of the city, through all the filthiest places where a man might have his throat slit, until he finds his fine, would-be sons-in-law slouched in their vomit, and he tries to sober them and bring them to the house. They wouldn't come of course. 'You don't like our ways,' they said to him, 'but what's wrong with a little drink? We'll see you tomorrow.'

They didn't come.

*

We went out of the gate as soon as it opened. Most of the sacks with our things, we left behind.

'There'll be need to hurry,' said the brown-eyed one. 'You mustn't weigh yourselves down.'

So we left almost everything, only Lot took the prayer mat rolled across his shoulder, with a cooking pot hanging from it, and I took my bag of dried herbs and the smallest of the sacks, which contained the bowl I loved and some cups, wrapped in a length of red cloth I'd been saving. Our daughters took their jewellery.

And we went out of the city. It was still dark. There was a tremor in the sky – dawn, not far off – and yet a crammed heat in the air that stuffed one's breath back down one's throat.

The brown-eyed stranger seized hold of my hand and took a firm grip on Lot's wrist. This green-eyed one held our daughters' hands. We glanced back often at the city, at its dark walls, until this green-eyed one told us, 'That's the last time. Have done with it now. No more looking back.'

And his friend said, 'Listen to what we're telling you. No more looking back.'

Good riddance, I thought.

Then Lot asked, 'Do you mean to take us to the mountains? I don't think I can walk that far.'

I stared at him. He's old, but he's strong. He's spent the greater part of his life walking. He can walk all day and ask for no more than one cup of water. When it comes to walking, he never complains.

'Put down the mat,' I said, 'if it's too heavy. We don't need the mat. Or maybe one of these young men could carry it. Let's get away from here by all means. What's the matter with you?'

Lot sighed. 'Have you still no understanding, woman? I'm weak,' he said, 'because of what's to happen.'

The sky was brightening.

'We must hurry,' said this green-eyed one.

But Lot moved very slowly, and all at once he said, 'Couldn't we go to Zoar? Surely nothing's going to happen there. It's such a small, unimportant place. It's much closer than the mountains, and the people there aren't entirely without merit. Couldn't we go to Zoar? Otherwise,' he said, 'I beg you, leave me where I am and save my family.'

'We'll go to Zoar,' said this green-eyed one. 'Only hurry.'

After that we walked fast, gulping like fish in the heavy stillness, while dawn came creeping from the east and shuddering with strange lights, purple and silver. A rumbling sounded.

'Don't look back!' The brown-eyed one tightened his grip on my hand. 'Whatever you think,' he said, 'and no matter what you feel, don't look back.'

A strange smell seeped into our nostrils, a burning, and the air turned yellowish –

'Keep walking,' said the brown-eyed one. 'Hurry –'

I could hear my daughters sobbing. They were terrified. From the corner of my eyes I could see them, this green-eyed one walking between them, straight-backed, while they clung to him, stumbling through the dust.

The rumbling gained on us. It came leaping at our heels in great bounds. Soon it was a roar that filled our ears, and with it came a wind that scorched and stung, while the sky over us darkened and crimsoned.

'Lot –' I said. 'Lot –'

I glanced at him, but he stared straight ahead. His beard was tossed. His eyes were narrowed. He looked grey and terrible. Tears caked his face.

And when I saw that Lot wept, the thought came, I don't know why, of the washing place, and the city women – especially the fat one with the smashed teeth and the amulets: I saw her big arms working in the sunlight and that fine head of hair of hers glistening. I saw her, and the others, and that skinny dog they liked to kick and shout at, and their wild children shrieking at some game in the gutters –

And I turned round –
My hand fell free.

This one came back for me. I don't know when.

Later. It was later.

He came and stood before my eyes, and when I saw him, I said, Don't ask me to move or to stop weeping. This is what I am now. The salt of tears is all my substance.

He didn't speak.

There should have been another way, I said. The evil in the cities was great, but even so, this punishment –

'It's a question of choices,' he told me.

I didn't answer. Weeping was all my argument.

'Time to leave,' he said.

I didn't move. I said, To be so abandoned. Not any living being should be so abandoned –

'What's this talk of abandonment?' He smiled. 'Now you must come with me,' he said.

But I told him, There's no one here to go with you. I've seen too much –

And then this green-eyed one laughed. It was a sound like water rippling in a brook I remember, many years ago, pebble-lined and clean, in the land I came from. Lot and I were young then.

And I began to walk.

He holds me by the hand, and I don't stare round at him. I'm not that kind of woman. Besides, there are his words, 'Look ahead, Lot's wife. Do it this time.'

And to make sure of that, I tell myself this story.

I've asked him, Am I dead?

The air is very pure. The stench of horror and destruction isn't where we are now. We've left that far behind. He holds my hand tightly.

SARAH, WIFE OF ABRAHAM

Lord, you're very great. I bow down to you. The boy grows strong. He doesn't smile often, but he's tall and can run like a lion, and he's dutiful. These are good things. I've fought for good things, and you've granted them.

Listen to me, Lord, I'm grateful, you know I am. So take away the splinter of reproach in me – if sometimes there is reproach, if sometimes when I'm tired I accuse myself because I ache to think of all the way I've had to come to where we are now.

What mother wouldn't act as I did?

And after so long?

It pleased you to keep me barren through years of promises and humiliations: the great journey from Haran, the time of famine when we first came into Canaan; you kept me like a wilderness while I was young and beautiful –

Yes, I was beautiful –

And always as I lay with my husband, I'd see the shining in his eyes of what he believed, how you'd told him his seed would produce a nation to honour you and walk in your sunlight. As he poured his seed into me, he used to cry out – cry to you – for a blessing on us, and through the months, the years, when no child came, he'd smile and tell me, 'I've been promised, Sarai my wife. Do away with your doubt.'

So full of promises, my husband Abraham, like his father, old Terah, who brought us from Ur – but more than his father: after Terah died at Haran, it seems to me, Lord, that you opened your hands and let fall on Abraham twice the power of visions, twice the force in his heart to drive him onwards for these promises of yours, across deserts and the lands of strangers.

We'd been comfortable in Haran. We came into the land of Canaan at a time of famine and you know all our journeyings, how in search of food we went into Egypt, where I was humiliated, the Pharaoh being a lecherous, grasping man, and Abraham, fearing for his safety, refusing to make known to him whose wife I am, so that Pharaoh –

But I'll not trouble you with such memories. You kept us safe, Lord. And then all our journeyings through the Negeb, to Bethel and to Hebron –

As for the wars on the plains that so endangered us, with great kings at each other's throats, and my husband working by negotiations and balancings and boldnesses to keep us from harm – again, you protected us, Lord. You've granted my husband sharp wits – I've never denied it – as well as his visions.

And always the promises, and my empty womb.

My feelings you knew. I'm your creature, and I'm a blunt woman, Lord. What paths you've led me on.

Even now, my belly tightens with cramp when I remember how it was, child after child born to Abraham by his slave women, and the fear in my heart that he might name such a woman as his wife, setting me aside. How I feared it, until my youthfulness had faded, and the monthly bleeding had dried in me, and I had no more hope.

Then I used to cover my head and draw the cloth across my face and sit and weep behind the tents. Yet when I walked, I held myself erect, even though the gourd-bellied slave women smiled as I passed and hid their mouths behind their hands.

And so the years passed, and we grew old, Abraham and I.

He with his visions. He's quieter now, but remember how it was, Lord. Sometimes he used to lie with his face pressed to the earth for most of the day, his arms about his head, and I would have the children raise a canopy over him, stretching it

34

out to keep the sun from baking him; and after those visions, his eyes were very bright, and he'd smile secretly – but he wasn't secret.

'What did the Lord say to you?' I used to ask, and Abraham would answer in a low voice and quickly, as if fearing to break the sky if he spoke too many words or too loud.

'Again the Promise,' he said. 'A great blessing on my issue.'

I used to laugh.

'Your slaves are as proud as great men's daughters,' I jested, 'you stuff them with so many blessings!'

Then Abraham would look grave and surprised, always surprised, no matter how often we spoke of such matters, and he'd tell me that my jokes were disrespectful.

'You're my wife,' he'd say. 'The blessed issue surely must be ours.'

And so I'd hold him in the nights as he did what he could to sire his impossible children on me, and remember, Lord, how I thought of him as a greater child than any, my husband with his shining Promise – until in the end, I heard a voice from my mouth tell him, 'Take a new wife, if the mother of this blessed offspring must be your wife. Take one I choose for you. Then in part the child will be mine.'

I chose Hagar. If a branch from the thorn bush must be grasped, better to grasp it boldly and firmly I thought, and accept the pain. I knew her quick smiles and pretty ankles delighted him.

He said she'd be his concubine, not a wife, but I answered, 'Fulfil what you believe. Beget your heir. And I'll rejoice for you.'

She was quick to conceive. I didn't rejoice.

I complained to you, Lord; and what I said must be held in your memory. I sat one night on a flat stone near the tents and spoke a great bitterness.

I heard no answer.

The next day, I slapped Hagar. She was fingering some trinkets of mine, and she said, 'When you were young, like me, these must have looked well on you.' Then, laughing, she held them to her ears and throat, and I slapped her.

Two mornings afterwards, I found her sleeping where Abraham had lain with her, and when I touched her with my foot to wake her, she stretched herself like a satisfied cat, and rubbed her hands across her belly and smiled. I kicked her and screamed. I would have pulled her up by her hair, but she sprang quickly to her feet and ran away into the bushes.

Later that day, Abraham came to me. He touched my arm. 'You scare her,' he said. 'She fears for the infant she's carrying.'

I wept.

'She delights in my humiliation,' I told him.

At that he flung up his hands and sighed.

'The squabbling of women,' he said, 'surpasses the nonsense of any children. You're my wife. Tell her so, and deal with her appropriately.'

I did, roundly. When I next saw her, near the well, while she stood quivering and staring, I told her her place, and to beware of me.

But she was cunning –

Lord, I'm direct in my ways, but that one was different. You know what came of my round speaking. She disappeared. For days, our people searched for her, but she came back at last of her own accord, calm-faced, quiet, and sought out Abraham.

'What did she say?' I asked him.

He was sober and spoke gravely. 'In her distress, she wandered about in open country,' he told me, 'until she received a vision. Her son is to be a great man, with countless descendants.'

'So there,' I said. 'You have your will.'

'It's not my will we speak of,' said Abraham.

I laughed.

I laughed often in the next years, Lord, laughter to fight the poison. Her son was poison to me. I smiled, for the sake of Abraham, at Ishmael's pranks and mockeries – childish mockeries, a disrespect sucked with his mother's milk. And Hagar and I came to an understanding: she feared me, especially my sharp tongue, and I tolerated her; and often, Lord, I sat down in the dust and lamented to you the bitterness of it all. Remember, you who remember all things, how I sat rocking with laughter, the tears pouring down, to think that Hagar's story of a vision had so eased my husband's heart and made all things seem right. 'What children, Lord,' I cried, 'the men of this people are, and my husband especially!'

And once I cried to you, 'Understand, Lord, that I'll sooner believe my husband's a duped fool than that you chose to speak to Hagar!'

Then I knelt and poured dust on my head, weeping and saying, 'Who am I to judge? What am I to think? I can speak of journeys through wildernesses, I can speak of ewes' milk and how to make cheeses, I know how to bake cakes of bread, but I know nothing of visions –'

Two comforts helped me through those years.

One was that I kept my health. I could still walk as fast as the younger women; I could work as well as any.

And the other comfort was Abraham, my husband. He spoke to me of all things in his mind. Hagar he treated well, he didn't neglect her, but he'd come to me and say, 'I think we must move the tents. I'll speak to the elders.'

Or, 'You're the companion of my youth. You'll understand how I feel. Our people need to set themselves apart from these strangers we live among. We need some special sign that shows we follow the God who brought us here.'

And a day came when, taking my hand, he said, 'My mocking, angry Sarai, listen to me! We're to have new names. From now on, call me Abraham. And your name shall be Sarah – Royal One – which suits you.'

It was late afternoon, and he'd spent that morning prostrate in the tent, laughing and mumbling in a way he had sometimes when the visions came, so I didn't make a joke of it. His eagerness to give me this gift softened me.

'Husband,' I said, 'if you wish it, let it be so.'

His eyes were very bright. He was pleased.

'There's more,' he said, 'but I think you won't believe me.'

'More promises?' I asked.

Then he said, 'You may yet bear me a son.'

I laughed and stroked his beard.

'Twenty sons,' I said. 'Let's begin at once.'

'Sarah mustn't mock,' he said, 'as Sarai did.'

And I begged you, Lord – remember how I begged you – *Keep this old man from going mad. Don't lay that grief on me.*

I bow down, Lord, who brought us out of Ur and out of Haran. You see how I am, how I always was. I've told you. I'm a blunt woman. Have patience with my slow understanding.

Three strangers came to our tents. At first, they seemed to me no different from many others. It was in the fourteenth year of Ishmael's life. Lines had deepened round his mother's mouth, although even so Hagar was beautiful – and then these strangers came. I thought they might have passed by, but Abraham, sitting at the entrance of our tent, got to his feet when he saw them and went running out, shouting greetings and offering them food, rest – as he often does; he gives lavishly, and if I murmur that a traveller might prefer a simple drink from the well and to be on his way, he only smiles, Lord, and tells me you've told him otherwise, so that I turn to baking more bread, and keep quiet.

The truth is, he loves to talk to travellers. That urge in his blood which drove him from Ur and from Haran – the urge you put in him, Lord – it needs news of distances and strange ways, which he uses, being cunning, to keep us safe. And for that reason, too, I say little.

So I baked for them. A calf was slaughtered, a feast was made, and these three strangers sat at the entrance of the tent with Abraham and spoke of rainfall and pasturage, and the cities they'd seen, and other things I didn't listen to. Inside, in the tent, why strain my ears to hear the men's talk? Doesn't Abraham tell me whatever concerns him? With that thought, I was content. The younger women laid out the food. Only once I stood at the entrance of the tent to watch, so that I could be sure they'd done everything as it should be, and as I did, one of the strangers turned and smiled at me with his green eyes.

Truly they were green. I looked away from them quickly.

So I went back inside; and I saw Abraham, as I went, eagerly handing the strangers my good cakes, his face bright with pleasure, and I smiled, because I saw in his eagerness his love of my cooking that neither Hagar nor any of the others could equal.

And then, Lord – how is it possible? How can a voice that's blurred and quiet suddenly be so clear, and yet no louder? I heard as if he spoke his words at my elbow, one of the strangers say, *'Sarah will bear a son. A year from now. I'll visit you again, Abraham, and she'll bear a son.'*

I laughed out loud.

They slept that night in our tents; and Abraham, coming to me late and lying beside me, was full of scolding.

'Why did you laugh?' he asked. 'They heard you. You shouldn't have laughed.' His voice shook, he was so offended.

'Who are these strangers,' I said, 'to say such things?'

'You've no faith,' said Abraham. 'Why can't you believe what my God says?'

'I didn't laugh much,' I answered.

'You shouldn't have laughed at all,' said Abraham, and he slept with his back to me.

The next morning, he went with the strangers down towards the plain, towards the cities down there. I watched him go. He said he'd see them on their way, and he walked with them, leading three of our barely tamed camels that he insisted they took, and I watched until the gleaming of the air played tricks with my sight, so that it seemed to me he walked with only two men, or even one –

Then I went to the stone that was my private place when I spoke with you, Lord, and I said, 'My body's become a dried stalk. Produce fruit from this, O God of Abraham, and for the future I'll believe that what my husband tells me is true, and that he knows your will.'

Hard months followed. When Abraham came back from seeing those strangers on their way, he looked tired and unsure of himself. It was evening. He came leading the camels. In the end, the strangers had refused them, but he seemed not to notice the insult. I watched the beasts being watered and tethered, and I said to him, 'What kind of courtesy is this? These camels you offered were a handsome gift.'

'They have no need of them,' he said. Then he glanced at me, and I saw his distress. 'Something's going to happen on the plain,' he said, 'but I think Lot will be safe.'

I'd never seen him looking so worn out, so collapsed inside his skin, and the mention of Lot irritated me. Over the years, how much worry that man has caused Abraham, and he's not even his son.

'Let your nephew take care of himself,' I said. 'It's time he did. What's going to happen? The plain's full of things happening, and no one the better or worse for them.'

'Something not imagined,' said Abraham. Then he added in a

low voice, 'We must move from here. Further away.' And as we walked, I thought he was going to stumble – it was as if I saw him stumble – but he didn't; and we went back to the tent together.

Journeys followed – more journeys, always more journeys – across deserts, towards Gerar –

The cities on the plain were destroyed. A fiery convulsion, such as no one thought possible, overwhelmed them – but I'll not speak of that. Many strangers came, we fed very many, and perhaps they came back to us again, those three, but if so, it was different, and I didn't see them: it was not a time for feasts, and so many came –

Then one morning, as I worked with the women, I found that they were staring at me. I looked up from the cloth we washed, and saw their faces turned to me, Hagar's among them.

'It's true,' I said, 'I feel it.'

'How can it happen?' they asked. 'At your age?'

'It was Promised,' I told them, and I knew then that truly a life had kindled in me, that the sensations in my breasts and limbs were not a sickness of too much wishing, but a late goodness beyond all hope.

That night, I told Abraham, and he prostrated himself. He thanked you, Lord. I watched him, and afterwards he reproached me, frowning and saying, 'Don't you also give thanks?'

'I will,' I said. 'Let me do it my own way.'

'Now you believe me?' he asked. 'Now you believe?'

'Now I believe,' I told him.

He was playful and stroked my face. 'My fruitful, handsome wife!' he said. 'If the king of this country hears of such wonders – fertile at your age – he'll take you from me! In fact,' he said, 'I think I'll tell him you're my sister. Then he'll feel free to carry you off, and afterwards I'll tell him his mistake and make him pay me a thousand pieces of silver in compensation.'

It filled me with delight to hear him rejoicing. I said nothing to remind him that such trickery had almost left me helpless once in the hands of Pharaoh. He was offering me that blunder as something not forgotten. It was a tribute to my worth. I knew it and we laughed together. Only as he turned to sleep, he said, 'You *will* give thanks?'

'I've good reason to give thanks,' I said, and I lay awake, and over and over until the dawn, didn't I thank you, Lord? Didn't I marvel at the quickening of seed in me, and the coming about of what had been said, and the smallness of this foolish, blunt woman, and the greatness of all that you are?

And at dawn, when Abraham had gone from me, didn't I prostrate myself in the glory of your sunrise, and say in my heart, *Now I know my husband Abraham speaks the truth, and I shall never doubt him again*?

You remember all things, Compassionate One. You know I said this.

The cities on the plain were swept away. They collapsed into ashes; the very stones melted –

And yet you saved Lot. It was months before we heard from him. Haggard-faced travellers told us of horrors and escapes, but of Lot they knew nothing. My husband said that we must trust his nephew was safe, and news came at last that he'd been seen with his daughters, though as for that wife of his, so proud and busy with her opinions –

But it's not my purpose to speak ill of her. The ruins of those cities smouldered in my dreams, so that often I pressed my hands against the roundness of my belly, and said to Abraham, 'We must do nothing to displease this God of ours.'

He smiled and spoke soothingly. 'Remember what's Promised,' he answered. 'Don't be afraid.'

Hagar walked through those days with her mouth thin and her head high. Ishmael was loud and full of laughter. He amused Abraham with tricks, clever shooting with his bow, antics on the back of a camel, and also with gifts – a staff for walking with, carved about its head with fruit and flowers – but like his mother, he showed cunning, and for all his laughter, he spoke often of his eagerness to learn. 'Tell me more, father. Teach me more about our people, father.' *Father.* Always, '*Father*'. And '*Our people*'. And he would look at me, if he had to, with clear eyes, bright with challenge, so that my joy clouded.

Isaac was born.

My son came, the child for Abraham's inheritance. My husband's eyes filled with tears as he held him. I felt dazed with completion.

And yet –

And yet –

I saw her standing there, Hagar, with a silence in her face that set my heart thumping, and at her side the smiling Ishmael as Abraham turned to him and said, 'See, Ishmael, here's your brother!' And at that moment, fear fell like a blade through the centre of my blessedness.

I said nothing at once. Hadn't I undertaken to believe what my husband believed, and trust as he trusted?

Yet I feared –

I feared when Hagar came close to the infant, or Ishmael, to Abraham's delight, lifted him from where he lay and held him laughing against the sun.

I slept little in those days, and often I spoke to you, All-seeing One, and begged you to keep safe what you'd given. I also whispered many fearful things to Abraham, who gazed at me with sadness and asked, 'Is it so hard to trust a blessing?'

He doesn't see, I thought. *No one can see, only I.* And I watched Hagar and her son. My gaze was fastened to their shadows. Their every move flowed through my blood.

On the day of Isaac's weaning feast, while the men ate, and the air was sweet with thanksgiving, Ishmael took my son from among the children; and he flung his knife into the sand, and stood laughing over Isaac while the child struggled to pull it out –

When I saw that, I would have scratched the eyes from Ishmael's head, but I was prevented. It took strong men to pull me from him, and I cared nothing for who heard: I screamed at Abraham, 'Rid me of both of them, mother and son! Honour me as I deserve! Can't you see? Won't you see? I'll not allow this slave-child to harm our son and take everything from him – even his life!'

'Ishmael meant no harm. He's fond of the child,' said Abraham, 'and just as Isaac's my son, so is Ishmael.'

He spoke firmly, in the voice of a man who leads his people and who speaks and they follow, so that I felt restrained, out there in the open, with so many gathered round. I left the feast. I took Isaac and went into the tent. It was later, when the sun had dropped, that he came to me and said, 'Sarah, what evil you've done today! Why must you create this enmity with Hagar and Ishmael? You trouble me deeply.'

'Send them away,' I wept. 'In all other matters I trust you, but your goodness blinds you to what I can see. I fear for Isaac's life.'

He sat by me while my tears fell. He watched them falling, but he didn't speak again. Neither did I; and after some time, he went out beneath the stars; and that night, he didn't sleep at my side.

When I woke, they'd gone. Hagar and Ishmael. I knew at once, before I asked or anyone told me. I went out and found Abraham seated with the elders near the well; and when he saw me coming towards him, he rose and came to me.

'We'll not speak of this,' he said. 'They've gone.'

I nodded. 'You've done wisely,' I told him, 'although for a time your heart may feel cold –'

He turned his back. 'Enough,' he said. 'It's done.'

Slowly he forgave me. Hagar sent word. She and Ishmael didn't shrivel into dry bones in the desert. They reached a friendly people in Paran and stayed there and lived with them.

I bowed down at the news, Merciful One, and thanked you for their safety. And I told Abraham, 'I prayed for them.'

'If their bones had been found in the wilderness, you'd have rejoiced,' he said.

'You're wrong,' I told him. 'You would never have forgiven me their deaths. I prayed that they'd live.'

Isaac grew; and in him I saw the beauty of my youth. Abraham also saw it, so that sometimes he touched the ruins of my face and said, 'Nothing's lost. What you think is lost is in our son.'

'And he's keen-witted and will be a leader of men,' I said, 'like his father.'

Then Abraham smiled. 'It's so,' he said. 'Is that not Promised?'

Years passed. We journeyed – always the journeys – but settled at last by a well at the place we call Beersheba. Abraham was thoughtful there and quiet. Our people planted a strip of land.

'My limbs ache,' he told me, 'and my eyes no longer see the high eagle. It would be good to stay here.'

So we stayed, and wasn't he as I've said, Lord – quiet, and thoughtful? *He's content*, I told my heart. I saw him gazing often at his son, Isaac. *He's content*, I thought.

How could I tell – I, who'd taken myself so deeply into believing my husband, Abraham, whatever he told me – how could I know that a strange torment lay behind his words in those days, and behind his silences, a thing not only unsaid, as many things may be, but also unsayable? Hadn't he told me, '*Trust the Blessing*'?

He's content, I said to myself; and I felt strong in the way of women who've held their menfolk and children through the twistings of many threats and difficulties, so that in the end they've reached a good place, a protected place where nothing will harm them.

Until Abraham said to me, 'There's something I must do.

I've been told to take Isaac up to Moriah. Up into the hills. It's necessary to make a sacrifice there. He and I alone. Our God wills it.'

'Moriah?' I said. 'Why so far? Isaac's very young. Spare him this journey away from his mother. Make your sacrifice here.'

'I must do as I'm told,' said my husband.

Then we lay down to sleep together, but I found I lay with my eyes open, and although I didn't look at him, I knew that Abraham also lay open-eyed. At last I asked, 'It's important, this sacrifice?'

'I'll never make one more important,' said Abraham.

'Will it bring a blessing on our son?' I asked.

'How can he not be blessed?' said Abraham. 'He's the gift of our God.'

At daybreak they set out. They went humbly. They took no camels. Abraham took firewood. 'In case,' he said, 'we find none suitable in the hills of Moriah.' He loaded it on an ass, and he chose two men to go with them, because I asked, 'How could an old man like you fight off robbers and any others who might intend evil to Isaac?' So he chose two of our strongest men to go with them.

I was blunt with Isaac when he left me. I hid my tears and said, 'Obey your father, and don't think it strange to be away from me. When you're older, you'll understand that a mother never truly leaves her child's side.'

He stared at me, and then he left.

After they'd gone, I sat alone in the tent. Women came to me and said, 'So young, to go with his father.' I ignored them. A question was rising in me. At our parting, my concern had been for Isaac to be calm, and also I'd been watchful of my husband: he'd leaned heavily on his stick, he was wheezing as he set out. He'd scarcely looked at me.

'You're sick,' I'd said. 'Put off this journey.'

He'd waved me away.

And so only in the tent, in the quietness afterwards, did I ask. What would they sacrifice? They'd taken no lamb with them, no beast worthy or unworthy except the ass –

No one offers his god such an unclean creature.

'So brave,' the women prattled. 'So straight-backed, setting out, the little one.'

After that, I no longer heard them.

I wished I could laugh. I wished I could rise up and cry, 'My husband in his old age has grown forgetful! Send after him! Let someone hurry after him with the purest of our lambs!'

But I sat silent; and I told myself, *His most important sacrifice. That's what he said. Maybe it's some new thing, some unseen offering, and nothing of blood –*

Yes, but the firewood, the firewood –

And then I told myself, *He means to buy what's needed on the way. In Moriah. So that they can travel faster, for the child's sake.*

And after that, didn't I whisper in the depths of my silence to you, All-hearing One, *If he's mad, make him well. Bring him home?*

What are men not capable of?

Five days. I remember little of the first one. Or the next. I remember only the fury, cold in me, at the ways of Abraham. I saw them walking together, the father with his hand on the son's shoulder to keep him from running and spending his strength – walking my child from me for whatever the father said must be done – and all the years, the lifetime's bond between Abraham and me, with the sum of caring and forgiving we'd spent on each other – all that seemed to become dust, and I thought, *What may this stranger not do to himself – or to Isaac?*

'*I must do as I'm told*,' he'd said, and I hated him.

I spoke to no one of what I feared. I didn't sleep. The second night, I didn't try. I stood at the entrance of the tent, staring out into the dark, willing them back – hating Abraham and willing them back – until, towards dawn, a small cloud that had hidden

47

at the very back of my fear and anger came closer to me, and I said out loud into the dark, 'I sent Hagar and Ishmael away. Is this punishment, Lord?'

No one answered. Only, as I watched the stars fade, a calmness came within a half-formed understanding that a thing done may wait inside the bud of what's to happen, crushed into its petals. So then I prostrated myself. I fell down at the entrance of the tent, and whispered to the dust, 'Because of me, he risked the life of Ishmael. Now he pays penance. Lord, Lord, we're imperfect. I'm a simple woman. I protected my own. It's how I am. Deal as you see fit. I'll obey you, God of my husband. I'll trust you and your Promise. Surely your Promise will save Isaac.'

Then I lay very still until the light gathered.

After that, for three days I fasted. And where in truth was I, Lord? I spoke to no one. I was so quiet within myself. I neither hoped nor feared. I was serene, like a still pool in a distant oasis, and people said, 'How she loves her child, to suffer so at this separation!' Far away I heard them, and I made signs that they should leave me as I was, and not be troubled.

I slept those nights, tranquil and dreamless.

But on the sixth day, I woke early; and it was as though a ripple of sunlight had fallen across the stillness in me. I no longer needed silence. At dawn, I went out to the well. I talked with the women. I laughed at the chatter of two small girls who told me their names for the fattest rams. I greeted the elders, and afterwards I sat in the shade twisting yarn – until the sun was high, and a shout went up.

Someone could see them coming.

I went on with my work, twisting yarn, but looking up from time to time, at last I saw them: Isaac riding on the ass; Abraham at his side, his head erect; the two men waving their staffs, and the women and children running out to bring them home –

I rose then, and waited –

I felt only peace.

Isaac wasn't smiling. He looked well and at ease, but like a child who's woken from a deep sleep, and looks gravely at all things. Abraham was smiling. He had words for the children who clustered round him, blessings for the women – and his eyes when they found mine were bright with tears.

I went to him and embraced him.

'So,' I said, 'you're back again, husband. And you –' I said, turning to Isaac, 'I hope you've behaved.'

He slipped from the ass. I held him close; and the peace in me faltered. Tears fell. The women round me sighed and smiled.

We made a feast for their return, a thanksgiving feast with an offering to you, Lord; and the young girls and young men danced until the moon was high. Isaac sat watching with great eyes.

I went to him, placed my hand on his shoulder, and asked, 'Are you truly well, my son?'

He said that he was. I told him to look at me. He smiled at that, quickly and softly, but I spoke to the seriousness behind the smile.

'Your father loves you,' I said, 'and so do I.'

He touched my hand.

'You needn't worry, mother,' he said.

Then he let me hold him and weep.

Abraham was quiet, very quiet, and later, when we were alone, we sat together and he smiled and touched my cheek. He was tender. 'Rub my back,' he said. 'Let me feel your hands on my back, taking the pain away.'

I obeyed him, and as I rubbed, he said, 'You ask no questions, Sarah.'

'Let it be enough that you've come home,' I answered, 'and that our son's safe.'

'Let that be enough,' he agreed, which angered me.

So then I said, 'I trusted the Promise. I know you've kept some secret from me, and my thoughts have been full of fear, but I trusted.'

My voice was sharp, and he glanced at me across his shoulder, a beseeching face –

'I also trusted,' he said.

After that, I rubbed gently but with firmness just as he likes, until he mumbled he would sleep. Then he lay down, and rolled his coat round him. I lay beside him, and discovered that my anger had worked itself away with the rubbing. I was peaceful again. My eyes closed. I was almost asleep when Abraham turned to me and pressed his head against my breast. He was weeping. I didn't question it. He spoke towards my heart, softly, as though the words were not for my hearing. I barely heard them.

'I almost killed him,' he said.

'But you didn't,' I told him. 'You're a good man, and you did no such thing.'

'It's our God who's good,' said Abraham. 'A God who keeps Promises.'

'Rest and sleep.' I patted his back. What are men, after all, but great children? 'Now there's nothing more you need to say,' I told him.

So he slept, but I lay awake with the weight of his head on me, and talked to you, High One. Didn't I speak roundly to you in my heart? Didn't I say, *My husband speaks the truth. You're good, Compassionate One, and I bless you. I know you'll not despise your creature's blessing, and I thank you with all that's mine?*

Those were my words, and so I say still on this day, as on all days.

Lord, you're very great. I bow down. Everything is well. And Isaac grows strong. He's a grave boy, it's true. He doesn't smile often, but he's steady and dutiful; and when he does smile, it's most often to show the affection in his heart, so that his smiling

quenches a thirst in me, like a draught of pure water, and whenever I see it, I hear my husband Abraham asking me again,
'How can he not be blessed? He's the gift of our God.'

That's so.

It's simply so.

It's so.

HAGAR

Listen, daughter, I grow weary of your long faces! You're a fine woman. You've born my son strong children. And didn't I choose you? I said to myself, *Let her be a woman from the Two Lands, as Egyptian as I am.* I chose you, and I wasn't wrong. You're a true wife for Ishmael, for a warrior. You're full of faults and hot-tempered, but you have courage and honesty. You hold your head recklessly high, I've often said so, but you have much to be proud of.

Only – end this venom.

Abram was his father.

Now the old man lies dead. What would you have? The secrets of Ur run through Ishmael's blood mingled with ours, the secrets of Egypt. Would you have my son deny that, and turn him into something base? Would you have him be a man who spits in the dust and cries, 'What do I know of fathers?'

Do you forget that they loved each other?

Every time you sneer, 'Now he's gone to bury the old fool who rejected him, and to kiss a brother who has nothing but contempt for him!' – you offend me, daughter. You offend me, and you flaunt a great ignorance. Ishmael had to go. By honouring his father, he honours also himself.

And I say again, haven't you understood that they loved each other?

As for Isaac – but I've seen it's nothing to you that he sent for Ishmael. You stared at the messengers, as if the dust on their coats stank like goat dung, and you heard nothing of their words beyond the fact of Abram's stopped breath. Or if you did, it was no more than you looked for: insult, humiliation.

But Ishmael heard other things.

Be reconciled, daughter.

I know you fear me. You think I mean to strip away that fierce spirit of yours, and leave you naked and powerless. You misunderstand. It would surprise you, if you could feel my love for you. I wouldn't trade that spirit of yours – not even for my own youth again, with all its extravagance. Men's lips used to part when I walked by. Their breath waited in their throats when they looked at me; but I wouldn't trade your spirit for all that I had.

Only – you must discriminate. Pride is a mere beginning.

Don't suffer as I did.

I was like you once, when I was young.

My father's debts ended my childhood before my height had reached his waist; but when he gave me away, I jutted out my chin and said to myself, *I'll kick and scratch anyone who harms me or insults me. I'll trust no one.*

Later, my owner took me with his household far to the north in Egypt, and there he exchanged me for sheep from some filthy travellers who were passing through that country; and when he said to me, 'This will be better for you. My wife says you irritate her because your nose leaks, but the truth is, you're too pretty, my lotus bud,' I answered him, 'I'll like it much better with the travellers!' And then I turned from him at once, although he was a kind man who'd treated me fairly.

I took refuge in pride.

And I looked at the woman I was to obey – old, so old, her skin cracked by the winds of the desert, and her clothes stiff with the dirt of many journeys. I looked at her boldly.

'You'll be safe with us,' she said. 'Serve us well, little one, and you'll learn to be content. I'm the wife of Abram. My name's Sarai.'

'My name's Hagar,' I told her, 'and I'm not so little.'

It took us time to know the meaning of each other's words,

but when the interpreting man had explained what I'd said, she laughed and ran her thin fingers through my hair. I smiled back, but only to please her.

You understand, daughter?

Those people separated me from everything I knew. I learned their words. I learned the sharp edge of Sarai's hand. I learned to move with my head bent against the dust, and walk and work and walk, and keep my voice low, and not to stare too much at boys and young men, and not to gape when the old man who was leading us, this Abram with his filthy beard and deep eyes, fell down and lay half the day in the dirt while we stood about waiting for him, then was helped to his feet, and the order went out that we must all turn this way or that way and start walking in a different direction. I learned not to mind the stink of sweat and the lice in my hair.

I learned all this and many things, sometimes laughing with the other slaves, women who came from many peoples and were caught up in this wandering; and sometimes I laughed with the women of Abram's kin – but not often with them. More truly, I laughed to myself when I spoke to them. They weren't like me. Their eyes weren't bold. None was as beautiful. I knew I was beautiful. I saw it in the faces of men.

Sarai was hard. If I burned bread, she ripped it into pieces, flung it into the dust and ground it beneath her feet. 'Now pick it up,' she'd say, 'every last morsel. This is your food – all you'll eat for three days. We're a people who don't waste what we're given.'

Her slaps were frequent.

'If you tried, you could please me,' she said, 'but your wish is different. This cloth will have to be washed again. Water must be wasted, because Hagar doesn't accept that she must work in life.'

Then I would hurry away and make a great show of diligence. But once I told her, 'It's true. My wish is different. I should want to please you, but sometimes I don't. My hand slips at the task.'

I was no longer a child when I said it. I stared at Sarai and expected a blow, but she looked thoughtful and even calmed. At last she asked, 'Don't your gods teach you to accept who you are?'

'I don't remember any gods,' I said.

'But there are others with us from your country,' said Sarai. 'Surely you know the gods of Egypt?'

'I don't remember any gods,' I said again.

Sarai watched me strangely after that. I noticed. And at times she smiled at me with a kind of twisted amusement which I didn't like. When she did it, I looked away quickly. I held my head higher at those times, and said in my heart, *I come from a proud people who own many cities. Think what you like!*

Abram was easier to understand, not as a leader and in his trances and visions – he had many visions – but at least as a man. He used to smile when I passed him, if my eye caught his. Somehow our eyes did meet. He was a man, after all.

Then a day came when Sarai had me called to her.

Listen to me, daughter. Over the years, you've heard many fragments, but now I'll tell you –

Sarai was sitting in the darkest corner of the tent. Her face seemed made of shadow, and before her lay a pile of gold, copper and silver.

'Come close,' she said.

I obeyed, and saw that they were her own necklaces, piled between her knees.

'Hagar,' she said, and slowly she began to finger the necklaces, 'you're a woman now, and I have it in mind to give you a gift. Which would you like? Would you like this one?' She raised a necklace and stretched it between her hands. 'Or this?' She raised another. She held it before her eyes, so that to look at it was also to look into the shadow of her face. Then she laid it down. 'Or would you prefer your freedom?' she said.

I couldn't see her eyes. Her voice was cold. I began to tremble. She stirred the pile of necklaces so that they made scaly, tinkling sounds.

At last I asked, 'Would you truly give me my freedom? Is that your wish, and your husband's?'

Sarai made a small, sharp movement with her head, so that I knew at once I had annoyed her.

'This is my concern,' she said, 'not my husband's. Wasn't it I who bought you?'

'You're my mistress,' I answered.

'But do you imagine that Abram and I don't share all things in our hearts?'

I said nothing, and again she stretched out one of the necklaces between her hands. 'This is the most beautiful,' she said.

Then I spoke. The words came sharply and quickly, and I said, 'If you wish me well, give it to me, and also my freedom. As your bondswoman, how could I wear such a thing when the others have nothing to compare to it? They would make my life wretched. But if you give me freedom – what's freedom without a dowry? So give me both.'

I felt sick with fear. It was a test. I knew it was a test, although its meaning I didn't know.

Sarai was angry. I sensed it, and I waited for her to spring up like a lioness. She was old, but she was swifter in her movements than many of the girls, and I could sense – always I sensed – the danger in her.

But she only said, 'Leave me now.'

So I went out of the tent with neither necklace nor freedom.

But I had passed the test. I lay with Abram. I bore Ishmael.

When Sarai told me I was to lie with her husband, her voice shivered with effort. 'I've chosen you,' she said, 'despite the shortcomings of your nature, because you're not a fool, and this is no meaningless coupling. This is for a great purpose. Abram and I have considered it deeply, with many prayers. For this purpose you must bear him a child – who will be free, and no slave. Respect Abram, and think of him as your husband. Do you understand?'

I didn't, and even as I heard her contradictions, I felt more in myself.

'I understand that you honour me,' I said. 'Your husband's a great man. But he already has children by bondswomen. How will mine be different? And if my child's to be free – am I then free? Am I to be a wife?'

'These are insolent questions. You're right to speak of honour,' said Sarai. 'Do as I tell you. In this matter, think of him as your husband, and be grateful that your child will be more than you can ever be. Isn't that enough?' she said, and she took from round her own throat one of the necklaces she wore and placed it round mine. I let her do it, her breath on my cheek.

'Then am I to be a wife?' I said again.

At that she became very still, as if absorbed in herself, deciding whether or not to let the anger out. In the end, she said, 'Don't try to make great matters small. Respect Abram always. I'll know if you don't.'

I thought he'd find pleasure in me. Often he quivered with anticipation. I wore perfumes. Sarai gave me perfumes. I did all I could to be pleasing to him. But as he lay with me, he chanted prayers, and kept his eyes closed, almost as though he'd willingly have closed all his senses if it had been possible. Briefly his hands wandered, but he'd bring them back, and afterwards he used to lie very still at my side, telling me about his god, and how the child that would be coming – our child – was to be no ordinary child.

'You must learn to trust my god, Hagar,' he said.

'I know nothing about gods,' I told him. 'Is it enough if I trust you?'

Then he used to laugh and let himself pat my belly.

Sarai hated me. A fire raged in her eyes whenever she saw me, and yet her voice was even, and when I told her that I'd missed my monthly bleeding, she took the news calmly enough.

'You've lost no time, Hagar,' she said, 'not because you're fertile, but because of our prayers.'

So I asked her, 'Shouldn't we thank this god of our husband's? Will we make a sacrifice?'

And then she was angry. 'Who are you to speak of such things?' she said. 'Abram and I will decide what's to be done.'

I left the tent quickly.

Who was I to speak of such things? I held my head high. I, at least, could conceive – a blessing no god had granted Sarai.

But, I tell you, daughter, fear grew in me, as steadily as the infant.

One night, I asked Abram, 'When the child comes, will I be his mother? Or will your wife, Sarai?'

He sighed. 'Let me sleep,' he said. 'You chatter so much!'

'I'll not let Sarai take my child from me,' I said, but I don't think he heard. He wasn't like many old men who lie awake and wheeze and groan through the night. He slept easily, while I –

I tried to reason out how matters stood. Sarai had chosen me. She hated me, because I was young and beautiful, and she was old and barren and many of the women said, 'The gods see some great fault in her. Why else has she no children?' She had to live with her fault, and the old man, Abram, accepting at last that she could never give him an heir, to ease her stricken pride had said to her, 'You must be the one to choose me a new wife. Let the choice be yours.' And she had set a test, and chosen me, because I had spirit and was not a fool. But whether or not she'd allow me truly to be a wife and keep the child, or whether she'd claim him for herself, I didn't know. She was dangerous. Only that much was clear to me.

But I thought I understood Abram's thinking. He didn't call me 'wife', because he feared Sarai's anger, and for that reason, too, he spoke of his god and chanted prayers when he lay with me, and made much of visions and promises, and how all this had to be, not because he longed to press himself into a young girl's flesh, but because his god insisted –

The follies of old people. And I, Hagar the Egyptian, was trapped between the needs of these two. And in the silence while Abram slept, I vowed to myself that Sarai wouldn't have my child. How could she be fit to raise my son if the gods had refused her any of her own? And if my son was to be Abram's heir – I never doubted it would be a son – then wasn't I fit to be Abram's wife? I was more fit than Sarai herself, and she would have to accept me.

These were my thoughts and I acted on them. So once, when Sarai saw me sitting in the shade while the other women worked, and came to me and said, 'Who told you to laze about like this? Get up, Hagar!' I didn't hurry to obey her. I stayed where I was. I shaded my eyes as I looked up at her, and said, 'The child inside me told me to rest. I was feeling faint.'

She said nothing back. She only stood stiffly, with her hands clenched, and I smiled at her, until she turned and left me.

After that, I often went into the tent and rested there, in a little space, out of her way, but in her presence. My heart bucked and shivered the first times I lay down in there, but Sarai only watched and said nothing.

As for Abram, his god didn't immediately forbid him to lie with me once I'd conceived. 'We must be sure,' he said.

'Am I your wife?' I asked him. 'And will you acknowledge me as this child's mother?'

'Questions, questions. You're full of questions, Hagar,' he said, 'and no understanding! Who can take from you the fact that this child grows in your womb? And he'll be a great man, isn't that enough?'

He knew it wasn't. He sighed and stroked me.

'Be respectful to my wife, Sarai,' he said. 'You're young. Learn from her. She's a wise woman.'

'She hates me,' I told him, 'and this life in me.'

'You fear her,' said Abram, 'and see hatred where more far-sighted eyes would see only pain.'

Some of the bondswomen also hated me.

'Is it such an unusual thing,' they asked, 'to have a child in your belly? Even Abram's child? Do you think you're the first – you with your finery?' They squinted at the necklace I wore, and yet I wore it, because I was a wife. To show I was a wife. And some of them said, 'Are you mad? Why should *your* child be specially chosen? Or if it is, you can be sure that the moment it's born, you'll lose it! It'll be snatched from your hands. Old Sarai will have it in her clutches. You'll have no say in the matter!'

I believed them, about Sarai, and slowly the fear in me turned to rage, hard and burning like a scorched rock. It lay in my womb together with the child, competing for space, and all the more fiercely I told myself, *I must in every way behave as Sarai's equal, so that she can't take my child from me. I must be strong. I must show her I'd make a powerful enemy.*

Do you hear me, daughter? Just as you are now, with your loud arguments and demands that Ishmael spit in Isaac's face, so I felt then. I chose defiance.

To me, equal with Sarai meant more than equal.

I began to wander about the tent, fingering things – Sarai's possessions, and speaking loudly to her of 'our husband' and how 'Last night, Abram told me such and such . . .'

She watched me, and said little.

Then one day, she was sitting with her hands in her lap, while I told some small thing – some small, deliberate thing: a remark of Abram's about my Egyptian ears – and when I laughed and stared at her, she lowered her eyes; and I became uncertain and began to tremble. Her silence frightened me. It was as if her hate was trapped in a hunter's net and beaten and quiet, but it was waiting its chance.

And suddenly I wanted to soothe her. So I said, 'I'm still very young. I know I've a great deal to learn.'

She didn't look up.

Then I saw what lay at her side. They were some of her necklaces that she'd shown me on the day when she'd tested me. Why she had them there, I didn't ask. I think she took them in her hands often in those days.

I squatted by her and reached for one. She didn't move.

'You were beautiful,' I said. 'I've heard that from many people. How lovely this must have looked on you.' I held the necklace up before her. She raised her head, and as she did – that rage in me, daughter – I brought the necklace closer to my own throat, and further from hers. It startled me that it happened, and I laughed.

She slapped me once, hard, across my mouth, and I dropped the necklace and ran.

Two days later, she kicked me. I was half asleep. She came to me before dawn. I hardly knew who it was who stood over me, but when I saw that it was Sarai, and the fury in her eyes, I smiled. What else could I do? I lay helpless at her feet. I spread my hands across my belly to protect the unborn life there, and rolled from her as she kicked me and screamed, 'Slut! Slut!' I got up at last and ran away.

I hid among the bushes shivering and sweating. I vomited and lay moaning to myself until the high sun forced me to go back and drink from the well. I waited as long as I could, but for the child's sake I went back.

Sarai was there, standing at the well, watching for me. Her face was very calm. She let me draw water and drink, the gourd trembling in my hands.

Then she said, 'Be certain about this, Hagar. My husband Abram needs me as he'll never need you. What do you know of

Ur and our forefathers? What do you know of our ways? Abram and I are one flesh, and we've lived your lifetime several times over together. Remember this when you look at me or speak to me. I chose you to serve our purpose. Remember that, too, and know your place.'

I stood trembling with the gourd in my hand.

Then she said, pointing at my belly: 'For my husband's sake and our purpose, you needn't fear for that one's life. But I warn you, Hagar – beware of me.'

'I hear you,' I said, and very carefully I placed the gourd on the ground, because I saw that I must submit, and to lay down the gourd bent my back. But it wasn't a bowing down, however she took it.

Abram didn't come to me that night; and before dawn the next day, I was gone.

I had filled two water-skins – but I took only one, so that I could walk faster. I went quickly from the tents. I meant to terrify Abram. I wanted him to wake and cry to Sarai, 'What have you done?' And I raged as I walked. Let him explain to his god what had become of me. Let him choose, and put aside Sarai. Let him send out his people to search for me while he examined his guilt – for wasn't he guilty? All this pain and evil – weren't they the making of an old man who hadn't the courage to stand before his first wife and tell her to respect his new one?

I kept up my pace. I thought they mustn't find me too soon . . . They needed time to grow anxious.

I myself wasn't anxious. I was testing Abram's god. How could a lion devour me, or any man violate a chosen one, whose son was to be the heir of a man who spoke with gods? All day, my rage kept me fearless. Let this Ur-god take care of us, my child and me.

My concern was only to walk fast in case I was followed. Too fast. I had to drink often, so that by the time the sun set, the water skin was already light. And yet no one had found me.

That made me thoughtful. And the cold and dark made me thoughtful. I crouched that night among thorn trees. They tore my clothes and scratched my arms, but it felt safer among them than out in the open. *Let his god protect me*, I thought; but I chose to hide among the thorns. Would a lion have knowledge of this god of Abram's? I crouched low, and sometimes hid my face in my arms, and sometimes put back my head to look at the stars. Their multitude oppressed me, and their silence filled me with desolation. One, I knew, was the Lady Isis. And in those stars shone also Osiris, and many other gods of Egypt. I remembered, long ago, standing with my mother in the night, and how she'd said to me, 'Bow down to the gods!' But after I'd been sent from my parents' house, and in all the years since, I'd looked up at the stars with cold eyes. What were gods to me, or I to them?

Only that night among the thorns, I looked up and asked, *Why are there gods if they won't help me? One must help me.*

I clutched my belly. At one time, I thought I heard some beast rummaging close to the trees – but it passed.

I talked to the life in me.

'Your father's a fool,' I told it, 'and I don't want you. Why should I care what becomes of you – or of me either? I've no real part in this. And you're no real child of mine.'

Then I talked to myself and asked, *What will you do if you're not found? Do you know where you are? Where to find water?*

'I'm never going back!' I said out loud to the thorn trees. 'I'll walk until I die.'

I set off again in the cool before sunrise; and that day I walked more slowly, but no one found me. I drank in single gulps, the one a long way from the next, and when the sun was high over-head, I rested and thought, *Turn back. Even now, perhaps there's enough water. You could still go back –*

Then I went on.

I drank and walked, and with each step I understood more

clearly that unless within the day I came to a well, we'd lie dead soon – the child and myself. And all the loneliness in my life spoke to me out of the stones and the hot sky and the dust, saying, *'There's only you, Hagar. There was never anyone but you. Who else could have saved your own life or the child's? And – see – you've acted unwisely, and soon you'll know it. No one will care. There's no one to care. Abram can make another son. Aren't there plenty of women to lie with him? But there was only you to protect yourself, and you've failed –'*

Well then, I said in my heart, *so be it. Better to die than to be so alone –*

But my eyes strained, searching ahead for green, for trees – or else for tents, some settlement – *Better to die,* I said, *or let his god bestir himself! His god, who laughs, no doubt, and even now shows Abram some new thought, a better plan, some different woman –*

I ached with walking. It wasn't the distance. What are distances to me? The years since Egypt had been measured in walking. It was the being alone that tired me.

A time came when the water-skin was almost empty. There were two, maybe three more swallows to be had from it, which I didn't dare take – nor could I think beyond them, except to tell myself that an empty skin would seem a useless weight, but I mustn't let the skin fall: if I found water, it would have to be refilled for the journey back – or onwards. If I chose onwards.

And yet the further I walked, the less I believed in directions or arrivals at one place or another. And after a while, I began to speak again to the burden I carried, heavy in my womb. 'Don't reproach me,' I said. 'Why should you, you who know nothing of life? I may have killed you, but what's death to you, or to me?

Peace. Peace. I'll save you if I can –'

I felt sick and faint. And as the day lengthened, a new thought crept into me. *How your pride has tricked you, Hagar! It taught you defiance, but, for the child's sake, you should have been humble with Sarai. It's robbed you of your chance of motherhood.*

I walked faster. The sun's beams were slanting, and it was barren ground, with little protection from whatever might prowl in the night.

'Save me!' I said – to the air, to myself –

And it was then that I saw bushes. A darkness of bushes in the distance.

After that, I had few thoughts. I offered up no thanks. I gave myself no more arguments about living and dying. I hurried, until slowly an image that had lain hidden in my mind ever since I'd left Abram's tents took shape where the bushes were. It was a pile of marker stones. They shone redly in the sunlight. A well. I had come to water

And someone sat there, by the stones.

I felt no fear. When I noticed him, I felt nothing. As I drew closer, he stood up. He was tall and young. His face was beardless. Slowly he came to meet me, and when I saw that, my legs shook, my strength vanished, and I sank down on my knees.

I wasn't afraid. It was because he came to meet me that I fell. It was his seeing me and not turning his head away, indifferent. That broke my loneliness, and my strength. I fell forward out of them, into the dust.

He helped me to stand. He took the water-skin and I leaned on him until we reached the rim of the well, where I sat, and he placed a cup in my hands; and all the time, I was speaking, babbling, but as to whether what I said was nonsense or great sense, I have no recollection.

I only know I spoke Egyptian.

'Rest,' he said, also in Egyptian. 'Rest.'

So then I was silent, and he sat beside me.

His robes smelled of spices. He was very still, but I shook and wept and could barely hold the cup. At last, I thought he must be waiting for me to speak again, so I said, 'I've run away.'

'Tell me,' he said. 'Tell me.'

His voice was quiet and calming. So I began in Egypt, in my

mother's lap, and told him everything.

The sun went down, and stars came out. At some time – but I know nothing of this – he must have gathered wood from the bushes, and he must have got kindling together, and lit it. I remember only the brightness of the fire, the warmth on my face, and his listening. No one had ever listened to me. Not in such a manner. It was a listening that seemed to lull me into a deep restfulness of telling – until I thought I had nothing more to say.

Then we ate. He unwrapped dates and cakes of bread from a cloth, and we shared them, wordlessly, our hands in the firelight, breaking the food. And when that was over, still we didn't speak. Why should we speak? I saw no more need – but he did.

'Hagar,' he said at last, 'listen to me. You must go back. Where else can your son be safe in his childhood? Where else can you go? Don't risk the child's life because you can't stand the pain of an old woman. She won't touch him. In your heart I think you know it.'

He smiled at me across the flames.

And I felt cold. I wanted to cry out. I wanted to fling dust in his face and shout, 'Is it for this I've told you everything? What right have you to instruct me?' But in his eyes shone a message that took my words from me. Respect. I saw respect. He was speaking to a power in me that I longed to deny, and I heard myself saying, 'Perhaps I should do that. Go back. Where else can I go?'

Then I spoke bitterly. 'I've no gods,' I said. 'I've told you that. Which of the gods cares about Hagar? I could stand here and howl to the gods for help, and in a full cycle of the moon, I'd hear back only silence. Whether this is so for most people, what do I care? I know only that it's so for me. But you –' I leaned towards him, and all my need rushed into my speech. 'I trust you. Take me with you!' I said. 'Protect me! Don't you find me beautiful?'

He didn't answer. He only smiled.

'I can please a man!' I said. 'I have talents. Take me with you, wherever you're going!'

He only smiled, and – a strange thing, daughter – I felt

shame. Sitting there beside him, a man almost as young as I, and sensing the warmth of his body, I covered my face with my hands, as if I'd spoken my words to my own father, or my son.

'You're right,' I said. 'I'll go back.'

Then I began to weep again, softly, because the decision was made.

'Be brave,' he told me. 'You must be brave. In that way, you'll teach your son courage. He'll need it. His life will be full of challenges.'

'You speak easily,' I said, 'of difficult things.'

He didn't deny it. He spread his hands in the firelight, and lowered his eyes. Then he said, 'Facing challenges can make a great leader. Such a man knows himself. He lets no one bind him or cross him. Give your son his chance. Think of it, Hagar. If your son becomes such a leader, and thrives, and one day stands at the head of a family – your family – what richness there will be then, if you can only accept this harshness now!'

'I'll go back,' I said.

At that he got to his feet and took up the water-skin I'd brought. 'I'll fill this for you,' he told me. 'Sleep.'

So I lay down at once, and my tears stopped. My eyes closed. For two nights I hadn't slept, and although I heard the dip of the skin into the water, and the sounds of water tumbling in the skin as he laid it by my head, I was too far gone towards sleep to thank him. But I remember his words. He spoke close to my ear. 'Why don't you call your son Ishmael?' he said. 'Because it's not true that you're not heard.'

Then I slept.

When I woke up, I was alone, which was as I'd expected: I didn't know it, but it was. The fire still smouldered. A streak of red shone in the east.

I wasted no time.

I took up the water-skin and started back; and some might say that I arranged matters to give myself courage – but as to that, people must think as they choose. What happened is this: the traveller's eyes moved with me. I found them watching me behind my own eyes; dark and smiling and unlike others, full of respect, urging me, '*Keep walking, Hagar.*' And I obeyed.

Before noon, three men from Abram's tents found me, and we travelled together. They were cold towards me but correct. They hardly spoke to me at first, but I was quiet and gave no trouble, and because of that, or because I told them, 'I was coming back!' after a time they softened, and round the fire on the second night, they even offered advice.

'Control that pride of yours, Hagar! You're a fine woman. Why make poison out of honey?'

And one asked, 'Why did you run away? Had you no thought for the child? You know, Hagar, a son of Abram might have great qualities.'

I looked at him. He was the sternest of the three. He was watching me with suspicion and desire in equal measures. So I spoke firmly to him and said, 'You're right. I carry Abram's son, and he'll be a man of authority, like his father. That's my belief, and that much I can tell you. But as to why I ran away, that's something for Abram to hear, not you.'

Then the man scratched his beard and asked no more questions. But one of the others said, 'Did you truly mean to come back?'

'I was told to,' I answered. Then I laughed. The eyes that still watched behind my own were smiling, so I laughed, and the three men looked puzzled and glanced at each other, but before they could ask me anything else, I lay down with my back to them, and slept.

Abram embraced me tremblingly.

'Child,' he kept saying, 'child –' His eyes were moist. He patted my arms.

When I could slip from his hands, I knelt down and lowered my head. 'Forgive me,' I said.

'You ran away,' he began, 'because you feared for the infant –'

'I was proud,' I told him, 'and your wife, Sarai, both insults and frightens me.'

Then he looked pleased, but also angry.

'Learn to know your place!' he said. 'You've been foolish and disrespectful. You've caused me great distress, and you've disobeyed my god.'

The words hurt. I looked up at him and spoke more boldly. 'As to that,' I said, 'haven't I come back? Ask the men you sent. I came back willingly. I've come for Ishmael's sake, and because I was told to –'

'And out of the duty you owe me!' cried Abram. Then he asked, 'Who told you? Who's Ishmael?'

He waited to be answered. I lowered my eyes again. I had hardly considered what I should say. I hadn't understood that I might prefer silence. Now Abram waited and must be told something. So I spoke towards the dust and described what had happened. I told him how I'd found a traveller sitting by a well, and how we'd talked together. And I told him, 'I see now that there may be greatness in this son of ours after all. The traveller spoke of such things. And he said, "Why don't you call him Ishmael?" So for me it's as if the child's already named. I can think of him only as Ishmael.'

It was a quickly told story but, even so, I had no breath for it. I spoke in gasps with tears, and my words stumbled out of me. I was amazed by this, and when, at the end of what I was saying, Abram stood over me and said nothing, I looked up to see if he understood my emotions better than I did, and saw that he was staring at me.

'The memory's powerful,' I said. 'Forgive me. I was desolate and alone. That traveller spoke to me in Egyptian. He reminded me of who I am. And he listened and understood.'

But Abram pulled me to my feet and hissed, 'Ishmael! That's one word that's not Egyptian! Is it in *your* language that it means *A god hears us* – or is it in mine? Ishmael! Truly a fitting name for our son! And a word to bring you back to your purpose – Don't you understand who was speaking to you?'

His fingers tightened on my arm and the spittle leapt from his teeth as he said this, while, although his eyes stared at my face, they seemed to see something more than me.

'My god has sent you a vision!' he whispered.

I didn't answer. What could I have said? I lowered my head again. Should I have argued, as I wanted to, that it had been a man and no vision who'd sat beside me at the well, who'd filled the water-skin for me, and built the fire that had kept me warm while I'd slept?

I thought it best not to speak. Besides –

There was a besides –

Abram's words reached deeper than thoughts; they reached my feelings, where they were too bold and foreign, and yet they weren't like strangers who'd mistaken their way. They spoke too roughly and in strange accents, but they'd arrived where they'd intended to arrive, and where they'd even been expected.

So I was quiet.

He frowned at me. 'You're very ignorant,' he said. 'You know nothing about the ways of this god. You don't even know how extraordinary it is that you're still alive.'

There, at least, I thought I could speak, and I said, 'It's true. I could have died in the wilderness.'

At that, Abram laughed – a short, irritated sound. 'You'll learn,' he told me, and he went hurrying off to see to other matters.

Sarai was furious. She slapped me. She spoke in something like a snake's rasp. 'So, our Hagar's seen visions –'

I lowered my eyes and forced up the necessary obeisances.

'I was foolish,' I told her. 'Very foolish.'

'Hah!' she cried. 'I'm the greater fool!' And with one hand she made a sign, as if to push away the air in front of her, because I stood in it.

After that, I was careful.

The child was born. They carried him to her – the women took him to Sarai – and I heard her screaming, 'Do I have milk? Do I have anything to do with this – this – ?'

They brought him back and laid him at my side, so then I closed my eyes and let sleep come.

He was strong and quick-witted. From early, I saw that he lacked patience. He snatched from other children what they wouldn't give him willingly. He took the lead in their games and tolerated no interference. And almost as soon as he could speak, he said to me, 'Mother, I'm special.'

'It's true,' I told him. 'But how do you know?'

I was with the other women, preparing the ewes' milk for the evening meal, and the women heard. They pulled faces at each other and stood with their hands on their hips, waiting for Ishmael to speak again; but he only pointed at Abram's tent. Sarai sat there, in the shade of the entrance, and I wanted to ask, 'What has she said to you?' but because the other women were listening, I shrugged. 'Your father's tent,' I said. 'He's a great man.'

Ishmael ran from me then, and found a game to play.

But sometimes when we were alone, I did whisper to him, 'Be careful of Sarai. She's an unhappy old woman. Children annoy her.'

Or I would ask, 'What has Sarai been saying to you?' Because although she often ignored him, sometimes she called him to her and spoke to him, or bent down to him as she passed, and laid her hand on his shoulder, and murmured things. 'What was Sarai saying?' I used to ask.

'She says I've my mother's eyes,' he told me.

'She says I must be careful of snakes. I mustn't prod about in the bushes.'

'She says I shouldn't shout so much.'

'She says I'm wilful.'

'She says I'm my mother's son.'

'She called me her pretty child, and told me to be obedient.'

All these utterances of Sarai's I examined for poison. I squeezed them and wrung out every drop of meaning. I tested them on my tongue.

Once, she slapped him. I ran to them, to draw him away, but she'd already turned and left him standing alone, blinking his tears back.

'Why did she do that?' I asked. 'What did you say to her?'

'Nothing,' said Ishmael. 'She called me to her and slapped me. That's all.'

I was delicate with her. I hated her, but I thought I'd learned from my time in the wilderness how dangerous my anger could be. So I went to her and said, 'Tell me Ishmael's fault, so that I can correct him.'

'The child's too proud,' she answered, and gave me a strange smile. 'Naturally,' she said, 'he has certain weaknesses of character, and my husband's very generous to him.'

I bowed my head and left.

It was true that Abram was kind. He often took Ishmael aside and told him stories of Ur and of his travels – and his dreams. The boy learned early that he'd been born because a god had promised it; and long before I'd have spoken of such things, he came to me and said, 'Tell me about your vision. Father says you had a vision when I was coming.'

I told him the story. He frowned. 'But was it a man?' he asked. 'Or was it a god?'

I spread my hands. 'When you're older,' I told him, 'these things will become clear to you. A small child can't understand everything.'

'You don't know which it was!' he said. 'But I do. It was a god.'

I often thought of that. I was lonely, daughter. Abram was kind to me too – but distant, so distant. He told me his 'necessity' was provided for and, out of respect for Sarai, he no longer entered my body in the fertile time of my month. He questioned me most particularly on this matter, and I didn't dare deceive him. I felt he came and lay with me only to recognise in me the mother of his heir, and if I seemed eager to ensnare him with womanly devices, he might despise me; he might accuse me of betraying the great trust of my vision, as he called it, and he might turn against Ishmael – or take my son from me. Such things were possible; and certainly, if I'd borne another child, Sarai's hatred would have increased – so I barely touched Abram; and although I could feel the strength of his desire as he lay breathing beside me – an old man's furious desire – I no longer tried to please him in that manner. I was matronly. I spoke always of Ishmael – 'our son', always 'our son'.

It was lonely.

And the other women were wary of me. What was I, after all? Free or slave? Only as the years passed and no more children came, they began to understand how I was placed, and gradually they smiled more easily with me, and even included me in their laughter and gossip. But, all the same, I was separate.

I bore the loneliness. Hadn't he said, '*Be brave!*' – the traveller by the well?

Almost every day I thought of him. I drew strength from him – his deep, complete listening, his eyes that still sometimes smiled at me behind my own; and slowly, over the years, I took to asking the shimmer of heat on the horizon, or the darkness in the well, down where the water lay, *Is it possible that Abram's right? That I saw a god and lived to tell about it? Could it be true?*

A time came when no one in me answered that it couldn't be. Instead, my questions found themselves confronted by another question: '*Who are you to say what's possible or impossible?*'

And Abram loved Ishmael. I knew that. His tired face softened when he saw the boy; and the boy, seeing this love in his father – how could he not love him back? Even when Abram was stern, as he often was, Ishmael loved him, and I told myself –

I told myself –

Peace! I said in my heart. *Endure Sarai and her bitterness. The victory is yours.*

But then –

When many years had passed, and Ishmael's head had almost reached my shoulder, and although his voice was still a child's it was beginning to deepen, and after journeys and settlings and more journeys, and after insults from Sarai too numerous to be counted, and all her airs, and demanding I call her by a new name, a royal name, Sarah – so that I truly wondered if I dealt with a madwoman – and Abram, too, becoming stranger, and wanting everyone to address him differently, so that often I heard murmurings that perhaps his age was weakening his wits, and were there no others to lead us? After so much difficulty, daughter, through all of which I guided and protected Ishmael like a hen with her chick, after all that –

Sarai conceived.

The ancient one conceived.

Somehow, I had known she would.

Three strangers came to our tents – three among countless strangers, but these were also among the privileged who were greeted with particular zeal by Abram, and entertained lavishly.

This happened sometimes. With his own people, Abram was strict. Even our feasts, if he and the elders decided we should have one, were simple and sparing. And to friendly neighbours who visited us, Abram was hospitable, but only within the bounds of correctness. Yet there were times when strangers came – unknown strangers – and the fattest sheep was slaughtered, and only the finest bread could be set before them.

It wasn't pride. I think now that Abram listened to strangers in a deeper way than others did. I think he believed that some of them were messengers from his god – only perhaps he didn't always know which strangers were messengers, so that to many he simply gave too much. You laugh at such an idea, daughter, and pull a face, but I think this understanding grew in several of us who were with him, because of the three who came in that year. Afterwards, they kept company in my mind, those three guests, with the traveller who'd spoken to me at the well, man or god; and often, when I thought of how Abram had received them, and set before them every delicacy, offering the food with his own hands, I thought also of how he'd immediately decided that the traveller I'd met was no ordinary mortal.

But those three who came, I hardly saw.

They sat with Abram by his tent, and slept one night with us, preferring the open with the stars over them to the honoured place in his tent that Abram offered. And the next day they left. Abram went with them a short distance – which wasn't his custom. He sometimes sent younger men as guides for part of the way, but this time he went himself, so that people said, 'They've told him something important. They must have brought important news.'

No one had heard of any.

One of those travellers had green eyes. Many had seen them, and so it was said, 'Those men have come from a country unlike any known to us. Perhaps a land of sorcery.' And it was also said, 'Abram's not like other men, after all. He walks at the rim of things, where there are greater mysteries than green eyes.'

I wished I'd seen those eyes. I wished I'd helped to serve the food, as was fitting. It was my place to do it, but I was sick. I sat that day in the shade of the bushes, and when Sarai came to me and said, 'Can't you see that we have guests? Get up and help with the preparations!' I groaned and clutched my belly. My head ached. My insides cramped. I sweated. She squatted beside me, and pressed her hand against my cheek.

'So,' she said, 'do you mean to give us a brother for Ishmael?'

I told her it wasn't that kind of sickness, and she narrowed her eyes. But then she shrugged.

'Rest,' she said. 'Keep in the shade, and perhaps tomorrow you'll be well.'

Then she hurried from me, and although it would have been wise to have spent the day in the tent, I preferred to stay where I was in the clean air, retching and shivering, until two of the women came with a brew of herbs, and when I'd drunk that, they led me to the shade of their own tent.

The herbs soothed me.

'Sarai told us what to make for you,' they said.

I closed my eyes when I heard it, and waited for death. But only sleep came, and when I woke up, I felt stronger. My belly was calm. My head ached less. I left the tent to feel the afternoon coolness, and sat looking across to Abram's tent where I could see him with the strangers, and the women there, setting down the platters of food; and standing in front of Abram was Ishmael – but it was only for a moment: then he was sent away. It was often like that. Abram would call Ishmael to him, turn to his guests and say, 'This is my son.' Then Ishmael would be told to go. My eyes closed. I was drowsy and I slept again. During the evening, someone helped me back into the tent I lay outside, and when I next woke up, the sky was bright with day, the strangers were leaving, and Abram with them.

It seemed so little.

My sickness had gone. Three strangers, one with green eyes,

had left us. People talked, as I've said, and Sarai was in a fierce, sudden mood, sometimes shouting with laughter at nothings, sometimes muttering to herself about patience, and how much nonsense she had to endure. She was brisk with me.

'So,' she said, 'you still live.'

'Your herbs cured me,' I told her.

'That, at least, is true,' she said, and laughed, although I saw no reason for it.

Part of what the strangers had said, we soon learned. Abram hurried us away from that place, because, so the whispers ran, something was about to happen there, or near there – on the plain. So again, a journey –

And not long afterwards, a day came when, in the early morning, the earth shook; the sky behind us, over the plain, bled into purples and scarlets; we heard the world groan, a horrifying sound, and a stinging wind sprang up, so that each of us huddled in our coat, and I think most jabbered to their gods. I held Ishmael close to me. Some of the tents blew away, like rags; but in Abram's tent, we were safe. Sarai crouched near me with her eyes closed, her lips tight. Abram lay prostrate, his hands stretched out in supplication. Ishmael breathed against my neck.

'What is this?' he whispered. 'This isn't like most storms –'

'Be quiet!' I said.

A bitter smell swept in with the wind. I held him tightly, and my thoughts fled for comfort to the stranger by the well, who smiled at me. '*Be brave,*' he said again, just as he'd said before Ishmael was born, '*so that you teach your son courage!*'

The kingdoms on the plain were destroyed. What to us, at our distance, had been a wind, for them had been a fury and a torrent of flame in which thousands perished. News soon came to us from those who'd fled; and many among us, who'd said over the years, 'Abram's god may be powerful, and Abram's a good man, but I pray also to this god or that god, because it's one god, at least, that I know is great,' now said: 'We were fools to doubt Abram. Who else would have saved us? And what other god would have sent messengers to warn us?' – meaning those three strangers.

So Abram gained respect. How could he not? And we sacrificed two bullocks – but with trembling and no rejoicing at our own escape. We knew too many people on the plain – relatives and traders. It filled us with horror to think of them. For months, we lived and worked in shadow, although the sun stood high over us.

Sarai was deeply affected. Her sharp tongue rested. She took little notice of me. She took scant interest in anything. Once, when some of the women asked her to decide the outcome of a quarrel between them, and both sides swore the other had wilfully overlooked certain facts, I heard her say, with wide eyes, mockingly, 'You come to me? I'm old. What do I know? Your heads are younger than mine. Reach your own understanding!' – which was not like Sarai, wife of Abram. It startled us all.

Then there were other changes. An unlooked-for gentleness entered her features. The lines of her face seemed to become less severe, so that there were times when, glancing at her in the half-light of the tent, I saw in a new way, more closely, that once she'd been beautiful. Also her body thickened. Sometimes, when a breeze blew against her clothing, I saw that; and the other women saw it.

I heard one say, 'There's a swelling in Sarai. Maybe she'll die soon. My aunt's stomach swelled like that. She died in great pain.'

But another answered, 'She doesn't look like a woman in pain. She looks pregnant.'

'It's not possible!' said the first.

Still, rumours started. Sarai, it was said, had been given a potion by some travelling sorcerer – perhaps the green-eyed stranger –

78

Yet even so – even with the strongest magic – could her years be cheated? And had anyone seen her retching in the morning, or heard a word from her or Abram about her condition? These things hadn't happened, and so, surely, the women told themselves, surely we misread the signs.

Nevertheless, one night, as Abram lay by me, which sometimes he still did, gravely and with many prayers, I said to him, 'Tell me. I know it's impossible, but if your wife, Sarai, conceived and gave you a child, would you still love Ishmael? You've called him your heir –'

Abram sighed. 'Woman,' he said, 'I've come here to sleep, not to indulge in speculations.' His back was to me, and he shifted his weight and wrapped his coat more tightly around him. He grunted and lay still. Then he said, 'Besides – have I no honour?'

So I didn't provoke him with further questions.

But I found in those days that my mind often formed the image of those three strangers sitting in front of Abram's tent, and the old man with them, and Ishmael being called to them and standing there, then being sent away; and when people whispered of green-eyed strangers and sorcery and potions, I took to laughing at them and telling them, 'That's not the way of gods. At least not of Abram's god – the one I met in the wilderness.'

At this, people stared and some, although they'd heard the story of my vision – or something of it: Ishmael's childish prattlings – whether or not they believed it, asked me, 'What do you mean? What do you know about those strangers and Abram's god?'

'More than you!' I told them. 'And I know what I've been promised!' But my heart shrank as I spoke, and all the time it was hardening, as if the fluids of life were draining out of it.

Then I complained to my traveller in the wilderness, so smiling as he'd persuaded me to come back to Abram. I summoned him behind my eyes and told him, *You tricked me! You and those other*

three you sent to Abram. You're tormentors. You've rejected Ishmael.
She's pregnant and you laugh at me.

And I began to hate Abram's god.

Then at last Sarai spoke. She told us.

It was one morning. There were several of us women at the well, and as she walked past, we stared – how could we fail to? – and she turned and smiled.

'It's true,' she said, placing her hands on her belly. Her voice rang at us. In that moment, she was indeed Sarah, Royal One. Her eyes sparkled. She lifted her head high. 'It's true.'

No one said anything.

'It was promised,' she told us. 'Always promised – didn't you know that? It's no secret. And you all saw the messengers who came to announce it. There were three of them. Some months ago.'

At last, one of the older women spoke up and said, 'We're happy for you, Sarah.'

And another, twisting her voice a little, added, 'There's nothing beyond the power of a god.'

Sarai laughed. 'Disbeliever!' she said, and walked on proudly – but not before her eyes had met mine and sent them a long, complicated message that in the end needed only one understanding: she claimed victory.

I told Ishmael that evening.

'Your father loves you,' I promised him. 'You'll not be pushed aside.'

He shrugged, and looked uninterested. 'He has many children,' he said.

'You know very well that this is different,' I said.

Again he shrugged. 'I'm special,' he said. 'A god sent me.'

I spread out my hands, as if to say that I knew nothing of such things – but how could he understand? Hadn't I always said that the story was true? Hadn't I come to think of the truth almost as

Ishmael did? He watched me, and I saw that he was angry.

'You're just a woman!' he shouted, and ran away.

I also tried once more to speak to Abram – a bitter moment.

'You must leave these matters to the god who leads us,' he said. 'You're very ignorant, and sometimes a very presumptuous woman!'

'But,' I said, 'everything that was promised for Ishmael –'

'My god keeps his promises!' The old man's face reddened. His voice shook. 'Do you question my god? Must you poison my joy?'

I lowered my eyes. We were standing near the cooking pots – out in the open, where everyone could see us. I had run and caught his arm as he passed: it seemed to me that he'd been avoiding me.

'I'm a mother,' I said. 'I must protect my son.'

'He's my son, too,' said Abram, and shoved me – he shoved me, an old man's irritation – so that I stepped aside and he could go on his way.

My nights stayed unvisited after that.

The baby came – a strong, round-faced boy. I helped deliver it – or at least I was there, with those who truly helped. Sarai pushed him out swiftly, and with a grimace, her teeth clenched. I thought her barely human. I had never seen such a birth, and in one so old we had expected long labour and a deal of shrieking and moaning –

Abram received his new son with tears and blessings and little broken smiles that reminded one of his own great age, he seemed so childlike. The elders were full of sober rejoicings. We were all told to rejoice.

I walked out a short way from the tents and stood with my face towards the sky, and spoke my thoughts. 'God of Abram,' I said, 'what have you done to me? I see now that in your eyes I'm nothing but a slave! All you have for me is contempt. Then know this. If I can find a way, I'll kill Sarai's son. If you've truly abandoned Ishmael.'

That's what I said. Then I went back to the women, who told me, 'Go to Abram. He's been asking for you.'

Abram was sitting beneath a tree that grew in that place, and he greeted me very lovingly. He told me to sit by him. He was most informal. He patted my knee. 'Be pleased,' he said, 'and don't be bewildered. You'll see, Hagar. If only we believe everything that's been promised, we can live in peace, and Ishmael and this new son of mine – I shall call him Isaac – will be able to love each other, as my sons should.'

I watched the dust between my feet. I kept silent.

'Trust,' he said. 'You must trust.'

He was very gentle and smiling. Strangely, I felt he knew what I'd been saying to his god, and I tried to conceal my feelings. 'You and Sarah,' I said, 'have waited a long time for this.'

Again he patted my knee.

'Be patient,' he told me. 'You'll see. All will be well.'

It was as if his god had answered my rantings – so I put aside my thoughts of killing Isaac.

And Ishmael –

I had it in mind to tell him: 'Be kind to the little one. It would be best for you if you can make him love you!'

But Ishmael didn't need my words. He found his own way with Isaac. Or perhaps, unknown to me, Abram spoke to him. However that was, he seemed to accept his brother. He carved beads and threaded them on wool and dangled them in front of him. He bound together sticks, making small figures of sheep and dogs for him; and he liked to work tricks with a piece of leather binding in his fingers, making webs and knots that Isaac was too young to understand, but liked to see and touch.

And all this Sarai watched suspiciously. She hated to see Ishmael laughing at the innocent ways of her son.

'Don't tire him!' she'd say. Or, 'Why do you laugh at him? Do you think you knew more at his age?'

Ishmael said little back. He was careful. He was always careful with Sarai. But one day he told me, 'She says she knows what I think.'

'Who?' I asked. 'Who can know your thoughts?'

Ishmael made a grim face. 'She says she knows me and is watching me.'

'Listen,' I told him, 'what's any of that to you? What does your father say?'

'He says he likes to see me amusing my brother.'

'So,' I said. 'Enough. What else matters?'

But in time I was answered.

She mattered. Sarai.

Two years passed. And I'll not lie to you, daughter, I didn't quicken into smiles and little cries of joy when Isaac took his first steps, or when he formed his first words, or did some small mischief that set the other women laughing. I didn't sigh at the beauty of his eyes and his thick curls, or pick him up and speak loving nonsenses to him. I watched him coldly; and I felt the coldness heavy inside me, so that sometimes, bowing my head, I'd appeal to Abram's god of promises, *Strengthen me! Help me to believe in equal blessings for this child and my own!*

But when I looked up again, there would be Sarai, her eyes fixed on me, as if I carried a spear, its tip aimed at Isaac's breast – or as if a spear in her own hand pointed straight at my heart.

Then the time came for Isaac's weaning feast –

And this part of the story you've heard many times, daughter: how we left Abram, how Ishmael and I were finally driven out. Your husband, driven out. From this springs your anger. This is the part that everyone seems to know, although for years I've hardly spoken of it, and as for Ishmael – but you see how it is with Ishmael. He has a complicated understanding. He loved his father. When he speaks of the past, he does so reluctantly, and now, as soon as he's heard of the old man's death, he's gone to grieve for him –

To your great outrage.

Listen to me, daughter. You think you know the story, but can all truths be held in 'this was done' and 'that was done'? When you hold sand in a bowl, heavy and still, and only so much of it – do you imagine you know everything about sand? Sand shifts. It has depths. It ripples in patterns. It swirls up in storms, forming clouds and moving walls. It belongs to more sand. And are our lives so much simpler that you can hold them in a bowl of 'this was done' and 'that was done'?

It's true. We were driven out. That day – the day of the weaning feast – perhaps because he needed to reassure himself, Ishmael took Isaac and carried him a short distance from the general rejoicing. Sarai seemed not to notice. She was queenly. She was receiving many compliments. She glowed like the evening sun, full of completion and glory. Everyone was happy. I don't include myself, but it was usual for me in those days to think of 'everyone' as if I didn't exist. There were guests and music and laughter. Abram allowed us fresh meat and fruit and other delicacies.

The day was cooling.

And Ishmael took out a knife that Abram had given him – a short bone hunting knife. He was proud of it. He wore it always in a belt he'd made for it – and he was showing it to the child.

'Look what our father's given me!' he said – he told me afterwards – 'This is because I'm nearly a man. Just see how sharp it is!' And he drove it into the ground. The child crawled to it, and tried to pluck it out. Ishmael laughed. 'It's not for you!' he said. 'You're just beginning. I'm old enough now to help our father, but you –'

And here the screaming started.

It was Sarai.

She ran. In my mind, her robe spreads: she's like a dark bird, an eagle swooping, or a great raven – and it wasn't her screaming, it was how she ran that was terrible, a murderous running, talons ready, so that after a moment of standing rock-still in bewilderment, people ran after her: not only women ran but several of the men, who outstripped us women and reached her just as she meant to fall on Ishmael and tear him to pieces. It took three of them to hold her.

Ishmael had leapt to his feet. He had stayed where he was at first, kneeling in the dust, watching her, but then he'd leapt up. He swayed in front of her, pale and gaping.

Isaac wailed.

Abram came hurrying slowly, leaning on the son of one of the elders, as if his strength had given out.

And all the time, struggling to escape those who held her, Sarai screamed madnesses, unsayable things – until, seeing Abram, she shrieked at him, 'Get rid of this slave-child! Him and his mother! Or will you wait until they slaughter Isaac? Honour me as you should!'

Abram gazed at her.

I stood nearby. I had run with the other women. 'Ishmael –' I said, but he didn't dare move.

'Get rid of them!' shrieked Sarai again, and Abram said softly, 'My wife,' he said, 'my wife –'

'Will you wait until he's dead?' cried Sarai, but this time less shrilly, as if she meant to reason with him, so that the men who held her loosened their grip. Then, in one pounce, she was free, and the life in me almost stopped – but she didn't fall on Ishmael. She snatched up Isaac. She snatched up her howling son, and ran with him to the tent.

There was silence.

Then I moved swiftly to Ishmael, and Abram said steadily, 'We have guests among us,' and turned away; and the feasting and music went on, as if nothing had happened. People even spoke of other things and laughed. It was their duty, so that Abram wouldn't be humiliated.

I sat awake that night, with Ishmael. He wouldn't leave me and go to sleep. He sat out in the night by one of the fires. Several of the guests lay round the fire, sleeping, so we spoke in whispers. No one took any notice of us.

'She hates me,' he said. 'I didn't know. I thought it was a kind of game.'

'The old are sometimes not to be trusted,' I told him. 'Their thoughts run this-way-that-way, like the wind.'

'She wanted to kill me,' he said. 'I saw it in her eyes!'

'You're strong!' I told him. 'Almost a man. And your father loves you.'

'That's true, isn't it?' Ishmael watched me as he spoke. 'He loves me.'

'He does,' I said. 'Sleep. Sleeping heals wounds. I won't leave you.'

In the end he did sleep, curled at my feet, with my hand on his back, so that he could feel that I was there – while I waited.

The night was half over when Abram found me. He could see that I wouldn't leave Ishmael, so he sat down where I was.

'Don't wake him,' I said.

The fire had almost fallen into ash, and I thought, *If he's cold, Ishmael will wake soon.*

'Speak quickly,' I said.

But Abram sat speechlessly beside me. It was as if he wanted me to tell him what he'd come to say. He smelled of sweat and oil and tiredness – as he always did, but it seemed different that night, as if he'd soured.

So I said, 'Something must be done – and be seen by everyone to be done. Tell Sarah to embrace Ishmael and speak lovingly to him. And she must make her peace with me. You owe us this.'

But my anger annoyed him. Abram clicked his tongue, and

then at last he spoke. '*Must*,' he said. '*Must* . . . Who are you to say *must*?'

Then suddenly his voice changed. 'Hagar,' he said, 'I have to send you away. You and the boy. For everyone's safety. I'll send two men to protect you, and I must think carefully where you should go –' And his voice went on, naming this place and that place, and on the other hand another place – but I wasn't listening.

I heard only her victory.

I heard only that we were cast out.

I heard only that Ishmael had lost his birthright, and that Abram's god had protected Isaac from my instinct to kill him until I could be the more thoroughly crushed.

I heard only that old men are weak, and don't keep their promises.

Abram was still speaking. I ignored him. I reached down and gripped Ishmael's shoulder, and shook him.

'Son,' I said, 'wake up! You and I have a journey ahead of us!'

'Hagar!' protested Abram.

I didn't listen. I got to my feet. Ishmael had woken, and he lay blinking first at me, then at his father.

'It's nothing!' Abram told him. 'Your mother's upset –'

'Stand up!' I said. 'Your father's sending us away. We'll go at once. I told you he loved you, but I was wrong. He's rejecting you – so you must come with me!'

'Peace!' said Abram. 'Peace!'

But Ishmael looked at him and asked, 'Is it true? Are you sending me away?'

Abram sighed. 'Soon,' he said. 'It's necessary. Tomorrow, perhaps, or the next day. To a safe place –'

I laughed, and Ishmael stared at me. 'Today, tomorrow – don't you see?' I said. 'We're not wanted here. Get up!'

Then slowly Ishmael did rise; and something playful and laughing that had always been his folded itself from him, deep inside himself, where he encased it. I saw it happen.

'Ishmael –' said Abram, scrambling up, but the effort of rising so fast silenced him, he was breathless; and before he could speak again, Ishmael said, 'We'll go at once. Why shouldn't we? You've chosen.'

Abram hesitated. He stood bowed and unsteady, and as he wavered, standing there facing us, I almost pitied him. It was dark, quite dark, but I could sense his tears, and I loathed him for them.

Then at last he said, 'It may be best, after all. Quietly and quickly. But someone must go with you. I must choose two men –'

'What do we want with your men?' I said. 'You've betrayed us. You speak dishonestly about your safe places. You're separating yourself from us. You've broken all your promises. I spit on your men.'

He seemed to stagger. 'No promises are broken –' he began.

'Ishmael,' I said, 'fetch two water-skins and fill them. Speak to no one. We're leaving.'

But Ishmael didn't move. He stood watching us – until Abram suddenly turned to him and said, 'Come, I'll help you,' and the two of them went together towards the well, Abram resting a hand on Ishmael's shoulder, and as they walked, he leaned on him, and said something –

Lies, I thought. *Pretty lies.*

The last trust in me seemed to shrivel as I watched. Then I followed them.

It was Abram who drew up the water. He laid a full skin at my feet. He seemed vigorous now that the decision had been made, and calmer since he'd spoken to Ishmael out of my hearing.

'Wait here,' he said, 'while I decide who should accompany you, and give them instructions. Draw more water, Ishmael. Then we must think of provisions –'

He went hurrying away while Ishmael busied himself. Ishmael did what he was told. But, as for me –

I seized the full water-skin that lay at my feet and flung it on my back, and began to walk. Ishmael called after me, but I didn't stop. I walked away into the darkness.

Choose! I was telling him. *Choose! Have you my blood in your veins, or not?*

He called to me again, but I didn't turn my head, and soon I heard him running behind me.

He brought no water with him.

So we left. We went swiftly – but not silently. Ishmael sobbed. I told him he whimpered like an infant, and that it disgusted me. 'I was many years younger than you,' I said, 'when my parents betrayed me, but no one saw me leave my home blubbing like you!'

After that, he was quiet. We walked fast – I saw to it that we walked fast – and without words. There were the sounds of our feet in the dust, and our breath, nothing else. Once, when dawn came, I thought I heard our names being called, far behind us. I wasn't sure, but I didn't want Ishmael to hear, so I walked even faster and began to talk to him. 'Are you afraid?' I asked. 'There may be lions, and other fierce creatures.'

'I have my knife,' he said. 'I came because you haven't one.'

We hurried. I wouldn't let him slow our pace. Already in those days, he was almost as strong as I; perhaps he could have stopped me, but he was dazed by what was happening, and whenever he slowed my fingers tightened on his arm and pinched him, and pulled him forward.

'You don't want anyone to find us,' he said.

I didn't answer.

At last he asked, 'Where are we going?' – which angered me.

'Do you think I've learned nothing?' I said. 'I'm no longer the young fool who ran away and had no knowledge of the country. There's a well just a day in a straight line from here. On a good trading route. For a long time, I've made it my business to know these things.'

'It's dry,' said Ishmael. 'I know the country better than you.'

'That's so,' I told him. 'You do. But I'm older than you, and wiser. That's why I've brought a water-skin with me, and you haven't.'

But in truth, I didn't know that the well was dry. And I had brought no food. And we had only the one water-skin. And after a long silence, when the sun blazed down on us, and we sheltered to drink beneath the bones of a tree, I said to him, 'How do you know that the well's dry? And which way would you have us take?'

He shrugged.

'Don't you want to live?' I asked him.

'We could go back,' he said. 'You shouldn't have run away like a slave. We could have left with gifts and camels. I'm Abram's son.'

So then I asked, 'What did he say to you? Last night, when he spoke to you, what was he trying to stuff into that head of yours?'

Ishmael wouldn't speak.

'I need to know,' I told him. 'Can't you see that?'

So then, slowly, he said, 'I'm his son. He told me to remember that. And one day I'll be a leader of men. It's been promised. He said that I must always trust the promise. And that he loves me.'

'Loves you – and flicks you off his skin like a tick!' I cried. And at that moment, my eyes suffered a strange blinding, as if dazzled by the sun; but it wasn't the sun: it was the past, my own childhood. I saw nothing. I only heard my father tell me long before, *'You'll no longer live in this house. Trust me. It's for the best. I've a debt to pay, and you're the payment. I'm giving you away. You must accept that, and know your place.'* I groaned and felt weak. I hid my face in my knees and rocked where I sat.

Ishmael watched – I felt it – but he didn't touch me. At last he said, 'If we go against the sun, we'll come to people who can help us –'

'Abram's friends. I'll not go grovelling to them!' I said. 'Think of somewhere else!'

'Where do you want to go?' he asked. 'Egypt?'

There was fear in his voice, and so I raised my head. I wanted him to see strength in me. I wanted him to feel safe. And at the word *Egypt*, strength was possible.

'Where else but to the Two Lands?' I said, smiling. 'You and I – we're Egyptian.'

He didn't smile back. He looked as if he'd gathered together all that he was and all that he thought he could be, and was listening to it very carefully, so that it could teach him how to behave.

'I think I can find the way to Egypt,' he said. 'And the safest wells. I've listened to more travellers than you have, because I'm a man –'

My child, Ishmael.

If I go back, I thought, *he'll be safe. Abram will save him.*

But – to see the triumph in Sarai's eyes, to hear excuses and double-talk from Abram, to have everyone falsely embracing us and sending us off at last on our journey with smiles and tears and words behind their hands: 'What else could be done? Hagar's nothing, after all, and Ishmael's little better than a slave himself –'

So much pain. How could it be borne?

I touched Ishmael's cheek.

'Egypt,' I said. 'Set us on our way. If you can, avoid those wells that belong to friends of your father's. Bring us onto a trade route. There, we'll soon meet other travellers.'

He got quickly to his feet.

'When we're safe,' he said, 'will you let my father know?'

I laughed as I stood up. 'You drive a hard bargain,' I told him.

At first, he succeeded. We reached a good well at dawn the next day, and he refilled the water-skin swiftly and joyously, but glancing round all the while, this way and that – as I did. No one saw us. No one came raging out of the bushes to call us thieves. And we hurried on.

That day, he showed me his skill with a sling. He killed a hare, and we made a fire and ate it half raw, we were so famished; and as I ate, I said to the emptiness of the sky, *What do I care for treacherous gods? Look! We've provided for ourselves!*

In the night, I slept soundly, while Ishmael watched. 'Tomorrow, you can watch,' he said. 'I'm not tired.'

I closed my eyes to show I trusted him – a poor mistake: he didn't wake me till dawn.

We found no water that day, and no food. And that night, as we sat by the fire he'd made, I said, 'This next well, which you say we'll reach tomorrow – perhaps we'll find other travellers there. Friendly people. If we do, there may be someone we can go with to Egypt. Or at least they may give us food, and we must beg for a second water-skin.'

He was silent.

'Are you sure,' I said, 'you know where to find this next well?'

'I'm sure,' he said, staring at the flames.

'Go to sleep,' I told him.

He seemed to obey me. He lay down and curled with his back to me, his arm under his head, but he didn't sleep until a short time before dawn. I knew it from the tension in his shoulders, and I said to myself, *Until we find fresh water, I'll take no more than one sip at dawn tomorrow, and one at noon, when the sun's at its height, and, if we find nothing, one at dusk –*

But he did know where the next well was. We reached it in the afternoon. Ishmael ran to it, laughing. He did this, although a tent stood by it, and several men watched us approach. I ran because Ishmael ran, in case they seized hold of him; but they only stood, grim-faced, watching, while he let down the water-skin, and they said nothing.

I spoke as soon as my breath came.

'Good friends,' I said, 'we thank you for allowing us to drink –'

Still they said nothing, not even when Ishmael put the skin to his lips and let the water flow into his mouth, not even when he spat it out, retching and gasping, not even then did they speak. They turned away.

'What is it?' I cried.

Ishmael flung down the skin.

'Who did this?' I cried. 'Was it you?' I ran at the men. 'Did you foul this water?' I wanted to kill them. I wanted to throw myself at one of them, and dig my nails into his throat. Already I saw my child dead, Ishmael dead and nameless in the dust.

One of the men grabbed my wrist. 'Woman,' he said, 'take care with your accusations.'

And another said, 'Our enemies have done this.'

I gaped at them. Their faces were hard. I didn't believe them. And besides, what was this fineness about their honesty or dishonesty? To me it was all the same. They were murderers.

I fell on my knees.

'Give my son water,' I said. 'Share what you have with us. Pour some into our water-skin, and I give you a mother's sacred word, only the child shall drink it –'

Again, they turned from me. 'Stop ranting!' they said. 'We've barely enough for ourselves!'

I stayed where I was, on my knees.

'Mother –' whispered Ishmael.

Then one of the men said, 'Leave the boy with us. We may have just enough to save the boy –'

But I saw into his eyes. I saw the evil light dancing there, and at the same time I heard Ishmael say again, 'Mother –'

I sprang up, and we ran. We ran like dogs, panting and scrambling –

They let us go. We ran whichever way opened up before us, and they didn't follow, but still we ran, until our breath had turned into knives in our chests and a darkness thundered in our heads. Then we flung ourselves down behind a rock and clung to each other.

When I could speak, I said, 'Don't be afraid. We're strong. We'll rest a while, and then we'll walk to the next well.'

'They may also go there,' said Ishmael.

'We'll be cunning. We'll creep past them in the night,' I said, 'and we'll use your knife if we must.'

He didn't answer. I stroked his hair. At last I asked, 'Can it be done? Can we reach the next well tomorrow?'

'I think so,' said Ishmael. 'I'm not certain.'

After that, we were silent. We no longer had a water-skin. We had fled without it.

We rested until the first star pricked through the blue above us. Then I pushed Ishmael from me and got to my feet. He stood up at once.

'We must go this way,' he said, pointing.

We walked all night.

And through the morning, with the sun pouring a kind of molten sand down on us. We chewed bark from dead trees, and sucked pebbles; and, taking Ishmael's knife, I cut myself across my arm and let the blood ooze, and we licked that. Also I cupped my hand when Ishmael passed a thin dark thread, scarcely to be seen, of his own water, and I caught it, and made him drink.

Peace, I said to whatever heard, if I was heard, deep within me. *Peace, all you gods, especially you, old man's god, Abram's god. Peace. Do with me as you will. Only let him live!*

And I told Ishmael, speaking in good time – what purpose would it serve to wait until my mouth was too dry for words – 'If we don't find the well,' I told him, 'and I fall down, as if in a sleep, you must cut out my heart and eat it. That will give you strength. And you must drink my blood. It will be a holy thing to do, and your mother's wish. You mustn't fail me.'

'We'll find the well,' he said. He wouldn't look at me.

'Give me your word!' I said. 'Or must I be ashamed of you?'

'You've always been ashamed of me,' he answered. 'You've never believed what was promised.'

He could hardly speak. I dared not argue with him, use up his strength –

And besides, I was dazed, so dazed. More than the sun and my great thirst, his words drained life out of me, so that it seemed a hopeless task suddenly, a greater and far more difficult task even than living, to tell him what I felt. Any part of what I felt –

I said nothing more, and as we walked, I began to long for the traveller who'd once lifted me from the dust and listened, and said, '*Be brave.*' I wanted to stare into his face and find there that I was wrong, that he was not, in the end, a tormentor, that I'd only misunderstood – but although I called to him, his face wouldn't come to me. Instead, a shadow formed, something featureless and predatory. I pushed it away, but it came back. It kept with me, step for step, although it was nothing, and I chose to ignore it.

And still we walked, Ishmael and I, creatures in a dream. Often my eyes closed, but very quickly I opened them again to be sure that Ishmael hadn't strayed from me or I from him, and that we walked, while my thoughts became faint and stretched, like traces of cloud.

Often he swayed. And there came a time at last when his knees buckled. I pulled him up. I slung his arm across my shoulder. I saw now that his eyes had closed, but still we walked, until his weight had so bowed me down that, in truth, we were crawling.

I laid him beneath a bush. It was naked and spiked with thorns.

He'll be cool here, I thought, *and he'll sleep sweetly. That will refresh him. He'll wake up smiling.*

I uncovered my head, and hooked the cloth among the branches to shield him –

From birds, from all things –

And somewhere – not far, but not there, where he was – I rested, my back turned, so that I couldn't see him. *Let me not see him!* I told myself. *Let me not hear him!*

I thought I did hear him – faint sounds, like a bird's – but, 'Let me not hear him!' I said, and a tearless weeping started in me, so that I shuddered and moaned.

'Let me not see!' I said. 'Let me not hear –'

Then I groped about in myself for one last barb of bitterness, one last anger to fling against the gods – all gods, and first among them, Abram's god, with his promises –

But found nothing.

Nothing.

I've killed my child, I thought. *Once before, when I was young, I tried to kill him, when he was forming in my womb. I was rescued. But I didn't learn. This time, it's done.*

Then I was still.

It was as if I'd stepped forward through the shadow – that faceless, ignored one that had been keeping pace with me, waiting to confront me –

I've killed my child, I thought.

And I was still.

My moans stopped.

Have you ever known such stillness, daughter? But I can see that you haven't. It's hard to find, although it's everywhere. It's in all that there is.

It's all there is.

That stillness held me at its centre. Most tenderly I was held, like a child in her parent's lap, where I was hardly I, Hagar was hardly Hagar, and I *saw*, as if I'd come into my sight from a lifetime's blindness: I saw each shading in the sky, although it throbbed cloudlessly blue; I saw every speck of dust on the stones and drifting in the sunlight, and each crack in every stone; they were all distinct, alive, and restful. And, in great calm, I saw the well.

It was there in front of me, at no more than a bowshot's distance. It was clearly marked, and someone had left a water-skin leaning up against the marker stones. And all this was so, and caused me neither joy nor surprise, since none of it could have been otherwise.

So then I got to my feet and went back to Ishmael. I lifted him in my arms and carried him. It wasn't, as you might think, a question of finding some final strength. I weighed nothing. Ishmael weighed nothing; and I carried him to the well and rested him against the marker stones. I let down the water-skin and filled it. I poured water between his lips and over his cheeks, and his eyes opened, and we both drank. After that, I sat down and held his head on my lap, and we slept.

It was there that the travellers found us – good people, who gave us food and were kind to us, the women holding my hands and saying, 'What will there be for you in Egypt? Stay with us. Let us speak to our menfolk for you. You're still young, and very strong. Come with us and live in Paran. Our people will protect you.'

I obeyed, because it seemed more than an offered kindness. I was being told what to do. And Ishmael, when I smiled at him and asked, 'Will it grieve you, if we don't go at once to the cities of Egypt?' – Ishmael answered, 'It doesn't matter where we go.'

He found it enough that we lived. It was a great wonder to him. He sat alone, watching the children, the dogs, the women preparing food. He watched as if his first breath had just been taken, and everything was new, and part of him still understood nothing but the womb.

So we went with the travellers, and lived in Paran.

Most of the rest you know, daughter. In Paran, Ishmael grew tall and strong; and when people said to him, 'Your father cast you out!' he held his head high. 'You have no understanding!' he told them. And when they laughed and said, 'Your father chose another son. The old man rejected you!' if they were boys like himself, he fought them to the ground, and if they were older voices, he stared until they fell silent because of the pride in him, so that often in those early years people said to me, 'He has your strength, and a leader's authority.'

I said little back. I seldom spoke of Abram, but the women I'd confided in at the start told others, who told others, until our story had spread through countless villages and settlements. And people marvelled at Ishmael. There was a seriousness in him where other boys were frivolous, while often he shrugged off matters that were generally considered important. He puzzled many. But, as he grew, he gained respect; and at last a number of the young men gave off mocking him. Instead, they found in him a leader. Despite his pride and sudden bursts of impatience, they wouldn't cross him. 'He has plans,' they said. 'This land can't support all of us, and Ishmael knows what it is to leave home. He has plans, and some of us may go with him.' So when others called him troublesome, they defended him. A few did find him troublesome – but just as many said to me, smiling, 'Your son's no outcast. He belongs to himself, anyone can see that. It's what gives him his power.'

He and I rarely mentioned the past. Sometimes I did ask, 'Are you content?' – but lightly, so as not to make too much of it.

He always said that he was. Or he'd tell me, 'I am if you are.'

'And if you are,' I'd answer, 'then so am I.'

Only once I probed more deeply. Gifts had come from Abram. There was a newly born lamb, there were blankets and, best of all, there was a fine bow for Ishmael. I watched him fingering the bow and, when he looked up, I asked, 'Do you blame me for what happened? When we left your father, you were angry.'

He didn't answer at once, but I waited, so in the end he shrugged and said, 'We've been taken care of. If we'd stayed, what would I have been like now? I'd have been different. How can I know if it would have been better? So how can I blame you?'

'Nevertheless,' I said, but he wouldn't listen.

'Let's test the bow!' he cried. 'Come and watch!'

So I stood watching, while he shot his arrows at a small tree by the boundary wall. Most hit their mark, and he was pleased. 'A good weapon! Father chose well!' he said. Then he glanced at me and added, 'Why talk about blame? Why think like that?'

So I never mentioned it again.

I never mentioned it.

But you, daughter – no matter what you speak of, in all your speech I hear the word *blame*. You imagine lost pastures, richer than any Ishmael could ever find for us. You imagine lost wealth, lost authority. The stronger and more respected Ishmael becomes, the greater you imagine his losses to be; and it's not only Abram you blame. You don't say it, but I too am blamed. Your anger jabs me from your eyes –

Have done.

You think this rage of yours pleases Ishmael – secretly pleases him – but it's your loyalty that pleases him. You weary him with your bitterness.

Learn gratitude.

In Paran, I practised gratitude. At dawn and evening, lowering my brow to the ground, 'Great One!' I said, speaking to the stillness – the stillness I remembered, that had come when I'd least hoped for it. 'Great One!' In those words I placed my thanks. What more could I say?

But over the years, I also spoke to the traveller who sometimes still formed behind my eyes, sitting by the well when I was young, on my path into the wastelands, the smiling one – and with him, I was more garrulous.

I doubted you! I said. *It hasn't been easy. It hasn't been easy. But now I can thank you. The advice you gave was sound.*

And the traveller laughed, and replied, '*Thank* you, *Hagar!*'

He still does – but these aren't things to speak of –

Time passed. At last I went to Egypt. I had a mind to find a wife for Ishmael among my own people. I searched the markets, and in your pride and that defiant toss of your head, I thought I saw –

I wasn't wrong –

Something of myself –

And of Ishmael.

And haven't I said, I love you partly for your pride? I love your fierceness. When the other women argue and start dragging each other into despondency, my heart sings to hear you tell them, 'Be quiet! Do you know more than Ishmael's wife? I tell you, we've nothing to fear!'

I love your strength. I love the beauty you lay down at night for my son, and the healthy children you give him –

Only be reconciled.

Ishmael and Isaac, standing together at their father's tomb: sons of a Promise. How could it be otherwise?

Who can afford to squander faith? What we believe, we must hold dear, which is hard; and what we hold dear, we must believe, although that may be even harder.

I kept faith with the child. Didn't I do as I'd said I would? I sent word to Abram. I said to the messenger, 'Tell him we're safe and live in Paran. Tell him I'm well.' I wanted to say, 'Tell him I'm no longer angry,' or, 'Tell him I've learned many things,' but simplicity speaks most deeply, and the messenger looked approving, although I hadn't said, 'Tell him his son thrives,' or, 'Tell him Ishmael still thinks well of him.' I spoke only of our safety, and then added what I added about myself. 'Tell him I'm well.'

So little said of Ishmael.

Who was I to speak easily of Ishmael? I needed the slowness of the years. I needed my watchfulness as he grew, and my bowing down to the stillness at morning and night until my hair was grey, before it rested peacefully in me to send word to Abram that Ishmael was content. And Ishmael, by then, had done as much for himself.

I think his father understood.

The gifts Abram sent, over the years, came wrapped in silence.

I think he understood.

To every one of us, our own understanding.

In mine, there's this.

A darkness stretched from my childhood. I couldn't trust. I was swift to be injured beyond the unavoidable measure. And this almost killed us both – Ishmael and me – before I saw it for what it was. I'd almost say we did die.

And yet we live.

We live –

But as to that, it was a great and necessary saving. What's promised is promised.

My father, Seti – may he shine in the Light of Ra – was not a tender man. You saw him once, and I know from what you've said that he was smiling and mild. But if you'd ever seen his anger, you would have more than trembled before him, Papnanyet. At one glance from him, you would have dissolved into a scattering of dust!

I should wake you. Nebta has drawn her lips into a thin thread. She profoundly disapproves. She takes care with her massage. My feet glow with her attention. The oil she rubs into my soles kisses my skin. Strange, to feel her touch again –

The red dye in her hair doesn't become her, and how much thinner she is! She used to be so stout –

She's very skilful. Despite all that's happened in Egypt in the past two years, Nebta's hands have kept their gift, and my feet receive it gratefully. Compared to this, Senen's efforts are mere blundering.

And how amusing it is, the twitching of Nebta's nose on account of the oil that Senen's so honestly saved and mixed from the last of my collection! It's staled, of course, and Nebta clearly considers it inferior, which it is – but what's to be done? It's what we have. And Nebta works so finely in any case. From a woman of *her* skills, nothing less would be tolerable: that's her belief; it's easy to see that's where her pride lies, whatever her other thoughts may be. Excellence is her duty –

Whereas you –

How artless you look. How simply you lean on that fan, crushing it – a fan worth more than the price *you* would fetch.

Those strips of cloth around the shaft were dyed by the Sea People. That particular colour is their great secret.

And are you so artless, Papnanyet? Or just stupid?

It was said to me once that *I* am stupid, that all trust is stupid.

Nebta frowns. Know, O my sleeping Papnanyet, that in her displeasure there's a considerable portion of pretence. She implies that, next to the oil, she disapproves of *you*, a mere slave, sleeping, dreaming, while the heat stifles us: I sweat, Nebta sweats – and one of us is of the Great House, and the other at least is virtuous and a free woman.

But in truth it's I who am the object of her disapproval. Naturally, she resents this summons. She resents it as much as I'm puzzled by it. Who told her to come? Why has Ramses allowed it? Or doesn't he know? Does Nebta herself know who sent her?

You in your sleep, Papnanyet, perhaps you have an under-standing of this matter? Perhaps sleep enlarges your knowledge – but I doubt it! Little ignorant one. Have you any comprehen-sion – of anything whatever? Even now, I think it might still amaze you, the idea that Nebta – whose people have neither fields nor influence despite her grand-sounding name: what was her father? Didn't she tell me once that he traded in beer and ox fat? – that such a woman could presume to be angry with me, the offspring of Ra, the daughter of mighty Seti, and not for what's happened in Egypt – at least, not only for that – but because I indulge you. Yet so it is. I suspect that every common person of the Two Lands has their particular judge-ments of me – their detailed judgements beyond their large one – of how I should look and sit and eat and behave. And each of them feels entitled to weigh my heart in the scales –

Ah, now Nebta wipes my feet, and pats the linen. So soon, finished. Her hands are firm and gentle, but the glance she gives me is hard and mask-like. Her brow's damp, but the cause of that is the heat. Certainly it's the heat. She doesn't fear me.

'You're as skilful as ever,' I tell her. 'You may go now.'

And see how she does it! So stiffly. If you could only see, Papnanyet, how she backs from me! How rigidly her spine is bowed, as if she might snap with the effort! How each of her steps says, '*And so I leave you, Traitoress. I leave you with your pet, your favourite, you who have ruined us.*'

I questioned her once – long ago, in my husband's house, before the Sorrow came. Perhaps that was when she told me her father's trade, about the beer and the ox fat. I know she told me she has only daughters – but that all her sisters were mothers of sons. I suppose those sons are dead now. And so Nebta, like many thousands, if she could speak her mind, would tell me I've forfeited my right to indulgences. She would say that an obligation lies on me to be stern with the likes of you, Papnanyet, an outlandish slave like you, as Seti my father was stern. She would say that after such calamities in Egypt, to let you sleep while she works – even she, ordinary and unimportant though she is – is one insult too many on the Two Lands. Or have I learned nothing? Now people must be kept in their place, or what will become of us? And she at least is Egyptian – and free.

I can almost hear her words.

And are they wise words, Papnanyet? Are you truly an affront to the grief of Egypt? Perhaps she's right. Perhaps I should call the guards and have you taken out and thrown to the crocodiles. It could be done. I think some of the guards would still obey me – in some matters –

Honouring my father, Seti.

At least you see they haven't killed me yet.

No one dares.

Ramses daren't. Too much has happened. So strange, this fear of me, his fear that I'm protected. And do you think that might be so, Papnanyet? As I tonight protect you, although the price I pay is that most valuable of fans, is it possible that the furious god of the Goshen Hapiru has fixed an eye on me, and willed that I'm spared?

Ramses daren't touch me. I live. They could come in the night. They could send away the few kindly guards with one word from Pharaoh, and dispatch me, and carry me silently from this place. But no one comes. They could poison me – and yet they don't. Senen, when she tastes my food, pulls such comical faces that I've seen you staring at her; and did you hear what she said when I asked her why she's incapable of swallowing anything without a grimace?

'Oh, Lady,' she said, 'I'm so frightened, I have to make a joke with myself, or I couldn't eat.'

'What joke?' I asked.

'Forgive me,' she answered, 'but I tell myself the food's a foul-tasting medicine that will make me the most desired of women.'

She's a plain little fool, but she has spirit. She doesn't fall asleep on me, Papnanyet. That is her charm. But then, that you do – that is yours.

I was the Favourite. Seti – may he rise strong and youthful by the power of Osiris – he indulged me.

Whatever I asked.

Did I fear him?

Certainly I feared him. And in all things, I endeavoured to be the most dutiful of daughters. But in one thing I failed.

'And where are my grandchildren?' he would ask; and when I said, 'Oh, you're blessed with so many grandchildren, father!' he would pull a face, not altogether unlike Senen's, and tell me, 'But it's *yours* that I wish for! Or do you intend to fail in your duty?' Then we would laugh, and, sick in my spirit, I would leave him; and every time I told these words of Seti's to my husband – as I did, because I was young then, and made many mistakes – my husband trembled for his life.

No child came – except once: that half-creature once, lost out of me, unripened. Not to be thought of –

My father, great Seti, he was not a tender man, Papnanyet, and we never spoke of that. Only he sent priests to me, young Iy, and the ailing Hekhemmut – the priests of his own choice – to perform cleansing rituals, and rid me – as Iy put it – of the *'unknown curse'* that lay on me.

I'd tried not to think of myself as cursed; and, I remember, I said to Iy: 'Is it truly possible? Who would curse me?'

He smiled.

'Your father,' he said, 'has many enemies. Not everyone wants him to be Pharaoh. Not everyone recognises, as I do, the divinity in him. Yet it's so. One day Seti will be Pharaoh in Egypt; and some of those who know it hate him for it. But your father's a god – he must be, since he will be Pharaoh – which makes him too strong to be cursed. So their curses fall on you, because he loves you.' Then he added, 'If you were stronger, their curses would fall away, like blades of grass. You must take care to obey the gods in all things. These curses have found out some weakness in you.'

And Hekhemmut, when I asked him, said, 'It may be so. One day, your father may be Pharaoh. Even now, isn't he among the most powerful men in Egypt? But I'm old. How can I tell whether a god lies waiting in him? He's not Pharaoh yet. Your family hasn't proved its divinity yet. Your misfortune shows us that nothing's certain.' And then Hekhemmut added, 'Make your heart clean. Make sure the fault doesn't lie in yourself. That would disgrace your father.'

And after these priests had spoken, I sat quietly and thought more deeply than I'd ever done, as if trying to see into an unburnished mirror and discover there what it meant, that my father, the son of Pharaoh's vizier, might one day become Pharaoh, that he might reveal himself as a child of Ra; that I myself might therefore be, in part, divine –

And if all this was so, could I also be cursed? Or if I was cursed – was that because it was not so? I sat trying to understand what I felt in myself – whether I was divine or cursed; and where to place the responsibility: was it mine?

But what do you know of such things, child? Do you blink about you in the daylight and consider what you are, and blame your gods for it? I think not. I don't believe you know how to consider anything. Your slavery rests gently on you, like the finest linen, or a kind of second nakedness. You're comfortable –

How could *you* consider anything?

I begged Isis and Taweret, *Turn this curse from me!* And secretly, so as not to offend Seti, my father, I sent for the priestess of Taweret, and after that, I sought out the High Priest of Isis – but he said little to me: he was timid and cautious. So I sent for Meru, who was newly a priest of Isis and unknown – and wasn't then as you see him now, greasy and lame, but strong and virile – and who wouldn't give me what I asked of him. How could it have injured my husband? But Meru wouldn't lie with me. Instead he said, 'You must trust. And give up this fear of curses.'

He came often – but never hesitated to reject my entreaties. 'Trust!' he repeated. 'Trust Isis!' Through many long months.

At last, it was my husband's sister, Aneksi, who came to me and said, 'It's well understood that if a barren woman raises an infant which isn't her own, sometimes the gods relent, and she becomes fruitful herself.'

It's so. She called me barren. I hurled a small, but most beautiful, ointment pot at her. You wouldn't have found me so agreeable when I was younger, Papnanyet. And yet I didn't forget her words.

Senen will come soon with the honeyed milk, to help me sleep –

To help me sleep.

Ramses shouldn't have followed them. He knows it. So many drowned. Even now, they say the Sea of Reeds is stiff with corpses –

Is there a woman in Egypt as hated as I am?

If there were a thought in your being, Papnanyet, you might puzzle over such a destiny – to be a slave owned by such as me. I've sometimes imagined that Senen finds herself bewildered but is too steadfast to show it. Then again, perhaps I overestimate her.

Neither she nor you, after all, can have kin among the Hapiru, certainly not the Hapiru from Goshen. Senen, whether or not she thinks of it, is Egyptian, which by now might have raised some outrage in her if she'd had brothers to die in the Sickness, or in the Sea of Reeds, but she had none; and, since she's an orphan and hasn't even parents to lament the state of affairs but was bought young, and raised by the most ignorant of my husband's servants – perhaps she has little awareness.

As for you, child, what can it mean to you that your mother came from the wild tribes beyond the Hittites – or so they told me when you were brought to me? Can you understand the word *free*? What have you ever glimpsed of freedom?

But the Hapiru of Goshen –

They never quite forgot. Faceless Ones. God-haters. Those we called by worse names than Hapiru. Always, beneath their servility, they half remembered that they were free, although Seti – may he be transfigured in the Light of Ra – saw to it that they were treated like true slaves, and how we're treated – doesn't that persuade us how to think of ourselves? So most would say. And from early in my life, when my grandfather was vizier, and my father went about on the vizier's business, he worked pitilessly to reduce the Hapiru of Goshen to a stupor.

Yet they wouldn't quite forget – which is why they were feared. And they were so many, and so industrious –

I heard him once, when I was a child, speak of the Hapiru. He came into the women's quarters, and at the door, the official who was speaking with him left him, and my father said to him across his shoulder, 'We must crush their spirit, or we'll have these foreigners of Goshen selling our own corn to us!'

And then he saw me standing before him, and smiled, and said, 'My fledgling!'

It's a vivid memory. I enjoyed how powerful he sounded. It made me feel safe. And later – years later – when the word went out to kill the Hapiru infants because there were too many, and it was said that my father, Seti, had first offered the idea to Pharaoh – I thought when I heard it, *Pharaoh must be strong. What my father has advised is for the protection of Egypt.*

But I lay awake at night and thought of slaughtered babies and the grief of their mothers, and my bitterness turned in me, in the stillness of my womb. I loathed the mothers for giving birth to babies that fell like waste to the earth, good only to be flung into the Nile, when I, who could have cherished a new life, and raised it in comfort, was granted none; and I wept for the infants, and said in my heart to the mothers, *I hate you, but you're my sisters in misery!*

And no child came.

The High Priest of Amun, when I mentioned my sorrow to him once, smiled and said, 'But what have you in common with such women? What are their offspring to you? These Hapiru have servile souls. Of course, they're also thieves. If they could, they'd take all our wealth from us. But they're contemptible. They're not our slaves. They didn't come here as a conquered people. And yet – see how they let us treat them! How can a daughter of Seti compare her destiny with the likes of theirs?'

And it's true, I marvelled at the time: no matter how stupefied they were by the hard laws of Pharaoh, why didn't they rise up and rebel? Better for all of them to die than to let their young be murdered –

They've become nothing, I thought. *The people of Goshen have finally forgotten themselves. Mighty is Pharaoh; and wise and terrible is my father. It's my father who's done this. He's crushed the Hapiru as he said he would. Their spirit has been trodden into mud and sand. It's completely lost.*

That's what I told myself. I was wrong, but it's what I thought; and I despised them, and wept and despised them.

And once I fell on my knees and prayed to Osiris: *These Hapiru in Goshen have no gods. Their slaughtered infants have nowhere to go. Make provision for them, Lord Osiris, because their souls stain the river, and my body aches.*

But none of this concerns you –

If I live, Papnanyet, I shall allow you children. I shall allow both Senen and you motherhood – if I can find you husbands.

And your children shall be free.

You will not thank me. It's not so comfortable, deciding for yourself – anything. Your children will learn that.

You, too, may learn it.

She was your age, the sister of Mose; and she at least knew what life was. Do you even know that, sleeping one? She ran and fell at my feet. Her hair fell into the mud. She pressed her brow into the mud.

'Let me fetch a wet nurse,' she begged, 'from among his own kind.'

I almost had her whipped. I knew what she was saying. She was speaking of his mother.

She understood life, that Hapiru girl. She was trying to save two lives – one from death and one from grief – and to do that, she risked her own. Not for her, this sleeping couched on feather fans. Not for her, Papnanyet, the art of dancing in beads and trinkets, and playful sessions sniffing her mistress's perfumes. Her arms, which she stretched towards me through the mud, were covered with scars. There was a gash on her hand, black and encrusted – and yet she knew the worth of life and, when I spoke, she came running from the rushes.

All I'd said was, 'Ah, if I could keep him –'

I hadn't even touched him. It was Takamenet who'd lifted the basket from the water's edge, a small wicker egg, daubed with fat and tar, and opened it, and –

How he wailed!

He wasn't beautiful. His face had purpled with rage. His eyes were bunched shut, and his chin was wet with vomit – the stench of the tar, or else the heat and being closed tight in the basket, had upset him – and he stank like the foulest gutter of Goshen, and his rags were soiled.

How could I touch him?

But *he* touched *me*. He reached into my heart, and there he touched me, so that I laughed to hide my tears, and I said out loud, 'Ah, if I could keep him –' And then the girl came – his sister: she didn't tell me so, and yet I knew, and later, as he grew, I saw how he resembled her in my memory – she came running and sprawling before me in the mud.

Did I mean it, my wish to keep him?

I think at first I meant it as if I wished we lived in some traveller's tale of a distant country, where all is simple and loving. I said it as a thing impossible in Egypt. But then, his sister's urgency – That so sharpened my sense of life, a new life, such as I'd begged the gods for; and I ached so, in every part of me, at the sight of him, and then those words of my husband's sister – Aneksi's words – came to mind so persuasively: *'If a barren woman raises an infant which is not her own, sometimes the gods relent'* – and at that moment, so heavily the truth pressed on me of a thousand such babies dead in the river, or consumed by crocodiles, or left abandoned on the road, or thrust into the hands of travelling merchants –

And all this so magnified the power of the creature that lay squawking in the arms of Takamenet, who wrinkled her nose and laughed at the stench; and all of it made my desire so reasonable, that I said, 'I'll call him Mose. What other name could he have? He shall be simply Child. But at least he shall be *my* child.'

Takamenet stared.

'My father will speak to Pharaoh,' I said. 'I'll ask this favour. One small life among so many – what can it matter? And yet, who knows? Perhaps some god has sent him to me.'

As for the rest, Papnanyet, as for the rest, I would bore you, even in your sleep, if I were to tell you all the twists of my anxiety in the years that followed. And one must take care never to bore one's slaves – not, at least, with too much truth. It's said that nothing corrupts a slave more thoroughly than too many secrets too freely given. First, the slave is bored, and then a creeping contempt is generated – which I would spare you, Papnanyet, you who care nothing for either innocence or corruption.

But I will say this –

My father was irritated.

'Are there no Egyptian infants?' he demanded. 'The Hapiru of Goshen are unwholesome. They're a threat to us, and they're polluted with strange diseases and customs. Why should we disobey Pharaoh? And isn't Pharaoh acting on my own suggestion? I'll send a guard to finish this creature.'

But I held his feet and wept.

'Why did I find him?' I pleaded. 'Some god must have wished it –' And then I said, 'Perhaps, when he considers how I found him, Pharaoh will see that, by granting this one child of the Hapiru life, he'll be showing respect to the gods. For who knows what the gods mean? It'll be a blessing on him!'

'Pharaoh himself is a god!' said my father. 'He has no need of lessons from you in these matters!'

Then he pushed me away, and hurried to leave me.

But I had my wish. Later that day, my father came to me, smiling but grudging, and said, 'Pharaoh has granted it. He's done this because he knows you're dear to me. But you must learn to ask for less in future! You've embarrassed me. I told him the truth. I said, "She's a hysterical woman with a fancy that this will help her breed." He had the goodness to laugh.'

So I kept Mose.

And the coils of anxiety began –

First, the silent dark woman, the Hapiru mother. I forbade her to speak to me. Someone else might have been found, but of course the child was accustomed to her, and, once I'd seen that, I feared to separate them until he was stronger. I had her sleep in a storeroom at the back of the women's quarters. I kept her there some twenty months. I wouldn't let her take him back to Goshen – what good was that to me, my child in their filthy hovels? In these days, people like to say that Mose spent his first years nurtured in Goshen filth. It's not so. When he wasn't at her breast, he was most often in my arms, and –

But I'll spare you, Papnanyet, the bitter language in that woman's eyes, watching me, handing the child to me.

And the many times my father, great Seti, when he looked at me, his smile suddenly sharp, said, 'Are you ready to give up your plaything yet?'

Or my husband, sometimes hoping, sometimes full of scorn, with his outbursts that were not quite jokes: 'Do you grow any rounder with *my* seed because you've plucked this Hapiru berry? Let me have him pounded into the flour and baked into bread. Maybe *then* your belly will swell –'

I was always anxious.

I shielded the child with every resource. I forbade the Hapiru woman to sing her people's songs, or murmur her people's words to him. I had her closely watched. Mose was weaned early, before she could tell him what he didn't need to know – what I thought he didn't need to know – and I hung round his neck and strapped to his chest the strongest spells against evil that the wise women, and the priests, and even the ladies of the court could give me.

The Hapiru woman didn't weep when I sent her away. At that time, I spoke to her.

'This child whom you've nurtured,' I said, 'will become a powerful man in the Two Lands. You can rejoice.'

Then I turned from her. Her face was empty. I said to Takamenet, 'Give her the silver.' I meant to pay her for her service, and in no less than silver, as befitted the wet nurse of a child who might one day be a prince. Then I left the room.

Later, Takamenet, who was honest, brought the silver back to me.

'The woman was impudent,' she said. 'She refused to take this.'

I said nothing. I took the silver – it was an armband of sufficient value to have made her whole family comfortable, a plain armband with a simple pattern of flowers stamped on it, but the silver was pure and heavy; and I placed it in a box which Seti himself had given me, may he shine in the Light of Ra. I still had it – until I came here. Through the years I kept it – the box, and, lying inside, wrapped in linen, the armband.

And I worked. I taught Mose how to run to my husband and call him 'father'. I taught him how to run to Seti, whenever he visited, and show him tricks, small tricks we women had taught him: how to work his wooden puppets, how to make clever puzzles with plaits of reed, how to make Seti laugh –

And I prayed, *Let him live. Let this child grow strong; and may no one whisper in his ear, or in the ear of Seti, my father, or the ear of Pharaoh, anything to harm him. Grant me this son, and I'll praise the strength and kindness of the gods all my life!*

Constantly I was vigilant; and Mose grew and thrived. I raised him to regard himself the favoured of Kings, born to a position of authority, and the obedience of lesser men. And he had charm, and cleverness – so much so that when he played with other children, even the children of Seti, my young brothers and sisters, they often followed where he led; and if there were times when they resented him, and told him, 'Go home to your mother! You're not truly one of us!' he used to boast to me that he shouted back, 'Seti may not be my father, but his daughter is my mother – and I, too, was sent by the gods! Isis hid me in the

Nile until my mother was ready for me. Just like Horus!'

Which silenced everyone. It was what I'd told him. As Isis had hidden her own son to save his life, hadn't she hidden mine?

'It was a vision,' I used to tell him, 'that came to me when you were born. I feared I'd never have a healthy child. And then I saw you lifted from the Nile. It was a sacred vision, so you can be sure that a deity protects you.'

No one mentioned his Hapiru blood in his presence. The children sensed that he was different: somehow they sensed it, perhaps from gossip in the kitchens; but I think no one spoke the word 'Hapiru'. Few had knowledge of the facts. And of those who did, most dared not speak – were they to criticise the decision of Pharaoh? – while the rest were loyal, and smiled at Mose, and willingly forgot.

As for my husband, except when he was alone with me, he was quiet. I, too, was feared in those days. Pharaoh was growing old, and my father was very powerful –

Until it came at last: the truth of my father's divinity. The old King died, and Seti – may he triumph in the glory of Ra – took the throne of Egypt.

On that day, Papnanyet, the Day of Enthronement, I stood in the robes they placed on me, and the heavy wig and the jewels; and as I watched the priests and listened to the chanting, and breathed in the perfumes of worship, I marvelled that I – I, with my tremblings for Mose's safety, and my precarious trust that the gods smiled on me, and my pain at the insults that my sullen husband delivered whenever he dared – I was seed of the Divine. The notion awed me; and yet it brought to me also a hush of recognition. As I watched the ceremony of enthronement, it was as if I'd always known, even from my earliest childhood, how closely I'm linked with the Divine; and it seemed to me that my confusion had lain not in ignorance but in a kind of mist across my mind – a blur of thoughts that had been lain on me by others, hiding me from what I knew of my own nature.

So Seti became Pharaoh. And I, his first and favourite daughter, saw new respect in the faces that turned to me. Our family held Egypt in the palm of its hand.

Such changes, Papnanyet. Such shocks and transitions –

At first, Seti didn't reign alone. His own father still lived, sick and fading. Of him I saw little. He had never found me interesting. For a year, they ruled together. And then Seti – may the Light of Ra enfold him – he solely reigned in Egypt. And it was then, in those days, when he was approaching manhood, that I spoke more fully to Mose. I feared that certain rumours troubled him, so I said, 'Now you see how important you are. My young brothers know you and trust you more than they trust each other. Over the years, haven't you played games together? Haven't you hunted and trained with them? Understand your position. Seti, my father, smiles on you. Some day, he may make you his vizier. Or perhaps not. But I know he thinks of several responsibilities to lay on your shoulders. And when at last he returns to the gods and one of my brothers – when Ramses – is Pharaoh, then I think you *shall* be vizier. You'll never be Pharaoh, but all your life you'll be one of the most powerful men in Egypt. So put aside any nonsense you've heard. I've told you. This story of finding you in the Nile – it was a vision. A sacred vision. You truly are my son.' Then I added, 'If she were still alive, my servant Takamenet could tell you. She delivered you. But she died when you were small.'

'And my father?' asked Mose.

'Of that,' I told him, 'what reason have you to ask? If I'm your mother, where else should you seek your father but in my husband? Let that be enough for you.'

And Mose seemed satisfied.

Oh, he seemed satisfied, Papnanyet. He was affectionate towards me and respectful; and he busied himself with irrigation plans and building plans that pleased my father, Seti; and how could we know that he also went often to Goshen, not for the sake of any such plans and necessary words with Pharaoh's agents, but to stare at the Hapiru there, and think about their lives and his own life?

He came to me one day. It was evening. He asked to speak to me alone. He seemed agitated, and I went out with him at once into the courtyard.

'Mother,' he said, 'I've killed an overseer. It was yesterday in Goshen. He was beating a man – one of the Hapiru.'

I was silent. I stood gazing at my hands, and the hands I saw before me were not my hands but belonged to Mose's Hapiru sister, spread out beseeching in the mud; and in my heart I saw the eyes of the woman who'd suckled him.

'They know in Goshen,' he said.

I shrugged. 'An overseer,' I began, 'who was no doubt disrespectful and raised his hand against you. This isn't so important –'

'They know,' said Mose again. 'They've always known; and I think I've known all my life.'

I didn't answer. I didn't look at him.

'Mother,' he said.

'It isn't possible,' I told him – but I knew it was.

I said other things after that. How could it matter, I asked him, what he might have been – or which people might have been his people? His destiny had made him Egyptian, as surely as I am. 'Chosen,' I said, 'by the gods.'

He heard me out. Then he embraced me. It was a strange action, not manly, but as he'd behaved when a child, with a great hug that was fierce and needing –

And he left me in the courtyard.

And he left Egypt.

Many said it was as well that he'd gone. And they spoke not only behind my back. A number of people told me as much; and so did my husband.

117

Seti forbade me to speak of him, but there was little need for such a prohibition. The slightest thought of Mose worked a sharp needle through my heart, threading me with pain.

I was silent.

In the long stretches of the night when no one saw me, when my husband slept – for during the day, our house was crowded with aunts and sisters and nephews, or else, when my father was in residence, often I spent my time in the women's quarters of the palace, as Seti wished – my father still preferred to have me near him: despite everything, I was still his favourite, and he thought nothing of my husband. What solitude did I have? Daughters of Ra, Papnanyet, are often possessed of no more privacy than a slave –

But in the night, when no one saw me, I wept. And I demanded of the gods, *What kindness is this? You granted me a child from the Nile – only to snatch him from me when he was bound to my affections by more than twenty years! And that I could accept if you'd taken him into the realm of Osiris, if I could pray for him, safely in the underworld – but where is Mose? You've cast him out into the desert. His name's been buried in a pit of ignominy. The brightness of his promise has soured into bitterness, and Seti frowns, and I'm humiliated. Oh, I'm humiliated, and my son's more truly lost than is the dead child of any beggar woman!*

I found no comfort in these tears and complaints. I grew sarcastic and proud. Seti, my father, may he shine in the Light of Ra, saw this change in me, and although he never spoke of Mose, he sternly said to me one day, 'Where are your smiles, Fledgling, and affectionate looks? If I want a block of granite for a daughter, I can send to my quarries. You're no longer young. You should acquire wisdom. You've squandered trust where only a stupid woman would have put it. You've been a great fool – but you'll be an even greater one if you forget how to smile!'

So I made an effort for him. I smiled – but, in truth, his warning came too late. I bored him. He was tired from his wars with the Hittites. He wanted freshness and joy about him. He himself was growing old. He was becoming stooped and thin. He slept badly. His teeth had crumbled into rottenness. He heaped titles and duties on Ramses. He liked to have his little great-grand-daughters play near him as he sat in his garden; and there, the noble and influential came to him for his decisions and conde-scensions. And in his garden he heard reports on his building projects, and devised cunning deprivations and unpleasant-nesses for the Hapiru of Goshen –

Punishing them, I sometimes thought, for stealing the smiles of his daughter.

So the years passed – as they will, despite pain, or pleasure.

How old are you, Papnanyet? Thirteen? Fourteen? How beauti-fully your breasts have formed! How rounded your arms have become! Perhaps Sabastet would marry you. True, he's not young, and it's said he's twice a widower, but his work in the garden is excellent. I've watched him. He's gentle with the plants. Also, it's work that keeps him fit. He's as lean and strong as any of the guards – and a better man. He speaks to me without awk-wardness or venom. He wouldn't mistreat you.

As for Senen, she shall have the cook, unless he finally poi-sons us. She shall be his second wife, so he won't mind that she's plain. Her steady nature and simple goodness of heart shall be his reward for letting us live. And since the cook is formed like a bull – didn't we see him once, naked by the river? – Senen shall become the most sated woman in Egypt, as she deserves.

Would these proposals of mine win your approbation, Pap-nanyet? Or would you be startled to find yourself a gardener's wife?

And your children born free –

Mose left Egypt.

The years crawled.

I gave up speaking to the gods. They had cheated me. I attended each festival and ceremony – am I not Daughter of Pharaoh? – and I uttered the prayers and phrases that tradition required of me, but in my spirit I no longer spoke to deities. I said to myself, *What do they care about us? They yawn at our hopes and heartbreaks.* And I said, *There may be traces in me of divine origin – but of what use are they? They're impotent traces. I'm in some way cast out from all the favour and power my nature should have given me.* And nothing I saw or heard, not the gleaming of the Nile, not the bright star of Isis rising through the darkness, not the music I loved, nor the silence of the desert, nor the prayers of priests – not even Meru's prayers – could turn me from my bitterness.

And then one afternoon, Meru sought me out. It was in the sixth year of Mose's disappearance. He found me in the garden of my husband's house – our house – where I was listening – and yet perhaps, in truth, I wasn't listening – to one of my husband's aunts as she delivered a long complaint about mouth ulcers and bleeding gums.

He sent her and the other women from me.

This happened sometimes. Through those slow years he visited me, although I didn't send for him. How could I send for him? Hadn't he told me to trust? And hadn't I reaped only sorrow? I never asked him to come, but he came nonetheless; and always he bore himself as a priest, with a priest's authority, which allowed us to be private despite the listeners in the household. But in any case, it was no less than the truth. Meru never casts off his priest-liness. He's not one of those who lays it aside when he's with a friend as though it were some tiresome formal garment.

And I welcomed his visits. I thought they meant little to me, but in fact I wanted them, which I found strange, because in my heart I blamed him. I had leaned so hard on his encouragements, always his *'Trust! Trust!'* I felt he had much to answer for; yet despite that, of everyone who came advising and coaxing, scolding and comforting, he offended me the least.

Of course I've always been fond of him.

He used to speak first of family matters: my husband, his relatives, the farm at Khmun – was all well? And only after that would he ask, 'And you?'

'I'm as you see me,' I'd tell him.

Then Meru would frown, and he'd say, 'Move a little faster, Daughter of Pharaoh. It's not good to try a priest's patience. It makes us gabble our prayers!' – Or something of that kind, so that I'd look amused, to show that, if I could have, I'd have forgiven him. He knew I blamed him, although I didn't say so. My words were more general. I used to tell him, 'Never speak to me again of trust! And spare me your thoughts on the nature of pain! Sit with me if you must. Keep me company. But no more nonsense. It won't be tolerated.'

And Meru would scan my face, as if taking measurements. I have seen the architects of Pharaoh scan a building with very nearly the same expression. And he'd shrug.

'It takes time,' he'd say, 'if you insist upon it . . .' Or he'd make some other priestly observation of the sort that lingers in one's thoughts for days, barely understood and refusing to disperse, like oil in water.

And before he left, sometimes he told me news: scandals and intrigues of the Temples, follies of ambition and jealousy – yet all of them harmless stories, full of laughter, as if we had an understanding between us that I knew of no other kind of story, or as if the priests of Egypt had become children again, and played games that both he and I knew were foolish and simple, because we had the benefit of years.

In the end, I used to tell him he bored me.

'As you grow older and more distinguished, you grow more tedious,' I'd say. 'At this rate you'll soon be a High Priest. You weary me.'

And then, smiling, he'd rise and take his leave. 'It's not my purpose to weary you,' he'd tell me. 'You need your strength.'

But on this day, in the sixth year, everything was different.

When Meru sat down beside me, he asked none of his usual questions. Instead, he admired the flowers – the lilies – although they were no longer at their finest, as I pointed out. The few poor lilies.

'Nevertheless,' he said. Then there was silence. I did nothing to break it, and at last he went on, 'Your father must leave us soon. He's old and weak.'

'Of course,' I answered. Everyone knew it, so why speak of it? By this choice of subject he annoyed me, but I remembered my duty and added, 'Ramses will be a powerful Pharaoh. Indeed, hasn't he already shown that, at great Seti's side? Egypt's fortunate.'

'Perhaps,' said Meru, 'but he's stubborn, more so than most; and he's determined to prove greater than his father. There may be difficulties.'

This was bold, even for Meru, and even alone with me. To make such remarks was incorrect behaviour, and I resented it. I also feared it. Part of me still looked to Meru for – what? Hope? Goodness? I couldn't say. But – for something. And when he'd spoken these words, I knew that if he showed himself in the end to be like so many others, full of schemes and conspiracies, he'd have betrayed me completely.

So I was harsh. 'Why speak to me of Ramses?' I said. 'You priests. You'd turn us all into sheep! Why shouldn't Ramses excel? It's his nature. As a child, he was always competing with Mose. Mose was bigger and stronger, but Ramses liked him, and so sometimes he accepted the situation. At other times, he behaved differently. He needed to prove best at everything – which is how it should be. A god must win. Pharaoh must win. I've no other thoughts on this matter. I'm old and Ramses is young. I'm one of many sisters, and, since Mose vanished, Ramses has hardly spoken to me. If you priests fear him, that's your own concern.'

Meru accepted this calmly. 'So you yourself are ready for change?' he asked.

'Quite ready,' I told him.

'Then why is it,' he said, 'that I see no signs of this readiness for change? You keep your eyes on the parched sand when all around you there are gardens. You've fixed yourself on grief – on Mose – and show no concern for your brother's future. I see not the least movement towards change in you, and no one watches you more carefully than I.'

At that, my suspicions fell away. Meru is cunning, but not devious; there's a difference. I saw that he hated my passivity and was trying to goad me out of it; and I said, 'Find someone else for these tricks!'

And I patted his hand. I respect him. And didn't I desire him once, long ago? But perhaps that small gesture of mine – patting his hand – was provocative, because at once he rose to leave although he'd barely arrived.

That didn't please me.

'Don't suppose you're in my good favour!' I said.

'I make no such supposition,' he replied. And then he added, 'You're like an angry cat. Once you snatched a fish from the marketplace, but on your way home you lost it, and now you scratch and bite at your own fur, and you're covered with sores. You let no one near you.'

Then he left me to my rage. I was deeply offended. I shouted after him, 'I forbid you to come again!'

Do you understand, Papnanyet? But, thoughtless child, how could you?

In any misfortune, our greatest anger is reserved for ourselves. That's what he meant. And to forgive ourselves for what has happened to us – that's the great requirement, before all others. In truth, I already knew it. In all my raging against the gods and the laws of Pharaoh, and my husband, and even the

Hapiru, I had discovered where the deepest pain lay; I had understood how little all this raging counted, great as it was, compared with the fury I turned on myself for having believed I might have happiness, and for having suffered the ruin of both the happiness and my belief in it. And Meru saw that I knew, and he judged I was ready to hear how I punished myself.

The man's a true priest. For years, he gave me riddles. But when he saw my readiness to hear – even though I knew nothing of my readiness – he spoke clearly enough.

So that evening, sitting in the garden when Meru had gone, I was very quiet. My indignation was short-lived. No one came to me. Perhaps Meru had spoken to the others in the house. I was left alone, and I sat watching a turbulence in the distance, deep inside myself. It was like a spiral of wind that moves across the desert, violent, and yet to one who watches from a remote place, seeming still –

And I thought to myself, *It may look silent and controlled, but it can destroy villages. It can pluck up living creatures and fling them down again with every limb broken. It's my anger, and I'm the first village, and all who live there.*

When at last I got up and went into the house, the sky was red over me. I smiled at my husband. I spoke pleasantly to his aunts, who studied me with inquisitive eyes. I ate a good supper –

And in the months that followed, I struggled with myself, fighting for peace.

Hadn't I known joy – the joy of a son? For twenty years, I who thought she could have no children? That joy was mine. It was stored in the deepest cave of my mind. It was sealed in the strongest and most secret of jars. Robbers would never find it.

And maybe he still lives, I thought. *Mose. Mose. Prosperous and well, far from here, but under the stars, nonetheless. The same stars. And if he lives, he carries in him some love for his Egyptian mother, whether he wishes it or not, because I raised him in love. There's love between us, even if he doesn't choose to remember –*

And slowly I grew calmer. A gentleness crept into my spirit, dulling my pain. I took considerate note of myself. I marvelled at my own skin, so finely stretched over bone and flesh, and no longer young yet still attending me; I spent quiet moments peering at my face in the mirror, offering it companionship – and I was gentle with others, and laughed when I could, so that Seti, may he rise in the might of Ra, as he lay on his deathbed, looked mildly at me and said, 'Well, Fledgling, are things better now? You look better. Will you manage when I'm gone?'

I wept over his hand.

Senen is late. I should call for her. She spends so much time in the kitchens, or running errands for the cook, and the guards, and whoever else asks her, that if she were anyone but Senen, I could easily believe she forgets whose slave she is.

But when she's here, sitting through the long aching times of the afternoon or night, rubbing my feet or playing her flute, or when she tastes my food with those comical faces –

Then I don't doubt her, my Senen.

You really must learn to play an instrument, Papnanyet. You're most unaccomplished. You dance well enough, but pregnant women can't always be exerting themselves, dancing for their husbands; and I feel sure that, despite his years, Sabastet can plant fertile seed! Senen must teach you. I must see to it. You must play the flute – or how will you entertain the gardener and keep his disposition sweet? I suspect he's not the most sociable of men. And I dare say you can't cook.

For five years, I felt gentle in myself.

I was no longer important. Ramses had no interest in me. How could he have? He had great work – he has great work – so many building projects left half finished by our father: the Temple of

Amun; and all the priests to control, and his wives with their bickering; and the final rooting out of heresy in Egypt; and the Hittites – always the Hittites to be pushed back with threatening letters and expensive expeditions; and that battle at Kadesh.

They called it a victory, but since you sleep and don't hear me, I tell you, Papnanyet, Kadesh almost destroyed him.

And in all this, how could I be of interest to Ramses? I was a nothing to him. And my husband, finding me less bitter, and feeling, no doubt, that Pharaoh cared little about the ancient folly of an ageing sister – my husband grew kinder. He resented me less; and we used to sit together in the evening –

But you know this, child. You had come to us by then, a late gift from Seti – sent, as it were, from his tomb. May he live for ever, by the power of Osiris.

The day his tomb was sealed – do you remember? It was evening. The ceremonies were over. You stood in the doorway of our house, as fragile as a sparrow. And old Henuttawi, Supervisor of the Dancers of Seti, haughty and stiff with her dislike of me, said: 'She dances no better than the others. Sometimes not so well. And she has no musical talent. But your father chose her. He pointed at this one and said, "On the day they seal my tomb, send her, as a gift."'

So you came to me, Papnanyet.

I took you into the storeroom. I broke open a jar of honey and dipped in a measure. As you sucked it, the honey dribbled down your chin.

And so you came to me, Papnanyet. And you saw how my husband used to sit with me in the evenings, in the room we called our own, where none of his relatives came, nor mine, the two of us listening to Senen as she played the flute, or my husband speaking of his lawsuits and the problems with his aunts' farm near Khmun, or his other concerns –

I was wifely and placid. And after so many years of not speaking, once or twice at dawn, or in the star-filled silence of the night, I addressed the gods again; and although I scarcely said anything except, 'Praise to you!' and 'Heal me!' I believe they were hopeful utterances.

Then Mose came back.

It's good that you sleep, child! Although you don't know it, you sleep for your mistress; and whether it's a dreamless sleep, deeper than the blackest pools in the Nile, or it's a sleep as colourful and crammed with incident as the greatest of our wall-paintings – what difference does it make? Unwittingly, your sleep serves me. It draws out these thoughts which are so far beyond your comprehension, and which, if you were awake, full of your chatter and your expectations of how your mistress looks and bears herself, could neither fully form on their thread, nor find a fit recipient –

Mose came back, and the months of shock began.

What did you think of him, Papnanyet, when he came to me – the bearded, straight-backed man of the desert?

He stood in the courtyard. You saw him. You, Senen – everyone – saw him, staring out at him. I sent away the guard who watched him so suspiciously, but I couldn't approach him. I stood at a distance. The porter's words had been, 'A stranger. He says he must speak to you. He speaks our language well, but he's not of Egypt. Maybe from the Sea People.'

But I knew at once that it was Mose. I knew before my eyes fell on him; and in that moment, all the bitterness and anger that still hid in me, together with whatever I'd thought I'd found of resignation, collapsed into a great need that was dumb and terrible.

I couldn't approach him. He stood in the noon light, in the fierce heat, and I waited in the shadow of the house, standing as straight-backed as he was: am I not the Daughter of Pharaoh?

He looked strong. He had gained breadth and weight in those eleven years; and he looked in every way foreign. How he stood was somehow not Egyptian; and then his clothes: they were rough, desert-people's clothes; and his hair was unkempt, and the thick beard that didn't become him stated clearly what he was: a stranger, who had more in common with the Hapiru in Goshen than with anyone else here in Egypt.

I stood in the shadow and didn't speak. And so we saw each other.

Then he came quickly to where I was, with decisive steps that, as they shortened the distance between us, widened it. A stranger's steps, for the doing of what must be done. And my breath stilled in my throat because of what was shining from his eyes. This was Mose but not Mose. I saw a Changed One, living from some inner understanding of things, beyond speech.

In Meru's eyes I've seen such a look sometimes. In Mose's it shone.

'Mother,' he said.

I found my voice. 'Don't mock me,' I told him. 'The Mose who called me Mother is long gone.'

He didn't deny it. His face was very grave, and it seemed to me – the thought came – that it was a leader's face. I wasn't speaking to the one man, Mose – at least not to him alone, but to someone who'd brought many with him.

'Nevertheless,' he said.

'Why are you here?' I asked.

'I've come to warn you,' he said. 'I mean to take the Hapiru of Goshen out of Egypt. They're treated shamefully, and they're a free people.'

My heart was weeping. Was it to be no more than this? Cold words, and all of them only for the Hapiru? What did I care about the Hapiru of Goshen? So I said, 'Ramses will never allow it. Why should he give up his labourers? There are so many building projects, which he regards as a sacred trust. He must finish them for our father. And he's forgotten that the Hapiru of Goshen were once free. Everyone's forgotten. They themselves barely remember –'

'Nevertheless,' said Mose again. Then he touched my arm. 'Let the sorrow pass,' he said; and immediately he walked away. He was almost across the courtyard when I called to him, 'Mose!'

He didn't stop; but a particular and astonishing thing, Papnanyet: he glanced back across his shoulder, and it was Mose the child who glanced back, open and ready to be smiled at and to return a smile for his mother's call; and even while it was the child, it was also this other Mose, this foreign man, who knew he looked at me in such a way, and permitted it.

And I was able to let him go.

For all that followed –

Oh, Papnanyet, how those months terrified you! How you shrank at the sight of the Nile when it was polluted and reeking! How pale and shivering you became in the ugly times when the land soured and stank with rotting snakes and maggots and those huge evil flies, and all the dead livestock. How you screamed with pain at the one boil on your leg, whereas Senen endured so many with no more than a grimace; and how you cowered in the Great Storm, whimpering as the hailstones pitted the roof, and at the lightning –

But you were dumb when the locusts came. While the rest of us struggled to beat back the swarm from the last green in the garden, you hid disgracefully in the storeroom, behind the jars. How useless you were!

The Darkness, I discount. Not one of us was braver than you, who were not at all brave. Three days deprived of light, that darkness oily on our skins, clinging to our breath, and the stench of our fear pasty in our nostrils; my husband so afraid, almost too weak to stand and refusing to move from the prayer niche; the women silent and horrified, creeping about, their voices quivering in the lamplight, and myself –

But as to that, folded in upon myself, with unspeakable

thoughts that I dared not even think and yet the worst of them I thought: that somehow all this horror was my doing –

And you, Papnanyet, your small fists gripping Senen's arm, or mine, or anyone's; and the barest of whispers from you.

And yet in the days between each of these calamities, how swiftly you recovered, thoughtless creature that you are, as bright and frivolous as ever! So delighted with the beads one of my husband's aunts gave you, so dishonest as to who spilled the oil on the linen, so quickly laughing when poor Senen fell over the bench –

You're wild, Papnanyet, although you don't know it, with scarcely more discretion than that little ape my father used to feed –

And what was it to you – what is it to you – that Egypt, as so many of his counsellors told my brother Ramses, was being ruined?

He sent for me twice.

The first time was when the livestock sickened. He stared at me and said, 'This madman, Mose, wants to frighten me into giving away my best labourers. He rants about the god of the Hapiru of Goshen. What is this god? I didn't know they had any gods.'

'I know nothing about this,' I answered.

Ramses continued to stare at me.

'Can you influence him?' he asked.

I laughed. It seemed the safest response, and the truest.

Ramses waved me from him.

The second time was after the locusts. You remember, Papnanyet? He sent guards to collect me. When I entered his presence, he was most formally dressed, and seated most royally, with men about him who had the look of tricksters – some of the worst tricksters in Egypt – and also cold men, like Iy, and one or two of our wisest men, but Meru wasn't among them.

And he said, 'What shall I do with you, sister? This Mose – this fiend of evil – lives because of you. You raised him. You cradled a curse on Egypt. I've a mind to punish you. For the sake of the Two Lands, I must placate our gods.'

I said nothing.

'I shall have you put to death,' he said. 'I'm advised by the priests that the gods expect no less. When you're dead, the gods will come to my aid, and then I'll crush Mose.'

I said nothing.

'This son of yours,' said Ramses. Then he added, 'The people fear him. Egypt fears Mose more than Egypt fears Pharaoh. The people look about at what's happening – all these disasters – and they say, "The god of the Hapiru of Goshen is very strong. How can such wretched, filthy labourers have such a strong god? Perhaps it's one of our own who's fighting for them: some god we've neglected – the god of the Heresy." Did you know that, sister? Do you rejoice to hear it? All the work of generations, stamping out heresy in Egypt, and then your Mose comes.' And he went on, 'Even if he weren't mad, even if he asked only to take his family with him, I would deny him. It's impossible for me to make concessions to him.'

Then he fell silent and he watched me. They all watched me – as if, it came to me later, I might somehow instruct them by my behaviour as to how to proceed – so I spoke slowly, treading with great delicacy on my fear, to keep it level.

'Truly, Pharaoh,' I said, 'something must be done. I'm full of grief. How can you suppose otherwise? As you say, the people are frightened. I've heard that in Goshen the Hapiru are receiving gifts of gold and silver even from the poor. Everyone's terrified of what's happening. They see dark powers in these labourers –'

'You hear reports from the Hapiru?' Ramses leaned forward. 'From your son himself perhaps?'

I told him I heard nothing from Mose.

'But you'll have to act,' I said. 'You must end this misery. If my death can save Egypt, kill me and be done with it. Can you suppose I wouldn't die gladly? But there's a great determination in Mose. It may not be so simple.'

Ramses stared; and it was then that I saw – I understood, Papnanyet – that he couldn't kill me, however much he wanted to. He was afraid.

He was afraid. So he said, 'You were his mother. Tell him to leave us in peace. Succeed, and I may spare you.'

I lowered my head.

'Then kill me now,' I told him. 'For even if I begged him to come, he wouldn't speak to me. And even if you sent me to Goshen, to fall on my knees and plead with him, it would make no difference. In this, at least, I know Mose.'

Ramses sent me home.

I had meant that I was powerless; but he understood my words differently. He thought that I supported Mose, and was under his protection.

Support Mose? What was it to me, this business of supporting one side or the other? I hated Mose. I hated his cold purposes, his turning from me, and his ruthless response to all the nourishment that Egypt had given him, demanding our Hapiru from us, ranting at us and dispensing evils. I hated him; and I wrapped that hatred in my love for him, in the finest lengths of it, and held it close to me where no one could examine it; and always I was busy adjusting my love around its sharp edges to keep them from cutting through, and always I was crying to him in my heart, *Stop this destruction!*

Support Ramses? Him, too, I hated for the sullen games that it was rumoured he played with Mose: games of *maybe* and *perhaps*, false hopes that he gave and snatched back. And my hatred of Ramses I wrapped in all my understanding of his nature and his obligations; and I carried it carefully hidden beneath my hatred of Mose; and to Ramses also I cried in my heart, *Stop this destruction!*

Meaning the destruction of Egypt, but not only of Egypt.
Of me.

Still, Ramses believed I supported Mose.

And what's your opinion, Papnanyet? But I've asked you before.
Can you imagine, as my brother did, that the fierce god of the
Hapiru had spread his cloak of protection over me, an Egyptian
woman of the Great House? And can you imagine that even now
it rests over me?
I'm alive. I'm here.

Ramses couldn't give in. How could Pharaoh submit to the leader
of his labourers? How could the living son of Ra encourage
heresy? How could the mighty Protector of Egypt send a signal to
the Hittites: *See how weak I am!* How could a dutiful son give
away the means to complete his father's building projects?
So those two grappled with each other, Ramses and Mose.
And the Darkness came; and after the Darkness, the Sickness;
and after the Sickness, the Drowning in the Sea of Reeds, which
they say is still stiff with corpses, even now –
And you and I are here, Papnanyet, with Senen, in these
guarded rooms of the palace, where my husband doesn't visit
me, and Senen jokes away her fear as she tastes my food –
Senen, who comes now, smiling, with my cup of milk.
How annoyed she looks to find you sleeping, although she
barely glances at you!
'Let her sleep!' I tell her. 'And sit and play for me. I'll listen all
the better without that little simpleton fidgeting!'
That makes her content. How easily Senen is rewarded. And
how deeply she tastes the milk!

And what else shall I tell you, Papnanyet? What else is there to
say of how it was in me, while Mose and the god of the Hapiru

fought Ramses and all the gods of Egypt?

The further we were dragged into the pit – that pit of horror – every one of us, the more clearly I seemed to understand a savage thing: that life is evil. A child's laughter, the beauty of sunlight on the river, or the rustling of leaves when a breeze stirs, or the brightness of the stars, or even the sweetness of Senen's melodies – all such comfort I came to value as nothing but a sneer on the face of a darkness that we are too stupid to comprehend; and a terror expanded in me, so that finally I was stumbling through those months, seeing – as I believed – truths that no one else saw: that everything is futile from its beginnings, and cursed, and all hope is a lie.

And yet I spoke of ordinary matters, and even smiled on occasion, and held up my head, and saw to whatever was necessary in the household –

Lonelier than I'd thought any creature could be. For everyone else was oppressed by horror but was ignorant, and in their ignorance lay their immeasurable blessing; whereas I knew, and wasn't I – as I've said – at least in part the originator of what was happening, and of my own understanding? That made me separate from everyone – yet everyone was affected by me. And I was hated. Many would have wept tears of relief to have heard of my death.

I dared not die, Papnanyet. I dared not find myself naked to the Nameless, the unspeakably horrible that seemed to reach through all things. And it was this fear of mine that had spoken so calmly to Ramses, since I had to survive, and against those who are themselves afraid calmness is the best defence. I dared not die. And it was fear that refrained me from provoking my husband, no matter how bitterly he taunted me.

'You disgust me!' he raged. 'I should kill you. That unnatural brat of yours has ruined us! But if I kill you, Ramses will have me done away with. He'll be pleased, but even so he'll condemn me because you're still his sister. Kill yourself, woman! If you had any honour, you'd have done it by now!'

'I choose not to,' I told him.

'You disgust me!' he repeated, and I bowed my head.

And so I watched what had seemed the one-time gift of the gods to me – my motherhood – twisting in coils of nightmare; and, believe me, Papnanyet, very soon I was far beyond enquiring even of myself, *Why through me? Why has such horror found its gateway through me rather than through another?*

In the deepest horror, there's a silence of false perfection. What is, is.

Then I was brought here, with you and Senen. When the guards came for me, Ramses sent a message. 'For safe-keeping,' he said. 'Because the people hate you.'

The guards were frightened. They wore many amulets. They avoided my eyes.

And that expensive fan, which you've crushed so prettily, Papnanyet, and which Senen snatched from the house as we left, along with my beads and ointments and her flute – the first night I sat here, you made use of that fan, although in the house it was never used, it was a cherished ornament. Do you remember? You waved it over me, since there was nothing else to do. Seti, my father, may he rejoice in the power of Ra, gave it to me on the day I married. It was heavy for you, but you waved it, while Senen played her flute.

And nights and days passed –

And all of them one night to me –

And somewhere out in the night, the dogs of Egypt howled, and the children died. And the grown men died: bakers and servants, scribes and barbers, teachers and weavers – even priests –

Then – again, the guards: they rushed in here and seized me; and how you screamed, Papnanyet! And how you whimpered and clung to me as we were thrust into a cart, myself with you and Senen, and taken out, before the first hint of dawn, along the road towards Goshen.

Ah, child, I almost wish I could tell you. I preferred your whimpering and snivelling then to the silent trembles of Senen. I was somewhere so dark that it's unimaginable, and the sounds you made were like a thin thread, holding me to reason.

And so, my little fool, you saw the great Ramses spit on his sister as he rode by; and you heard what he said: 'Look well, malicious bitch. See what you've done!'

But I think you were too terrified either to see or to hear.

The sun came up. Our cart stopped. And in the distance, in the direction of Goshen –

A great cloud.

It was dust.

They were leaving. The Hapiru, with their cattle and sheep and carts of home-things, and their ancestors' bones: in their thousands, with their children and old people, their angry god and their leaders. Mose. They were leaving Egypt.

We saw only the dust – but such a cloud of it, powerful, muscular –

As we watched, it reddened in the strengthening sunlight, and reached out eastwards along the horizon; and very faint – I suppose you didn't hear it – there was a blur on our silence, a rumbling like the sound of a storm passing, as those Hapiru trod down the stones of Egypt and drove their livestock over them and pushed their wagons over them –

Leaving us.

We watched.

Then we were carted back.

And I have no recollection of anything.

I think I sat here. How can I ask? How can I say to you, Pap-nanyet, or to Senen, 'When we came back that time from the road to Goshen, how did I conduct myself, and for how long – was it for the next two days and the bridging night? Tell your mistress. Did I lie on my bed? Did I sleep? Or did I sit here? Did you oil my hair? Did you guide me to the place to pass water and raise my skirt for me? Did I speak? Did I eat?'

I have no recollection. Only in the end I remember Senen offering me a cup of milk. The milk gleamed on her upper lip, and she was looking at me not as she should, but frankly, and with curiosity.

'Lady,' she said, 'will you drink?'

I took the cup. My hand was steady. I acted in a great quiet that was barely anything. I seemed numb; and yet, Papnanyet, I think that I'd returned from somewhere. I think it was a kind of homecoming, because suddenly I could see most particularly everything around me, as though with young eyes – the small hairs that grow from the mole on Senen's cheek, the grease marks on her neck, the soiled edge of her tunic – and I remember I said to her, 'You have Goshen dust on you. Wash yourself, child.'

The horror had gone. I was numb.

Even when our troops went out to stop the Hapiru and reports came back and were brought to me by Senen from the kitchen, Senen shivering at my feet, and whispering of how the Sea of Reeds was crammed with our drowned men – and even when Ramses burst into this room and gripped me by the shoulders and hissed, 'What did I do, what evil have I ever done, to deserve such a sister?' – even then I was numb. I seemed to be suspended in my mind like the dust cloud of Goshen –

I saw always the dust cloud: how it rose on the horizon, gathering, until it seemed a thing of great power that had been approaching us for thousands of years, and I saw how it moved slowly towards the boundary of Egypt, and the sunrise flooded it with colour, so that the light and the dust together seemed to make a statement, wordless and secret – yet somehow expecting to be understood.

Then Iy came to visit me. He came at a time when he'd recently refused the appointment of High Priest of Amun. He told me his reason. The god, he said, had placed a voice in his head, telling him: 'Stand apart. You'll serve me better if you watch over and guide a younger man.'

'And Amun must be obeyed,' said Iy bitterly.

'Even so,' I said, 'who is more respected than you? All the priests of Amun fear your opinion.'

He was silent. He stood in front of me, leaning on his staff; and then, pointing a finger at me, he said, 'Daughter of Seti! Our sons rot in fields and ditches and in the Sea of Reeds – and all this is because of you! You're a woman of no moral substance! Long ago you disobeyed Pharaoh. You saved a child from the scum of Goshen. You defied Ra. You acted out of malice, because the gods knew you were flawed, and had sent you no children. Now see what's happened! Your disobedience has brought all this evil down upon us. The gods have permitted it because of you. You should be whipped through the Two Lands and abandoned in the desert, where your bones can't pollute us. I've made this recommendation to your brother.'

'Do as you must,' I told him.

But the months passed, and I'm here.

And I found I no longer feared death. I no longer quailed at the thought of nakedness to some unstoppable darkness; and as the numbness has passed, I've been strangely content, although grief has scorched me to the bone –

How can that be, Papnanyet? How can such grief be borne? And yet I bear it, and these days I sometimes seem to step out of myself and watch it, as one might watch a fire raging on the far bank of a river –

For many months, I thought little about anything. But when you danced, Papnanyet, or when Senen played her flute, or when I walked in the garden that Ramses, to appease the god of the Hapiru, permits me to use, I began to notice moments that were strangely different, when my mind felt weightless and cleansed and unscarred; and as soon as I noticed them, they were gone.

And still they come; and when I notice them, they've already passed –

Leaving behind – what can I call it? A kind of expectancy. But what is it I wait for? You who sleep, child, in your sleep can you tell me this? What is it that we listen for in our darkness, what snatches of song? What lamp do we watch for in the cramped corners of ourselves?

The sleeping may be closer to the answers than most of the wakeful. I sometimes suspect it.

And isn't it extraordinary, Papnanyet, how robust I've become in this detached state? How able to laugh and scold, and to watch the judgements and hatred in the eyes of such as Nebta when she looked up from rubbing my feet? And how I can set an edge to my tongue, or tease you and Senen and make plans for you, and hold myself as the Daughter of Seti, and all this while in my heart I'm so peculiarly expectant, waiting for I don't know what?

Small things touch me. You, Papnanyet, the way you sleep now, crushing the fan. And how you like to waste my perfume, with not a hint of thought for the fact that when it's gone, there'll be no more of it –

And yet who can tell? Gifts come. There was that broken cone of scented wax –

Do you remember how Sabastet gave it to me? So correct – When you're his wife, Papnanyet, try to teach him some frivolity – How, when he saw her with me in the garden, he thrust it at Senen, his hands dark with earth, the cloth around the wax grimy with sweat.

'I'm no thief,' he said. How gruff he was! 'I found it in the main garden, and I can't take it home. Someone must have dropped it.'

I was touched.

And Senen, winning delicacies for me from the kitchens –

And do you remember the day when she brought from the kitchens that blue bowl, filled with figs?

She set it down without words, and in the way she released her grip on it, I knew how hard she'd fought for it – and that it was because Iy intended to come that day, Iy, the Wrath of Amun, and she knew; and also Meru was being permitted to visit me – and Senen had fought for my dignity.

They came together. It couldn't have been as Iy had planned. Iy was frowning as usual, and cold-eyed. Meru greeted me calmly, and almost smiling. It was like a sunrise to see Meru: the only time he's been permitted here –

I suppose you haven't noticed, Papnanyet. The only time.

They sat one each side of me.

Iy spoke first.

'Daughter,' he said, 'Pharaoh's been merciful to you. This is because the people fear the god of the Hapiru more than Ramses fears Amun. And as I've told him, that's a shameful outcome.'

I inclined my head. 'My brother's very great,' I said. 'He wishes to spare his people further distress, even fear. Surely Amun loves Egypt, and understands my brother's restraint.'

At that, Iy was incensed. 'Who are you,' he shrilled, 'to say what Amun understands? Even your divine brother fails to see the understanding of Amun! You're as presumptuous as you're corrupt. If Ramses punished you as you deserved, Amun would shower blessings on Egypt!'

I spread my hands on my knees, an expression of weariness, but Iy ignored it.

'And do you mean to make threats?' he demanded. 'Do you mean to suggest that Amun himself cowers from the evil of the Hapiru – and that if we dealt with you, he couldn't protect us?'

'I make no threats,' I said. 'But you puzzle me, Iy.'

He waited in furious silence, so then I looked at him plainly and said, 'You claim that Ramses fails to see the mind of Amun, but isn't Ramses himself a god? And if he is, mustn't he follow his own divine nature? If so, in all that he's done in this matter of the Hapiru, in how he resisted Mose and made promises and broke promises, in how at last he let the Hapiru leave us but only to send thousands chasing after them, as if they'd left like thieves in the night – in all this, was my brother mistaken? Although a god, is he a god naturally opposed to the will of Amun? Or is it only in this particular matter – the treatment of his sister – that he fails to know what Amun wills for Egypt?'

Iy sat very still. He stared at me, most like a cobra or some other deadly serpent; but Meru, sitting on my other side, was relaxed: I didn't look at him, but I could feel no tension in him.

Meru said nothing.

Then Iy said: 'Gods clothed in flesh have moments of blurred vision. The function of such dedicated mortals as myself is to clarify those moments. For that I was born, and the likes of you could never understand! As to what you ask, from the start, Ramses should have trusted Amun more. At the first demands of Mose, your brother should have thrown him to the crocodiles! Then Amun wouldn't have punished us so severely for *your* misdoing. He wouldn't have so greatly withdrawn his protection. But Ramses was cautious –' Iy lingered on the word. 'He was cautious. And yet I don't say he was mistaken. I say he should have trusted more, not that his dealings with Mose were mistaken. Your mind's too gross to see these things. Who can separate Amun from Pharaoh? He himself may have wrought your brother's caution as a test, to bring us all to greater punishment for allowing your blasphemy – you, who raised scum of the Hapiru on the threshold of the Great House! This may be so, but even I can't see all things. However, this I know clearly –' His voice rose. 'In how

Ramses deals with you, he's in error! His people's fear has set weights upon his eyes. He fails to see how Amun longs to smile on us and end our punishment. I tell him, "Be rid of her, Pharaoh! Let Amun be pleased and Egypt shall prosper again!" And he answers, "Be silent. Let me concentrate on my building projects, and the business of finding new labourers!"'

Iy stopped. Whatever emotions rose in his throat, they could find no further utterance.

'Ah!' I said, 'You who know the mind of Amun – not, as you say, completely, but so much of it – how it must vex you to see Pharaoh so obsessed with trivial matters!'

And I heard that my voice was mocking, and I marvelled at it, Papnanyet, and I thought to myself, *This is because Meru's here. In his presence, I can find a sort of gaiety to ward off Iy's passions –*

Then Iy found more words, and started ranting. 'Daughter of Seti!' he cried. 'In the great Truths lie many seeming-con-tradictions! Don't take me for a fool! You mustn't take me for a fool! I see how dark you are, how distant from the gods you are, and perverted! Believe me –'

And truly, Papnanyet, I saw in his eyes such a hunger to be believed, to be understood beyond the antics of words: an old man, dangerous and tired, and frightened of being laughed at –

'This wearies me,' I told him. 'When have I ever called you a fool? Isn't it as I've said? You command great respect in Egypt. But there's a wretchedness in you that wants to make me wretched beyond all endurance. What's to be done? We need guidance, you and I, as to how to speak with each other. Perhaps by prayer –'

'The gods won't hear you!' he hissed.

It was an infantile response, and so full of spite, and dealt so quickly, that I think I smiled. I think I did, I hardly understand why; and I raised my hand, meaning, *Enough! Are we urchins hurling mud at each other on the river-bank?* – and Iy watched my movement – I merely raised my hand – he watched it, Papnanyet, and I think he flinched. Truly I think so. And a darkness fell across his eyes, a swift flickering. And that was how I learned that even Iy, the powerful Iy, is more than a little nervous of the god of the Hapiru who's said to protect me.

What else could it have been? In myself there was nothing to threaten him. I was so surprised that I could turn at last to Meru.

'And you?' I asked. 'Have you also come to revile me?'

Meru shrugged, and I thought I saw merriment in his eyes, but I warned myself, *These are not the old days. Since I last saw Meru, the Two Lands have suffered greatly. He's my friend, but what he has to say will be difficult.*

'Speak!' cried Iy. 'Condemn her! Or are you not a priest?'

Then at last Meru said, 'Egypt's like a child that's coughed up and spat out a fish bone – a bone that for too long festered in its throat. The process hurt. Our throat bleeds. But it will heal. Perhaps in future we'll eat less greedily.'

There was silence.

Then I laughed with relief. I felt giddy with relief. Can you understand that, Papnanyet? Have you ever feared a scolding with even the faintest trace of the dread that I'd gathered in myself? And I began a strange chattering: 'Why do you talk so much about fish?' I asked. 'You told me once that I was like a cat that had lost a fish –'

And while I spoke this nonsense, there was a rustling and a scraping of a chair on the floor, and Iy rose. He stood rigidly, looking at me. I stared at him, and he said, 'I came to offer you rituals of Penitence, Daughter, that might in time take away some thousandth part of your guilt. But I can see that this isn't the occasion for it.'

I said nothing. I let him go.

He left the room without the barest courtesy. I turned back to Meru.

'Do you also think I require rituals of penitence?' I asked.

'I'm full of grief. Tell me the truth. How am I to assess my responsibility? All these disasters that have fallen on Egypt. If I hadn't raised Mose – tell me the truth –'

I wept. Meru sat by me. And although I'd asked questions, there were no questions between us. It was a questionless silence, which I ended when I said, 'At times I feel I'm waiting for something. What is it I'm waiting for?'

Meru smiled; but then, instead of answering, as if a shadow had passed from the sun with Iy's departure, he said how good it was to see me, and how well I looked – or must look when the kohl wasn't streaming down my cheeks – and he asked: did I walk often in the garden? He recommended it. 'Haven't I always', he said, 'insisted you pay attention to the garden?' And so he went on, mildly joking while I composed myself.

And he spoke of you, Papnanyet, and Senen.

'Are they behaving as they should? That pretty one, and the steady Senen?'

'Meru,' I said. I so longed for reassurance. I stretched out my hand to him. 'Meru.'

He took my hand and held it firmly. Then he said, 'You may gain greater freedom yet.'

'What?' I asked. 'Is Ramses relenting?'

But at that Meru laughed; and suddenly he let go of my hand, and began to admire the size and plumpness of the figs in the bowl – the figs that Senen had contrived to win for me – and I knew it was an unmistakable sign that he refused to discuss any serious matter – any of it – any further.

Somehow, I could accept it. His presence comforted me so. And, almost in jest, because he made so much of them, I offered him the figs.

'You must take them with you when you go!' I said. 'If you think them so wonderful!'

At once he rose to leave. It was abrupt. In my heart, I cried out to him, *Not yet! Not yet!* But I rose too.

'A short visit!' I said. 'One of your short visits!'

Perhaps he wasn't permitted to stay longer. But as to that, I don't know.

'One of your short visits!'

'But long enough!' said Meru.

I embraced him.

And then – oh, Papnanyet, if you'd been watching and hadn't been banished to the garden, you'd have found it very natural! He seized not only the figs but the bowl as well, although I hadn't offered him the bowl. Still, I allowed it. I didn't reprimand him. He's not only a priest. He's a very mischievous old man –

Besides, isn't he my friend?

And a remarkable gesture: do you remember, Papnanyet? The bowl was returned to me later that day – one of the guards, awkward and unsmiling, brought it to the door; and how you laughed and clapped your hands –

It was filled with the most exquisite lotus flowers.

MARTHA

It was late afternoon. I was preparing the food, and through the open doorway I could hear his voice, the calm of his voice, but as to what he was saying, I couldn't make out the words. And when I turned from the pots and the hearth, through the doorway I could see them, the Teacher and his followers and my brother sitting out here in the yard, the Teacher explaining some deep matter, and my sister sitting close by in that quiet, rapt way of hers.

The vegetables were not yet washed and peeled. The chickens needed feeding. So I came out – wiping my hands on my skirt and pushing my hair back so that I looked respectful – I came out, and stood where the Teacher could see me. Then, when he paused and looked up, 'There's work to be done,' I said. 'Don't you think Mary should come and help?'

My sister looked at me vaguely, as if I'd spoken in some foreign tongue; his followers gawped, because I'd interrupted; as for my brother, he went red in the face; and the Teacher gazed at me.

'Martha, how busy you are!' he said. 'But why cook a big meal? That's not what's needed. Keep it simple. The part that Mary's chosen is good,' he said. 'It'll not be taken from her.' Those were his words, or something like. So then I turned, and I went hurrying for the house. Oh, I went straight back. I couldn't trust myself to speak. Too much pain. Too much pain. How could he have spoken to me like that?

And as I began washing the vegetables, his voice rose up again, talking, telling things – I almost burned the meal for them. I wanted to. *But he's a great teacher, after all*, I thought, *and that has to be respected. A teacher who wants his belly filled, no doubt.* Every moment hurt, I can tell you.

Then, when the meal was cooked and the men came in at last, Mary came, like a woman in a dream, and helped me carry their supper to the table, exactly as though she'd shared in the work; and a bitterness settled on my heart. Even so, we sat together in the outer room, she and I, as was proper, while the Teacher and his followers and our brother ate their fill.

Then she said, 'Let's go in and listen!'

'Suit yourself!' I told her; and although I followed her, it was only to bring out the plates and dishes, while she settled down again near the Teacher's feet.

'*Giving* . . .' I heard him say, and '*selflessness* . . .' I bustled past. I could hardly see for tears.

I brought the plates out into the yard. I set them down, and then I grabbed hold of the pitcher and went to the well. I met no one. Amos was sitting at his door. I nodded and so did he, but I think he saw I was in no mood for chatter. He didn't come after me. The sun was about to drop. It was orange. A strip of rosy pink shone behind the trees. The rest of the sky was already darkening, but I was glad to be outside – bitterly glad. When I came back into the yard, I splashed down the water into the washing dish as though it were some filthy slop. Then I squatted to wash, thrusting my hands in among the plates and the slime of the supper; and I was thinking that the chickens still had to be fed and it was Mary's task, so why should I do it, when there were footsteps behind me. Someone had come out into the yard. Then whoever it was came and stopped in front of me, very close –

I didn't look up. I went on with the plates. I'd felt he must come. He's a great teacher, after all, and it seemed to me that I was owed a word or two.

He squatted down. I still didn't look at him, but I could see the movement as he pushed his sleeves back. Then his hands reached down into the water, closing round mine along with the plate I was holding, and the cloth. It didn't feel wrong. I let my hands rest there while I drew a breath. It was good, my hands being held like that. Then I pulled free and brought out the plate from the water and set it down on the pile of clean ones; and after that, my hands were in the water again, wiping the grease from another plate, and his hands were in the water, too, and he also had a plate and he was using the same cloth – and so we worked together, silently, sharing the cloth.

If he wants to do a woman's work, I thought to myself, *who am I to stop him?* It was a thought that made me smile – not the kindest smile, truth to tell – and I looked up at him. He smiled back.

'Thank you for supper, Martha,' he said.

'You're welcome,' I said.

And just at that moment, it was true; he was welcome, his smile melted so much of my pain – and yet not all of it.

'I do what I can,' I said, thinking of that *'good part'* Mary was supposed to have chosen. 'I'd like to listen too, you know. Only, someone has to feed you –'

'And wash up afterwards.' He laughed. Suddenly he laughed, like a shift of the sun into higher sky. It was like that. Then he straightened up, wiping the water from his arms, and he looked very slight, standing there with the pink of the dusk around him, smiling at me while I squatted by the washing dish.

He said nothing else. He turned, and went back into the house.

As to what happened next – it's not a thing for words, but what else do we have? A shutter opened. I crouched there – over there – with the cloth in my hands, and I waited to take offence. He'd left me to go back to the others. I waited for the anger to come – but instead this shutter opened. I don't mean one of the house's shutters, this was a shutter in my understanding – and merriment came streaming out: a silent mirth at no one's expense; and everything the Teacher had said since he'd arrived that day, everything I'd heard only in snatches and blurs – I understood that I already knew it. It was alive in my being. And I folded my arms, and, as I crouched by the washing dish, I could smell my own warmth caught in my skirt, I could feel my own strength, and I saw how –

But I won't speak about that. I have the bread to bake.

I told someone once. Do you remember Joanna? The Capernaum woman. The educated woman. You remember her? How she used to walk – remember? – pulling her skirt away from the chickens and turning her head from the stench of the mules!

That husband of hers was a great fool. What place was this for such a woman? He sold the house again within a few months. He had business in Jerusalem, but Jerusalem's rents weren't to his liking, and so he brought her here, both to save himself rent and to make sure she squandered nothing from his purse in Jerusalem's markets. A bulky, small-eyed man. He kept her in the village like a pearl in a sealed box. Don't you remember? It was the weaver's house. Micah's house. After Micah died. The son didn't want it – Nathan. He had settled in the north. He came back only to show respect, and sell everything. Joanna's husband saw the house and bought it. I think he'd rented out their home in Capernaum. She was trapped here, and she walked with a tilt to her nose, and she made friends with no one –

But I suppose, you didn't notice that, did you? You seemed to notice so little in those days – I mean, of such things: vanities, snobberies. When she first arrived, you took her honey. And once you left some figs outside her door. She wouldn't open to you, so you left them there. And sometimes at the well, you smiled and chattered to her, as if she might be any of us. I heard you admire her hands once. They were pale and very delicate, and you said they were beautiful.

She stared at you. I don't think she liked you much.

But then, she liked none of us, and yet I told her – at least something: more than I told anyone else in those days, including you. Especially including you.

I know. You think I'm abrupt. You often say that it's been hard for you, how I keep my own counsel, and that whenever you ask me what I think, I simply say what I think – not what you want from me, which is more than what I think: you want the feelings behind the thinking. And you say it's hard for you that even now, with lines deep in your face, I judge you as a child who plays with emotions.

Well, it's been hard for me, too.

We've said it many times. It's been hard for both of us.

Put more wood on the hearth. Why be cold? Before you leave tomorrow, you can find some more. You used to know where to look. Or James will find it.

And that's something we must talk about. James. He misses his parents. That's natural. And sometimes he looks at me, and in his eyes I see the question: *Why does she still live?* I don't say he's not fond of me, but he watches and asks himself: *Why did the sickness take my parents and not this old one?* It unsettles him, and it poisons his respect for me.

Speak to him. Ruth may be dull, and not so pretty as some, but she has strong arms made for hard work, and anyone can see the promise of those broad hips. One must be practical. And she's honest. I can tell from her smile. He shouldn't be ogling around, over her head.

Speak to him. If you lived here, he might find things easier. Or if you came more often –

He'll be home soon, and then we won't talk like this.

You spend too much time – everywhere but here. You should have married. Laugh all you want, it won't change anything. Wandering about, spending nights in strange houses. You and your good part. '*Mary has chosen a good part.*'

Your clothes are filthy. When did you last wash whatever that is you've wrapped round you? And you're thin.

I know. I know. '*Mary has chosen a good part.*'

And later that evening – remember? – you came to me and said, 'I didn't feed the chickens. I'll go and do it now.'

And I stopped you. I put my hand on your arm. We stood in the doorway, and I wanted to say that I was content – more than content – to be who I am, and for you to be who you are, but somehow I didn't speak. Then you said, 'It's late, but until I've been to them, they won't settle.'

So I told you to go and be quick about it.

You meant, I suppose, that they were waiting for their scraps and wouldn't be cheated out of them; but you meant, too, that those chickens loved you, or you loved them, or some such notion. I could hear it in your voice. Love, before we wrung their necks and served them up as suppers. And I laughed, but even so, I was angry: all this business of loving chickens, and being so sure – you've always been so sure about it, haven't you? – about the business of loving and your right to it? But I didn't want the anger. After what had happened in the yard that evening, it was coming back too soon, just like a tax collector trying to push in at a wedding feast. Remember Neriah? So puffed up with importance and bad nerves – and so greedy? The anger felt like that and I didn't want it. So it turned into tears, and I stood there by the door, laughing and weeping, and when you came back, you saw it.

'I'll work hard tomorrow,' you said. 'When the Teacher's gone.' Then you said, 'I never mean to displease you.'

I patted your cheek. You had tears in your eyes, too, which was irritating. You've always wept so easily. Tears for everything.

Nothing changes. Look at you now! Blow your nose.

I patted your cheek. You were very young.

'Go and sleep,' I said. 'We have nothing to quarrel about.'

And I didn't tell you –

I didn't tell you, in case you said – or somehow outshone it – told me what was greater. Not that anything could be More. And what was there to say? But you –

There's a way you have of being so full to the brim, and I feared my own fullness might be lost in yours.

Besides, as I say, what was there to tell you?

I told no one except Joanna, a stranger, and one I didn't care for, that conceited woman –

Oh, and not some enormous story. Now you expect stories! You, who have so many! How hungry you look for one more, still one more! And what can I tell you? Only that, in the yard that evening, I'd learned something to laugh about in this living out of who we are. Not that it's easy, but then, the best jokes – the simplest – come out of what's difficult. Haven't you noticed?

In any case, you know what I know. At least as much as I.

I changed, didn't I? After that evening? When the Teacher left in the morning, that basket I gave them – Simon and the others – fruit, bread and our best oil: didn't you see my hands as I packed it? But I suppose not. You had eyes only for him. The Teacher. My hands were trembling. There were matters I'd have liked to have discussed with him, but prayers had to be said, and then there were people – too many people – who kept pushing into the house, demanding to see him, and there was Lazarus for him to talk to; and so all my wanting went into that basket, into the things and the packing.

And I was quiet afterwards. Remember? We were all three very quiet, for weeks.

But Lazarus and I talked sometimes, just the two of us – you were so young – about you, for instance.

Lazarus used to say, 'When she marries, it'll be different. For now, provided she does her work in the normal way of things, where's the harm? He didn't find fault with her, and he's a great teacher. You can't deny that.'

I never denied it. And one evening, when we'd heard some news from a traveller, some small news of him, Lazarus said to me, 'I believe he may be greater than I've understood.'

You were asleep.

I knew you would have thrown your arms round your brother's neck if you'd heard him: hadn't you once whispered to me, 'The Teacher's no ordinary man. Can't you *feel* that?'

And can you remember my reply? I folded my arms and looked at you. 'Whatever you think,' I said, 'be quiet about it. That's best,' I said, 'because *he's* quiet about it.'

And so that evening, I said to Lazarus, 'Be careful what you say.'

'You don't agree with me?' he demanded, pale and staring. You know how he was – so passionate.

I went on with my sewing; and I heard him get up and come across the room.

'Martha!' he said. 'Martha! What troubles we would have without you. I'm not sure that Mary and I deserve you, dreamers like us. You should marry again.'

'I expect I shall,' I said, pushing the needle. 'And don't fool yourself. I have my own dreams. And understandings.'

He stood close to where I sat, almost where you're sitting now. I could feel his gaze on my fingers and the thread.

'Then you agree,' he said, 'that he's greater –'

'All I'm saying is be careful!' I told him. 'There's no need for many words.'

I know. I know. He spoke more freely to you – and I dare say, more often. Young though you were.

I used to see you, your heads together, out there in the sunlight in the yard, or even as winter came, out there, your breath and his frosting together – or when I came into the house, the pair of you caught in some web together: a silence like a web, the words barely gone from your mouths; and you would turn to me, both of you, your faces open as though to say, *'We don't mean to keep you out!'* And wasn't there an understanding in how I always accepted that? Didn't my silence tell you, *I'm content?*

Don't weep.

Lazarus loved us both. He was a good brother. He was wise, treading that path between us. Saying things when he called us to prayers, not as though I might disapprove: he knew I didn't – but as though he and I – and you – had spoken equally about everything, each one of us as fully as the next.

Lazarus.

That was strange – how at first you didn't weep when he became so ill. Remember? Sharing the long watches by his bed. Obedient. Going, when I told you, curling at once by the hearth, and then, coming again, gentle, concentrating, with whatever was right and sensible: a bowl of water, the juice of squeezed lemons with honey, and cool presses.

No tears.

I was grateful. So grateful. How I loved you.

Only when you said, 'Let me send for the Teacher!' your eyes turned into great pools. And when Lazarus smiled and said, 'It's too dangerous. Don't forget his enemies. Recent events –' you said, 'I don't care about the danger!' And only then you wept – wept for shame, because you'd thought first of danger to ourselves, and that wasn't what Lazarus had meant.

I know. I know. It was an easy mistake to make. You found it unthinkable – danger for *him*. I know.

And didn't I half agree? Remember my words. Lazarus was sleeping. You and I were eating at the table. I mean that I ate, but you – your tears fell into your broth, you gaped and sobbed into your broth, and I said, 'Perhaps it isn't so dangerous. Who are we to decide this? He and Lazarus love each other. We'll not ask him to come, but we'll send a message. He has a right to know that Lazarus is failing –'

You sprang up. 'Joel will go for us!' you cried. 'I've already asked him!'

'It's Joel I have in mind,' I said. 'He's solid and unexcitable. And Hannah can see to everything while he's away. Go and fetch him. We must make sure he understands that we don't ask –'

You had already left the room.

So Joel went for us. And was that honest, do you think? That '*not asking for anything*'?

You knew he'd come. You were calm. Sitting by Lazarus, or moving about the house, you were wrapped in expectation. Lazarus sank. His breathing burned down into whispers of breathing, his skin yellowed; but you were calm.

'Lazarus is dying,' I told you.

'He'll come!' you said. 'You know he will!'

And that was true. I did know.

'But too late,' I said. 'It may be too late.'

Can you remember the first time I said that? I can still see your astonishment, and hear the breath – the gasp that came from you, almost a laugh at such an idea.

Then Joel came home again. He had hardly slept since he'd left the village. Straight there and back. He stank of sweat. He had borrowed that horse – remember? – that flea-ridden creature from the desert near Bethabara. Some old friend's. Joel, who'd never ridden any beast greater than a mule. And so he came back before we thought it possible, in half the time.

'He's coming!' he said. 'Most of them say he shouldn't. It's too dangerous. But he's coming!'

You smiled, and said, 'Of course.'

The house was crowded, and we spoke softly. That was hard, wasn't it? So many would-be comforters and helpers, advisers and well-wishers, and some tight mouths when they heard who it was we'd sent for. All that intrusion.

I took you out into the yard. We stood by the herb pots. It was a crisp afternoon, the last cold day before that mildness came, that strange mildness –

'How can he come fast enough?' I said. 'He'll be on foot.

And if he doesn't come tomorrow, he'll be in time only for the rituals.'

And you said, 'Nothing can go wrong now.' Then you said, 'All these people –'

'Most will go soon!' I told you. 'They won't wish to be here for the uncleanliness of death.'

You gaped at me. I suppose you have no memory of it. And I thought to myself, *She thinks I'm mad, speaking of death. She thinks I've lost my senses –*

I thought *you* were almost mad.

Then we went back into the house, and I sent everyone away. I was blunt – remember? I told them that they took too much air from the room. Some were angry. There was that man – who was he? – the one who said as he left, 'You're his family, so I won't argue with you. But I believe his wife, if he had one, would have shown us more respect.' He never came to us again.

So then we were alone. And before dawn, I touched your arm, and said, 'It's over.'

He lay naked –

Lazarus –

Oh, there was the coverlet over him, and the cloth across him – but naked: all that suffering lifted from him, all that longing for – what he longed for – all lifted.

And no colour left. Haven't you noticed? Almost anything has colour in lamplight – but he had none. And the tension had gone from his face, like a mask taken off.

'Now we must wash him,' I said. 'And you must fetch the men. We must send for a priest –'

You ran out of the house. I heard you in the yard, wailing and arguing. I didn't hear the words, but the sound was terrible. It woke Hannah and Joel. It woke Simon and Micael and Abigail –

I sat by Lazarus. What had been Lazarus.

'Well,' I said, 'you see how it is, brother. She doesn't understand. She expected a miracle.' And a weight, something I'd forgotten, you could call it the sorrow of everything, returned like an old comfort. I felt it settling in my belly.

'We'll manage,' I said. 'You didn't want to inconvenience the Teacher, and now look. It's too late. And will you find now what you hoped for? And what am I supposed to say when he comes? He will come. Or should I send and prevent him? But there's at least one of us who couldn't bear that.'

After that, I was quiet. I didn't want Lazarus to hear me. Perhaps I was more than half mad. But in my thoughts I said, *He could have saved you, my brother. And somehow, if he'd wished it, he could have been here. But he didn't wish it. He had business elsewhere. That's how it is with Teachers. They expect everything from us.*

Then you came in, bringing help, and saying that Micael had gone for a priest, and you spoke so steadily and quietly, although your cheeks were wet, that I felt scolded and childish.

You don't believe me? But that's something you've never understood. You say I judge you as a child, but often you've made me feel foolish and clumsy like an infant, breaking things and upsetting things –

And with you to look after, even so.

Lazarus was closed in his tomb.

What days. Cruel days. Was it any easier for us that he'd so often told us his health might not sustain him into old age? Did it comfort us that he'd left everything prepared, his ledge ready in the tomb, and his fields tended and his business interests in Jerusalem so well protected – all that thought for us, which you'd barely noticed, and which, whenever he'd mentioned it, I myself had smiled at and said, 'If only my husband had been so careful! You're a good brother!' And then I'd moved on quickly, because I'd known he saw that I approved, and what more was there to say? I fed him carefully. I saw to it that he wore light woollen clothes in winter, warm, but not too heavy, I scolded him if he overexerted himself in the hot months. And I said to myself, *He's sensitive like our mother, but he doesn't cough and grow breathless as she did. His health may be weak, but it's not the poor rag that hers was. Why shouldn't he live a long life?*

All those arrangements for us. His care, breaking open like a honeycomb, the sweetness pouring out. So many friends hurrying at once to sit out the mourning days with us, and assure us of promises made to him for our welfare.

To be grateful, and with our tears – I did weep: you say I hardly ever weep, but in those days you saw it, if you saw anything through your own tears – to find words of thanks and understanding of kindnesses, and to be sure they were comfortable, all those good people who packed into our house –

Not to mention the others: the sour ones, who came for propriety's sake, suspicious and sharp-nosed, fearful of scandalous goings-on, because – how did our aunt from Bethcar put it? – 'Your brother sometimes kept such strange company'?

That was hard. It grazed the bone of our grief. You think I don't know? You look surprised. You think, because I spoke sharply to Hannah, and I suppose to several other neighbours, if the food ran low, and because I spent worry on blankets and places to sleep, you think I didn't feel the cruelty of it? That Lazarus had gone, and there was no sign of the one friend he'd have wanted here, who might have saved him, and who, they said, was coming – but when? When? And for what? While there were all those others to house, feed and thank –

And you, weeping steadily and calmly, a kind of dream-weeping that people took for resignation, so that they said to me, 'Losing her brother will make her more responsible. One can see the woman in her now.'

More responsible. Don't laugh. It's what many thought, and it angered me – that hint that you were not as you should be. What right had *they* to judge?

But it was hard. To find the right words was hard, or to say nothing.

And you were difficult.

Can you remember?

At one time, I was in the yard: I was watching the women wash bowls and platters – squatting there, with the water splashing on their skirts, and their hands were red with the wet cloths in them; I was standing there, I had lost what it was that I'd gone from the house to say, and you came up behind me.

'He'll bring Lazarus back!' you said. 'You'll see.'

Don't you remember?

I thought not. There are times when we speak and hardly know we speak. The knowing is all somewhere else.

And now are you surprised again? Did you think I have no inkling of that – how we sometimes speak without knowing it?

Or am I unfair?

Oh, it's true: I'm unfair. It's not that you think I don't know such things: it's just that you think I don't notice – much as I often think you don't notice a great deal that matters, as now, when I look at you, and not only are your clothes filthy, but those shoes: don't you see they need mending? That thong – that one – might snap, and will you like that, out on the road somewhere?

'*He'll bring Lazarus back,*' you said, and you went wandering to the gateway, looking out.

The sunlight lay on you. *Such a child,* I thought, *such a child!* And I felt fear.

There. I was afraid.

What will become of her? I thought. *Lazarus can't come back.*

Then I came in again to our guests, and the prayers, and the weeping, and, *Let her be quiet,* I thought. *Let her not say too much with all these people here! If she shocks them, they'll think she's mad with grief – the kind ones. But the others will say she's been corrupted by our brother's strange friends. They may expect her to undergo disciplines –*

And I looked round our inner room, crowded with faces – settled faces – each one fixed in its own business with death, and duty, and whatever else can't be avoided, and I thought: *Isn't this enough? All this weight of so many faces, and Lazarus dead? Isn't it enough, but must I also carry the weight of a sister who won't see the inevitable? Lazarus rots in his tomb. His friend, when he comes, can speak kindly to us and comfort us. He can show us that nothing's happened that shouldn't have happened – but – bring Lazarus back? That's a child's dream, and only because it's a child's dream can one hold from crying 'Blasphemy!' The dead are not to be summoned. The will of Who Made Us is not to be rebelled against –*

Then you were standing in the doorway. You had come in from looking down the road, where, I saw at once, you had seen nothing. Pale and weeping, you came and sat by me, while the prayers droned on, and I thought, *I mistook what she said. It's true. She spoke a child's dream, not a belief. I needn't worry.*

So we sat there together, until late into the night, and in the end – remember? – because the house was crowded, we lay down so close to each other here by the outer door, we shared one blanket, and you slept, and your breath – but how could you know this? – was deep and steady, while I stared at the roof and asked myself: *Can anyone ever be brought back? And if he came, what would I say to him? What questions? But how could it be right to question the dead? And what food would I cook for him? And what would the priests say about it? And those with whom he'd made arrangements – to whom he'd left gifts and the running of his business affairs? Would they tell him, 'You're no longer alive. The dead shouldn't walk among the living. Get back to your grave'? And would he, in fact, be Lazarus?*

Oh, you don't know. I lay chilled with horror, and your breath on my cheek so trusting and deep.

You see.

It's not true that I feel less than you. You see it now.

I couldn't close my eyes, lying there with your weight pressing on my back, and, truly, you weighed on me – until, towards dawn, I drifted into a memory: it was evening, and the sky had pinkened. I was crouched in the yard, washing supper plates. My hands were in the water. I was rubbing at a slick of grease with the cleaning cloth and, as I did, there were those other hands in the water along with mine, a man's hands, rubbing at a plate with the other end of the same cloth.

And I fell asleep after that.

Well, he came. Not that next day but the one after. And his whole wide-eyed, empty-bellied flock with him – Simon, James, Thomas – they all came; nothing discreet about it.

I was called to the door. It was Amos, who had passed them on the road and came scrambling to us. He whispered something. He snatched hold of my arm and pulled me out of the house. He was panting. Old Amos. Oh, you laugh now, but he was very frightened. He shook as he told me, 'That person's coming!'

Then he said, 'Is this wise? We don't want trouble here! I know your brother – may he be at peace – thought well of him. And you've been waiting for him. But this man's far madder than he used to be. You must have heard –'

'I'll go and meet him,' I said, taking Amos's hand. He was quaking like a small bird. 'Tell no one yet,' I said. 'I'll go and warn him that all these people are here!'

'Tell him to behave himself!' cried Amos.

So I went quickly. I walked out of the village. I thought of you, weeping in the house, the comforters round you, watching you, and how, if you'd known what I was doing, you'd have sprung up. But one of us, I thought, should remain with our guests, and which of us should break the news that Lazarus was dead? Surely the elder of us. And I knew that I could be calmer than you, which was as it should be –

*

He was waiting.

Over the years, have you considered that? I suppose you don't need to. But I have. He had stopped by the broken wall, where the track leads off towards the tombs. He was standing there waiting, and the others around him looked nervous and watchful, as if they meant to lift him up and carry him off at any moment, so that I might have thought, *They're not sure that it's safe in the village. They want me to reassure them –*

But instead, because of where he stood by the track, I thought, *He knows!* and I spoke in a rush.

I didn't welcome him; and I didn't mean to reproach him. *He knows everything!* I thought, so I let my words hit the point.

'If you'd been here, you'd have saved him!' I said. 'Somehow.'

He didn't answer. There were murmurs – regrets. Thomas, I think, spoke awkwardly about God's will, but he soon lost what he was saying and fell silent like the rest. They were embarrassed – I saw that – and confused. And suddenly I felt that their nervousness had to do with more than safety and threats from Jerusalem, or even with coming too late. There was a secret in it. It was as though I'd walked into a Test that involved them all. They were stricken with some Teaching – one of his difficult Teachings – and they were watching me as if I might make matters worse, whatever it was that he'd been telling them. Or as if I might make him appear foolish – and not for coming late. That's how I felt. And something was expected of me. And still he said nothing.

What could I do?

I hadn't meant to reproach him – and yet, *Why shouldn't there be reproach?* I thought.

Why shouldn't I be angry? Had he rushed to comfort Lazarus? Had he borrowed horses, or walked through the nights? But the anger in me wasn't free to stab about as it might have done: there was this other thing – this Testing thing – and so I hardly knew what to say. I was annoyed, and I flung my hands up.

'Oh,' I said, 'I understand. Even now, even though Lazarus is dead, you can comfort us. God listens to you. God blesses what you do. I haven't forgotten.'

Meaning – that time in the yard: I hadn't forgotten. *He's a great Teacher after all*, I thought, *and I haven't forgotten.*

Then he was speaking: 'Lazarus,' he said, and he spoke about the dead, and of life beyond death, and I was saying, 'I know, I know.' He made it sound – as he made so much sound – simply a matter of patience; and I kept saying, 'I know. I know –' until he asked, 'Do you believe that?'

Quite sharply: *'Do you believe that?'*

It was like a rap on the wrist; and when I think of it now, I see our grandmother. Of course you can't: she died before you were born. I see her hunched by the yard gate, smiling and nodding at passers-by, and if anyone – as many did – stopped to gossip with her, she would listen to their news with little cries of interest, and repeat the names they mentioned, and sigh, and offer observations. 'The young have hot tempers!' she'd say. Or, 'A wise man values his wife!' so that people thought that she was truly listening; and even she thought she listened to them. But it wasn't so. And whenever our mother sent me to speak to her, she used to say, 'Ask her if she's seen Micael go by –' or, 'Ask her if she's thirsty – And, remember, touch her first, or she won't know she's hearing you.'

And there, by the track that day, it was much the same. *'Do you believe that?'* he asked, and I knew I'd almost not heard what he'd been saying, and yet I had heard. His eyes waited. They were wide open, and they left the question open –

But I had heard.

'I believe that,' I said. 'I know what you are.'

It was no surprise – to myself, I mean. You smile. Not for *you*, the rap on the wrist. But some of us –

It's one thing what he'd done in the yard that evening, how he'd opened an understanding in me; it's another thing to speak plain words against the common order of what we see, and expect them to be heard. Some of us have to be desperate before we can be touched, and know what we're hearing. But when we do know – where's the surprise? It's simply so.

I think he understood and allowed that. That I was desperate.

Once I'd spoken, he smiled. He was fond of me. Oh, he loved you, and Lazarus – but he was fond of me, too, in his way. I'm not talking about that great Teaching love –

He was fond of me.

'I do,' I said. 'I believe it.'

Then he sent me to fetch you.

That's how it was. I had been touched. I'd heard – and yet you frown. It's that word, isn't it – *desperate*?

Why is it like this? I know you trust me, and yet sometimes you and I, when we try to explain, we miss each other.

Aren't there two kinds of desperation? One kind could make us swear that chickens talk, or that Jerusalem is made of cheese – anything, if that would only save a sick child. Then there's another kind that could keep us walking for three days without water, or make us able to lift a slab of rock that not even strong men could shift – lift it up quickly and lightly as though it were a basket of eggs, if a trapped child lay beneath it.

One is a lie. The other is a reach beyond what seems the limit. I didn't lie.

And so I came back to you.

'Come out,' I said, 'into the yard.'

Remember? You sat weeping. Our aunt from Bethcar had her hand clamped firmly round yours, as much as to say, 'This is as it should be!' And after days of peering down the road and gazing through the shutters, you didn't see what was obvious. You wouldn't come out into the yard. Wasn't it in my face, what I had to tell? But you just stared, until I whispered –

And then –

How like you that was! Nothing discreet. You sprang up. You tore away from the hands and the eyes, and you ran –

Our aunt shrieked, 'The poor child! She's going to weep at the tomb!' And the men rose, and out they came, pushing through the doorway into the daylight, shuffling and murmuring.

'She shouldn't be alone!' they said. 'She scarcely knows what she's doing!' they said. 'Poor child!' And, 'Ah, Lazarus!' they cried, and in each of them – in the kindest as well as in the sour ones – strange to say, there was that thing like satisfaction. I saw it, and do you know what I thought? I thought, *People feed off death.*

Then I ran after you.

He was still waiting, by the track.

As I ran, I didn't concern myself, as I should have done, with how many of those people following us were hostile to him. I didn't even ask myself what you would do – something too much that might make things dangerous for him –

Well, it's your way –

I didn't think. I only ran.

You flung yourself at his feet, and grasped his ankles.

'If you'd been here,' you said, 'Lazarus wouldn't have died.'

Hadn't *I* said that?

You and I – but why talk of it? It's hardly important, what I thought. Except that you want to know. If I tell you, will you promise to eat more? And will you wash those clothes more often? And talk to James? If he loses Ruth, he deserves to go to bed with a scorpion, and he has so little sense, he probably will.

What did I think?

Your tears on his feet. His tears at the sight of you –

I thought, *These two don't need words.*

I thought, *Why are my eyes dry? Why have I always said to myself, 'Be strong!' so that she can be weak?*

I thought, *He showed me that evening . . . Didn't I understand?*

For me to be me, and for her to be what she is – it's a play of patterns.
And in the end, coming to what's behind them, there's only –

But at that moment, I couldn't remember the thing behind them that had made me laugh so. And, truly, it's hard to remember. Instead, there was only the sight of you weeping and him weeping with you, and the need to cling to what I'd said to him there on the road – how I believed what he'd told me – and everything I half knew but had half forgotten that he'd shown me in the yard –

Which leaves me no choice, I thought. *If I have a sister born closer to the Truth than I am – what's to be done? I must accept it.*

And then I thought, *I've twisted things. He tried to show me. It's nonsense, all this asking which of us is closer –*

But it was hard. Why you and not I?

And why could you not be I?

The questions refused to be rubbed away. They are stubborn stains.

Then he said, 'Take me to the grave.'

So – Well, enough! All this holding and hugging. When you were small – remember? – I used to push you away, you with your arms open, wanting everything. But then, just as often, I held you. And I was stronger, so when I had a mind to hold you, you couldn't have run away even if you'd wanted to. But you didn't want to.

Fetch me a cloth – that green one on the hook by the door. Perhaps it's as well you don't come more often. I know for you it's nothing, all this weeping. But I don't trust it. You know I don't.

Why not? You ask me, 'Why not?' Haven't you understood anything? What is it you think I'm talking about? It's not that I'm angry – but do you listen? You are you. And I'm your sister, Martha, not you. Not like this, at least –

*

166

So we took him to the grave. Remember the mob of us scrambling up the slope, the flies buzzing – a mob, what else? All those noses for grief and gossip. All the quick sympathies, the 'Too late!' and, 'Ah, how this fellow must have loved Lazarus!' All our fear for the Teacher's safety, and of what might happen, and what was happening. And you, with your vast – whatever it was you felt, trailing it with you, and me, with all my tossed-about ideas. And I was saying in myself, *Brother, would you have wanted this, what he's going to do? I know what it is that he's going to do. I know. And all these people. And you, such a quiet, private person.*

Then we had reached the entrance. The stone. Someone slipped. Remember? I don't suppose you do. He fell flat on his belly down the slope just as we got there. He was hauled up, grabbed beneath the arms and hauled up, but no one paid much attention, because the moment he was on his feet, there were those words: '*Take away the stone.*'

I felt very weak. I was shaking and wanted something to hold on to. There was nothing –

'He'll be stinking,' I said. 'He's been dead four days –'

And where was everyone else? You, and the followers – Simon and the rest – and the aunts and the business partners, the friends and cousins, and our neighbours – where were you all then? For me, it was as though every one of you – even those grunting as they pushed at the stone – had been swung out in a great net from where I stood, quite suddenly, all of you in some strange dream, where you hung, peering through the mesh, waiting to be lowered to the ground again. But I was *there*, and my voice cracked, but even so I said what had to be said. This was for Lazarus, after all.

'The weather's been mild.' I said. 'He'll be stinking.'

At that, he smiled. The Teacher. And he spoke to me softly. He said something about belief – I couldn't follow it. I only knew that what he meant was terrible. He was talking about power.

And I felt it.

As he spoke, I felt it – the power of belief. It seemed to turn the very air into a muscle that set to work on everything, shaping and reshaping, and I, too, was gripped by it and, as the stone shifted, I thought I'd crumble into nothing, into fine dust –

Tell me – we've never spoken of it –

Did you feel horror? I suppose not, netted in your dream, you with all the rest.

Lazarus, crawling out. Our careful bandaging – Blind and bound – trying to right himself – wriggling like a worm – levering himself, his back against the wall, onto his feet – swaying there, and none of us moving, no one. It failed me then, didn't it, the part in me that does the sensible thing? I couldn't move – until I heard that sharp instruction: 'Let him go! Untie him!' And you –

Were you there first? Which of us? Fumbling with the bindings –

Who helped us? Have you any idea? I have none. I only heard you whispering, 'Don't be afraid, Lazarus. It's us!' and I was thinking, *Why would he be afraid?* And I heard myself, too loud, saying, 'Stand still, brother, or you'll fall over. Breathe slowly. You must stand still.'

You lifted the cloth from his face. It was you, wasn't it? I don't think I did.

And behind us, and all around us, silence. And there in front of us, silence. The silence of Lazarus.

Then I said, 'You don't stink. I thought you would. But you must wash –'

And at that, a hubbub broke out –

You took his hand. You led him through the shouting and fainting, the praying and arguing –

I must go home and heat water, I thought, but I sat down. There, by the tomb.

Someone came to me and said, 'Aren't you going to thank the Teacher?'

And someone else said, 'What you did was an honest mistake, burying an ill man. It happens. Don't blame yourself.'

A great deal was said.

I felt sick. I heaved up lumps of bread there by the stone. My head buzzed. And then – but when was this? – some women standing nearby started to yammer about blasphemy and demons. And someone else stood by my ear, saying in a cold, unsteady voice: 'My wife was young. She was so very much younger, and I have no children. Was your loss so much greater than mine?' And again, someone else insisted: 'It happens. Trances sometimes last for days.'

And it seemed to me that all these sounds built up into a wall around me, through which, squinting through the chinks, I saw sunlight, and men and women silently weeping and embracing each other, and their faces were the faces of children.

Then I felt a hand on my shoulder, and I was calm. *It's him*, I thought, *the Teacher* – but when I looked up, it was only rough, simple Thomas. His eyes were wet.

'Back to the house,' he whispered.

He helped me to my feet, and I started to say, 'I must thank him –'

'Just walk,' said Thomas. 'That's enough.'

Stir the broth. You've forgotten it, haven't you? Stir it. Why shouldn't you cook for me for once? I've cooked for you often enough!

Should we be laughing? Add the herbs.

You wanted me to talk. I'm talking.

It's true. My bones grumble. If I bend or stretch or try to hold the smallest pot, they grumble –

It's good that you're here.

Lazarus would want us to laugh.

A time of secrets. You, of course, never asked Lazarus, 'Were you really dead?' I'm sure of it. Why would you?

Neither did I, although once I came close to it. He was so quiet. And warm. Weren't you relieved that he was so easy to touch? So living – the veins blue and thin, his breathing like anyone's, only – remember? – every breath seemed to be for us. A kind of gift. I don't mean that he suffered. That's not what I mean.

If only he'd spoken more.

One night, you were out in the yard, I could hear you talking to Hannah – I touched his hand and asked him, 'Are you truly here, brother?' And when he didn't reply, I said, 'Where were you?'

I thought he might say something then. I think he almost wanted to, but he changed his mind; and I felt I should brush my questions out of him, so that he kept his feet on the good ground. So I said, 'We must keep you safe. Not everyone likes what's happened. You mustn't go into the city.'

At that, he looked amazed, and then he started to laugh.

'I won't have you taking risks,' I said, and he laughed all the more, a mouse-like, wheezing sound, the water pouring down his cheeks. At first it scared me, but soon I found that I was laughing too. He thought it absurd, this talk of taking risks, and I laughed with him.

You came in and found us laughing together, and Lazarus said, 'Don't worry.'

You rushed to him. You held his hands, and you two – your eyes were on his face and his on yours, and although the three of us were laughing, I thought to myself, *Their joke is something more. And he feels more at ease with her.*

I got up and fetched my mending.

Always more. How you sat with him in the yard, how you ran errands for him, or went with him down the road as far as the sycamore, encouraging him, feeding his strength with little words that would have sounded laughable from my mouth, and how you talked to him, telling him again – and yet again – how his friend had come, and wept, and how we'd all gone up the track to the tomb.

And Lazarus spoke to you, didn't he? About – I don't know what. Neither of you ever told me.

I asked you – bluntly, remember?

'Has Lazarus said anything? About those days in the grave?'

And you stared, and said, 'It's not like that. He asks me what colour I think a stone is, or a chicken's feather. He says I should learn to look at things.'

'What did the Teacher say to him,' I asked, 'before he left here? What advice did he give? That quiet talk they had in the yard. It would help to know.'

I've always thought you knew – that Lazarus told you – but you wouldn't say, and even now, at the mention of it, I can see that closed look on your face. You're never going to tell me. I don't know why. Your only answer was, 'To live peacefully and avoid becoming a spectacle. I think it was something of that kind.'

And nothing else? Nothing?

You say not, and if you say not, I suppose I must believe it. But I've always thought –

You seemed to know more.

He used to smile when you came near him, and together you would smile when I pushed the bowl of oil and the bread at him and said, 'Eat. It's good bread, freshly baked, and with the herbs you like. Eat. You're too thin.'

I pretended I felt included in your smiles. That I should bake and urge him to fatten up, while you and he murmured your other things – I held myself as if I knew nothing was more natural.

Which I did. I did –

And yet it hurt.

He understood that. And so did you.

Pushing visitors away – that was my part. Sending gawpers

packing. And those business associates – the ones who came to ask about legalities, and would he approve of this or that arrangement? I used to watch Lazarus, smiling, polite, and – it seemed to me – lost for words. And then – remember? – I'd go smartly to where they sat, and tell whoever it was, 'You're tiring him. Can't you see? It's enough for one day.'

He never spoke against that – and do you know what I said to those associates? When I had them on the road – remember how I used to walk them briskly from the village? – I said, 'In the days when his life was like any man's, my brother trusted you, and you and he came to understandings. Don't trouble him. Just honour those understandings, as though he were in his tomb, because his life now is like no one else's.'

It moved them. They looked tearful and relieved.

'You're a good woman,' they said. And one or two told me, 'It would be for the best if I spoke to you when there are business matters. Just as if you'd survived him.'

'It would be for the best,' I said.

Then I would walk back to the house, thinking, *This, at least, I can do.*

And Lazarus –

Once he said to me, 'Martha, you hold on to our roof for us!'

'I can understand business as well as you!' I said.

'Oh, better!' he said. 'That, and many things.'

I was scrubbing the table when he spoke, and I was glad of it – the strong, good action. His words meant so much to me.

Another time, I was beating a mat in the yard, and he sat watching the dust rise, and how I beat the mat against the wall, and I knew – I felt it – he had started to weep as he so often did; and I meant to ignore it, as I so often did, usually it seemed the kindest thing, but instead I turned to him and asked, 'Is it this? Do you weep because I beat the mat?'

You smile. But I'd noticed he could weep for the strangest reasons.

Lazarus laughed. There he sat, sobbing and laughing, so that I went to him and put my hand on his arm, and wiped his face on my skirt.

'You'll get stronger,' I said.

'You're the strong one,' he answered. 'Remember that.'

Well, how motherly you look! How very motherly! It touches you, does it, that I treasure these little praises?

But then you –

Oh, there were days when you used to vanish, walking out in the fields, somewhere, anywhere, or sitting in the yard at night, or silent, in the corner of a room, hugging your knees, or even doing what you should be doing but with not a word all day, distracted, as if you weren't really here in the house –

So that sometimes I thought, *If it weren't for Lazarus, caring for Lazarus, where would she be?*

And at other times, your eyes were too bright. You spoke too happily –

And then the next day you would be normal again – normal in your own way – and it was at those times, when you seemed steady and cared so well for Lazarus, that I would ask you my questions.

And you would answer with your nothings.

Do you blame me for needing praise?

Also you grew sad. When you weren't bright, you were often in the other direction. You wept secretly, when you thought I saw none of it. So unlike you, such deliberate secretiveness, such efforts at hiding what you felt; and about that, I didn't ask. It was enough. I had enough. As I worked, I complained to the cooking pots, and the kindling.

'My brother,' I said, 'can hardly find his footing in this life again. And my sister – she and I share the chores, but she's another who's scarcely here in Bethany. Most of the time, most of her lives somewhere else.'

Then those strangers came from Jerusalem. Sharp-faced men, clutching stones and lengths of wood. They arrived wordlessly in the yard, gaping at you and Lazarus, and you and Lazarus – I watched you from the window – you ignored them: you went on quietly speaking with each other, until one of them said, 'Lazarus, come with us!'

And then the pair of you just stared at them, like children.

It still grieves me. You were hard on me that day.

What would have happened? If I hadn't come to the door and laughed at them, wouldn't they have butchered him there on the spot? If I hadn't shouted, 'Madmen! Dreamers! How many more of you are coming? Can't you see he's just a sick man who falls into trances? How many nights have you sat up, plotting this? How many penances have you promised? I spit on you!'

And I stood there, laughing.

And if I hadn't?

They left. Then you came to me and said, 'How could you speak like that? Don't you understand anything?'

I shrugged, and went back to gutting the fish. The accusation in your eyes had struck a cruel blow. My hands were all bloody, and the blood smudged my face, wiping the tears off. Also, I was afraid. You meant that I'd been treacherous. I knew what you meant. You ran out into the fields, and a tension fell on the house, as if a calamity had happened –

But Lazarus was kind. He came to me. He stood watching me slice the belly of a fish, and said, 'They make a clever defence, questions. So does laughter. But you'll have to let me go some time.'

'Are you upset?' I asked.

Smeared with the fish, the blood on the plate, and holding the knife, I asked, 'Was I wrong to protect you? Have I betrayed – anything – saying what I did?'

'You asked questions,' Lazarus answered. 'You're always asking questions! But if those men had asked *you* certain questions, what would you have said?'

Then he turned away, so that I could weep and get on with the cooking, but I called after him, 'Lazarus! *You've* never asked me what I think!'

'It's not necessary,' he told me.

And when he said that, I wanted to run to him. I wanted to say, 'But it *is* necessary. We must talk. We must talk.' I wanted to chatter about all manner of hidden things, but he looked so tired, and so accepting, as if the burden of my need – and yours – all weighed on whatever had come with him out of the tomb, that – what was it? – that defenceless peace in him, and I couldn't go to him.

'She's not angry,' he said, meaning you. 'She's just different.'

He went outside again after that, and I sat down on the stool and sobbed loudly.

Because I knew you were angry.

Gradually, you let the tension drop. It took days, but at last you brought me flowers. I think they were from the rubble behind the weaver's house, where that old wall had broken down. I saw you up there, as I came from the well. You brought them to me. I was sweeping, and you laid them on the table.

'For you,' you said. Then you took the broom from my hand. You swept and washed the floor, and sang, the way you used to when you were much younger, so that I'd know you felt affectionate.

And I was noisy. I made a fuss of shooing Micael's dog from the house –

I trembled with your forgiveness, and almost let the flowers wilt.

You kiss me now – but it was hard.

Well, it's good, being sisters. It's comforting to have another linked to us, through the same womb, whatever the pain, and even if we *are* born into what we are – alone.

And yet – I suppose you know this but even so I'll say it – I've learned just the opposite: no one can ever be alone. What I am is also part of you. What you are is part of me –

Oh, I know some may say, 'If, in truth, there's only One of us – all of us – then isn't that One completely alone?' but that's a poor sort of cleverness, and I think a dog makes better use of it, chasing his own tail.

Laugh then. It's as I say, isn't it? I surprise you. You still think I've nothing in my head but stews and clean clothes –

You know, that night in the yard, when the Teacher came out to me while I was sulking over the supper plates – that night I told Joanna about –

I saw something then. I keep trying to tell you. I lived something then. If I could still see –

If only understanding didn't fall into a memory of itself, dulled, like wet pebbles losing their colours as they dry in the sun –

There'd be no talk like this talk.

The weeks brought us close to Passover, and that message came: he was coming back to us, on his way to Jerusalem. The Teacher. He and the others.

Thomas told us. He was sent ahead, and when he brought us the news, you and Lazarus accepted it calmly, neither of you showed emotion; only, when I objected, you left the room, and Lazarus said, 'Be quiet!'

'Be quiet!' As if I were a child.

He looked down at the floor when he'd said it. 'Be quiet!' indeed.

But Thomas understood.

'You're right,' he said to me. 'It's dangerous. Madness, as you say. A kind of madness. He says it's all necessary. He has to go there – so what can we do but go with him, and die if we must?'

'It can't be as bad as that!' I said. 'But why must he always look for trouble?'

Then Thomas asked, 'Don't you want him here? If you think it might bring danger on yourself –'

'She's already in danger,' said Lazarus, 'because I live here. But no harm will come to her. She knows that. She's not the fool she sounds.'

He was smiling, so I pretended not to be angry.

Perhaps I wasn't.

I wiped my hands and went out into the yard. I seized the big pitcher and set off for the well. Thomas came after me.

'How is he?' he asked. 'Lazarus – how do you find him?'

'He's full of simplicity,' I said, 'and just when I think he's an innocent, with as much guile in him as a newborn babe, he comes out with something like that. Calling me a fool.'

'He didn't,' said Thomas.

We walked on in silence.

Then Thomas said, 'I'm worried too. But what can be done?'

'At least he'll eat well in our house,' I told him. 'After that, we must trust he knows what he's doing!'

He came – with all the rest, and the commotion – the crowds at the door, gawping –

'*Is he that one, the thin one?*'

'*You're mistaken. That's Lazarus. The ghost. Look how pale he is!*'

Forcing our shutters open, falling over pots in the yard, creeping in and squatting, uninvited, by the wall, staring and whispering –

'Everyone's welcome!' said Lazarus. 'That's how he wants it!'

'And who'll replace the broken pots and the stolen blankets?' I asked.

'We will.'

'And what about peace and quiet?' I asked. 'I thought he came here for those!'

But no one was listening.

And the supper I'd cooked – we'd cooked: I know you helped – shared out in the end among twice as many as we'd planned for that first night, and all the baking and sweating the next day, to feed more and more mouths –

And all the time I was thinking, *Is this what he wants? Should I, too, sit and listen? Who will feed us then?*

And all the time I was deciding, *This is my part. He showed me. I am I, and this is what I do.*

And that second evening, I cooked more simply: what else could I do? Slaughter every chicken? Or give him finer food than could be given to others? I cooked simply – bread and vegetables; and while Hannah and some of the other women helped to dish it into bowls and ever more bowls – where were you?

The scent of spikenard filled the house. It came spreading out across the food, mingled with the good rich smell of beans and oil and bread; and in the other room, there was a hush –

I knew that you had something to do with it. I knew.

I pushed my way to the door. I saw you on your knees, and how you massaged his feet, and your hair was loose; you had untied the braid so that your hair fell forward, hiding your face from me. Your hands moved on the Teacher's feet. I didn't stay to watch.

I came back to dishing out food.

'What is it?' someone asked – Hannah, steady Hannah, with a ladle in her hand.

And I turned to her, meaning to say – I meant to say – 'Nothing. Just my sister.' But instead I said, 'My sister's massaging the Teacher's feet. She has a spikenard ointment. I think she must have sold her jewellery for it.'

Hannah stared. 'Spikenard?' she asked.

I took the ladle from her. 'Go and look,' I said.

I didn't go in again myself until the voices had blurred back into what was normal. Judas objecting to what you did, and the Teacher's answer – all that: his distinct words in the hush, I can imagine the hush – I missed it. I was out in the yard, squatting by a toothless old rogue who'd found one of my best blankets. Wrapped in it, he sat gulping down the broth of vegetables and he winked at me across the bowl I held for him, and in the end he spattered out, 'Haven't you got anything more tasty?'

'Not I,' I said; and looking at his miserable, greedy face, I began to laugh, silently with sudden happiness. It wasn't like the first time, there in the yard. It was quite different, smaller, and mingled with knowing. *This slippery fellow will go away grumbling*, I thought, *and take my blanket with him! And I'm out here with him*, I thought, *while my brother sits at table, and my sister –*

Yet it was the same.

I patted his head, and he grinned back. He didn't seem to mind my tears.

'Give me some bread!' he said. 'More bread!'

You and I – that was another night when we slept here, squeezed by the outer door, our backs against the wall, heads on our knees. Where else was there for us? The chill air crept in through the door's chinks, and yet this room was stifling.

All over the village, the crowd slept, in almost every house. And by most of our neighbours, too, chickens had been slaughtered, vegetables cooked and pots of preserves broken open for too many guests – or else for those who grab and don't ask.

Our village had become a meeting place of forces that might have seemed common enough, but we couldn't calculate or run from them; so we were still and watchful in ourselves, like startled hares. There were the gawpers, and there were those sent to hurry back with hostile reports for others who sat thinking and criticising in High Places; and there were those who followed the Teacher about and listened and stared at what was happening with their untellable hunger and their fear that time was running out – that he might end up jailed or stoned to death; and there were those – there was the Teacher himself – who knew and measured all these forces.

And *we* were there too: hungry yet nourished, understanding yet bewildered, and watching – at least I watched.

What will happen? I wondered.

I felt vulnerable and gentle. You were also awake, so I turned to you and asked, 'How did you afford it? The spikenard?'

'I sold our mother's earrings,' you said.

I had given those to you. She had said to me, 'You're the elder. Keep what you want for yourself. But I know you'll deal fairly with your younger sister.'

They were so beautiful.

'Do you disapprove?' you asked.

I squeezed your hand.

I won't worry about this now, I thought. *With Lazarus for a brother, what kind of man will take her in any case? The dowry's not important.*

The scent of spikenard rose from your hands and spread from your hair. I breathed it in as I slept.

They tell that story often, don't they? How you knelt down, only days before what was to happen, and rubbed spikenard into the Teacher's feet.

And the Purse-carrier objected. Pale, observant Judas, who hardly ever spoke, and never smiled. Unknown Judas. Did you notice how the others didn't tease him as they did each other?

What did we know of him – Judas? Only that he liked to feel responsible, and considered himself educated.

He objected. Such a waste, he said. That expensive ointment. And the Teacher said, 'On the contrary. With this ointment, she's preparing me for my grave.'

So I'm told.

You didn't speak of it. The visitors who come – *they* tell me, and then they ask, 'Did your sister understand? When he said that, did all of you understand what was about to happen in Jerusalem?'

I spread my hands. What answer can I give? No one told me the talk of graves. Your quietness and your tears in the following days, the strange, listening silence of Lazarus – how could I know what to make of them? We were all worried. No one spoke to me of graves. Only Thomas, when they left in the morning, smiled at me and said, 'We'll do our best. But you see how it is. How he talks.'

'Keep your wits about you!' I told him, and I took his hand and pressed it, and he smiled all the more –

So what can I offer these visitors?

Only the truth. 'I was outside, serving food,' I say. 'We were all aware of the danger if he went into Jerusalem. But I didn't hear what was said.'

They listen, and look serious. Then often they say, 'What your sister did must never be forgotten. It has significance. It has the nature of a sacrament. What can it be like to have such a sister – one granted such grace? It must be very wonderful.'

'Oh – wonderful!' I tell them, and I laugh. 'Very wonderful!'

'Tell us more!' they say. 'How did she respond? When he spoke those words – about preparing him for burial – surely she must have said something?'

And I explain again. 'If she did, I never heard of it. And I wasn't there. I was outside, serving the food –'

Sometimes, you know, they doubt me. Their eyes narrow. They look for signs – little signs that I have resentments tucked away in the fold of my sleeve.

'Your sister's so strong,' they tell me. 'So sure of what's happened and its meaning. Her reputation inspires us all. And *you*,' they say, 'are you equally sure?'

'How do you measure certainties?' I ask them. 'I'm Martha, not Mary. How will you place my beliefs in a balance and weigh them against my sister's?' And then I'm blunt, and I say, 'Your own doubt – or fear of doubt – asks the question. But you must find your own answer.'

Most of them understand.

Oh, there's a great deal of understanding.

Most people are not fools.

And they ask so little of the worst part. The horrors. I'm grateful for that. They spring to: 'And *you* – did you see him, after his death?'

As for Lazarus, they worry about Lazarus. They lean forward and lower their voices. 'How can you explain it?' they say. 'Your brother, brought out of the grave – only to be found dead a year or so later, lying by the roadside?'

'Explain it?' I ask.

'What sense does it make?' They breathe on my face: they would climb into my head if they could. 'To be brought back, only to die again so soon?'

'My brother had giddy spells,' I tell them. 'He must have tripped and fallen. He smashed his head on a rock. Is that so unnatural? He was a living man, and living men can trip and fall if they don't watch where they're going. What other sense do I have to make of it?'

They stare at me. Then they repeat, 'And after his death, did you see him?'

'Who are you speaking of now?' I ask.

'The Teacher. The Master. Did you – do you see him?'

But there I disappoint them. *In my own way* isn't the answer they want.

'What do you mean?' they cry. 'Has he come to you? Here in this room? Has he sat at this table? Does he stand by your bed at night?'

'Those are other stories,' I tell them. 'Other people's stories.'

'And *yours*?' they cry.

But I say, 'Find your own.'

How else should I put it? You – you're the one with stories. Enormous stories. What have *I* to say? I didn't even tell you – the small, great thing, about washing the supper plates that evening in the yard, and how he came and crouched beside me and dipped his hands in the water, sharing the cloth with me –

Doing women's work, I thought, and then he thanked me for supper.

I told only Joanna.

I wasn't ready.

And are *they* ready, those questioners, to be told so little? I have no great stories. But if they look crushed, I try. I say, 'My way is in common matters of the house. In the cleaning of plates and dishes. That's all.'

Sometimes they're pleased. 'And that's when you see the Master?' they cry. But others are offended. One man said to me, 'Don't think I chase dreams. I've had a hard life. I need no reminders that in this world our portion is to work. But I respect visions. And you're wrong to mock them.'

I told him he misunderstood, but he didn't listen. He began to speak in a loud voice about certain dreams he'd had, and shortly afterwards he glared at me and said, 'It's true what I've heard. You're not at all like your sister!'

Then he left.

Not like you.

Well. Haven't I accepted that? Don't I tell myself, *In the end, what of it? I know that, in the end, after all our difference, we're the same.*

But the difference matters.

Remember what it was like, when the news came that in the night the Teacher had been arrested and was answering charges? It was mid-morning before we heard: everyone was too shocked to remember us. And you ran out of the yard. You left Lazarus and me and the poor child who'd been sent to tell us – you left us all without a word, and only your brother calling your name stopped you – Lazarus, for a moment his voice strong, so that you stopped and waited for me.

'We must make preparations,' I said, taking hold of you. 'Come back to the house. We'll eat first, because this could be a long day. Perhaps tonight we must stay in Jerusalem, and in any case, it won't do to faint in the crowds.'

'How can you speak of such things?' you said. But even so, you let me lead you – pull you – to the house again; and you ate the bread I placed in front of you, and drank the strong wine – the best wine – and watching you, I thought, *Even with the wine, she looks weak enough to collapse before we reach the first marker stone.*

And as you ate, Lazarus came in from the yard and beckoned to me.

'Put some food in a basket,' I told you. 'There'll be others who may not have eaten. This at least we can do for them.'

Then I followed Lazarus out to where a man stood by the gate who had come from Jerusalem.

The man wept. And Lazarus spoke so quietly, I could hardly hear him. They told me the judgement. Lazarus said it, as if he followed an overgrown track in his mind, where words lay like small stones, each formed and laid in its place long ago, waiting to be found.

And finally he said, 'I must go with this man. You – look after your sister –'

'Wait!' I called, but Lazarus was already hurrying – slowly, carefully hurrying, leaning on the other man's shoulder.

And I? You remember – I came inside. I barred the shutters, as if to make the house ready to leave it.

Then I went out again and rammed the broom across the inner room shutters, and the washing pole across the outer room shutters. You didn't notice. At least you didn't question it. You stood impatiently in the yard with the basket, looking out along the road.

'Hurry,' you said. 'Won't you hurry?'

'Fetch your brother's coat!' I said. 'He went without it. It may be cold later, and who knows where we'll sleep tonight?'

You obeyed. I suppose you trusted me.

I followed you in.

I barred the door. I told you the judgement. What sentence had been passed. The Roman sentence. And you sprang for the door, but I stood against it. You bruised me. You screamed at me, your fists smashed against my chest. What else could I do? You would have gone running to the horror of the nails being driven in, and the groan of the cross being hauled up –

It counted then that I'm different.

You ran from room to room, banging on the shutters. You came back, weeping and pleading. 'For pity's sake!' you cried. 'For pity's sake!' Beating me, clinging to me –

And I stood there thinking, *Not yet. A little longer. So she won't see the nails going in –*

'If you love me!' you wept.

And you were strong, and as fierce as a bandit, and running against the shutters, you crashed them open at last – so that I knew it was time. I unbarred the door. I stood aside, and you ran headlong out, and I followed you – we carried nothing, neither the food nor the coat – to Jerusalem.

I was breathless – remember? – All that beating you'd given me. By the time we came to the place of horrors, I was so faint that you were half carrying me, and I was shaking like a child. But you were calm, steady, and only days later it came to me – did I ever tell you? – in your face at that time, I saw our mother.

That night we sheltered in a rich house – Joseph's house. You and I huddled on a pallet beside Lazarus. It was like that: such turmoil – men among the women – and none of us sleeping.

There were so many of us. Some wept. Some whispered complaining prayers into the darkness. Lazarus lay on his back, his eyes open, and his hands folded on his chest, as if he'd gone with the Teacher into the grave. You lay with your back to me, your knees drawn up, and I kept a tight grip on you, because you're what I had, and I thought, *We could have done nothing. I wasn't wrong to keep her from being there earlier. What we saw was enough.*

But a wordless voice in the silence said, *'For you, perhaps. Don't you speak for yourself?'*

Was I wrong?

You've never reproached me.

But I bowed down in myself to that voice. *For me*, I said.

No sleep came. How thin you were. I felt the bones of your spine against my breast, and I lay burdened with a future of your grief, and Lazarus creeping through his days, trying to weave his secrets into a covering for his nakedness – left alive, while that one died.

And then the voice asked – abruptly, clearly, yet with no words: *'Do you believe that?'* – the tone, without the words, that I'd heard on the road when they'd come to the village, the Teacher and all of them, after we'd shut Lazarus in his tomb.

How can I know what to believe? I asked back. *There's been a great slaughtering of love and hope here. The world's both cruel and mad. And who will hold this one, my sister, and Lazarus together if I don't? There may be nothing left, but I tell you this: I'll fight for these two.*

'You're presumptuous,' the voice said.

You're hard on me! I answered. *Always hard on me.*

And I soaked the back of your coat with my tears.

'Martha,' the voice said, *'Martha.'* It was gentle and strange. I didn't know how to speak to it.

Take the broth from the hearth. Surely James will come soon. We'll wait. I suppose he's where he shouldn't be. You must talk

186

to him. You know nothing of marriage, but he thinks of you as a woman who's seen the world; you must say a word for Ruth. You've as good as promised me, remember.

He's so restless. He feels born too late to know what to think. It's not easy for him. A great-uncle who walked out of the grave but was dead and gone before he could be met. A grandmother who knew another – a Teacher, who, people say, walked out of the grave – and yet his parents and his grandfather all sickening and dying in his infancy. He's restless. And he finds me too exacting.

Talk to him –

That Passover. That day we blundered through – let's not dwell on it –

You hardly moved in the morning.

Lazarus said, 'Let her sleep. She's carrying too much.'

I think he knew you were awake. I sat by you. The old man, Joseph – he came out into the room where we were. He stared about at us – his guests, his collected shocked and broken. He was unkempt, distracted, but still the host, murmuring about food, and since we'd eaten no supper –

How could any of us have eaten supper – a Passover supper?

Lazarus rose and went with him.

I sat by you. Some of the other women busied themselves. It was the Sabbath, but – what was the Sabbath? They busied themselves. There were children, even children. Water was fetched, and meat, and the plainest wafer-bread, and all of it was done in silence, or with few words that faded quickly.

I told several of the women, 'She's asleep!' although your eyes were open. They understood. They touched my arm and didn't speak, and so I sat, hearing Lazarus say again in my heart, '*She's carrying too much.*'

And isn't it I who carry her? I thought. *So which of us, then, carries more?* But it was a small thought, and it fell against something rank and dark. The base – I knew what it was – of a Roman cross.

The scummed base, the splintered grain of wood, and the muck. My mind saw only that. It couldn't look higher. It hadn't the courage.

Strange. The night before, my head had been quite clear. But in the morning – that grain of wood, and all the muck, and I didn't dare look up.

Sometimes, I touched your shoulder, to let you know that I was there – and to feel that you were there, too, in your own way, with me.

Then at noon Lazarus came back.

'You've been praying,' I said.

He looked waxen and very distant, but mild, like a man who's just heard a better version of his own argument.

'Take her out into the courtyard,' he told me. 'You need to breathe daylight, both of you.'

And his voice reached you. You stood up. You let me lead you out. We sat with another woman in the vague sunlight. Two children played at our feet, and she said, 'Look at them. It's nothing to children, what we've lost.'

'We must find his mother,' you said. 'I want to be with his mother!'

I pretended not to hear. 'In the morning, at first dawn, we'll go home,' I told you. 'That's the best we can do.'

You stood up. 'I must visit his mother. Where's his mother?' you cried. And – remember? – at that, I let the anger burst. I leapt to my feet. I grabbed you and held you roughly. 'When will you consider others?' I hissed. 'How much more selfishness? Do you think his mother hasn't enough, without you and your antics? Must you always be the centre of everything?'

And you gave me back a look of – what was it? Pity? Hatred? It seemed in part almost animal. Something wild and cornered –

'I must go and comfort her!' you cried.

'*You?*' I laughed in your face through my tears, and you watched me –

I remember how you watched me –

I remember laughing – and laughing –

Then I was sitting on a stone bench by the wall. I suppose you'd led me there. And you brought me a cup of wine, and sat by me while I drank it.

'We'll wait here today,' you said, 'and at dawn we'll go home. That will be best.' You patted my arm. 'That will be best,' you said, and you stroked my hair, and took the wine from me, and pulled my head forward until it rested on your shoulder.

Well, I thought. *Well, if it keeps her here –*

Then I fell asleep.

At dawn, we came home. You sang on the way, and looked back often at the city. I didn't question your singing. You're too different. You sang childish songs that you'd learned before our mother died. They irritated me, but I said nothing. Lazarus had stayed with Joseph, and I was thinking, *Couldn't he have spared us such a dismal homecoming, us two on our own?*

'Why are you looking back?' I asked. 'There's no point.'

You shrugged. 'It's hard,' you said; and again you looked back. 'Someone's coming!' you said.

And, turning round, I saw several people at some distance on the road behind us. So then I hurried you on. I thought I saw how it was. You imagined a messenger running after us, his face wide with joy, to tell us that everything hadn't happened, the facts were not as they seemed, or the days had spun backwards –

'Home!' I said. I longed for this good strong table, and the smoke-stained pots, and the broom by the door. I longed for their simplicity. 'Home!'

But when we reached here, you wandered from the house.

You stood by the entrance to the yard, looking out along the road, as you'd done that other time, when Lazarus was ill. And when I reproached you and asked, 'What good will this do?' you asked my forgiveness. 'Forgive me!' you said, quite clearly, so that I brought out my mending to sit near you –

Until the messenger came.

And now is that enough? Have you heard what I hadn't told you? Can you see now what you missed in me or feared I'd missed in myself?

That's your secret, isn't it?

You feared I'd missed in myself –

Oh, laugh. Laugh. You know it's true, you feared it, because the words don't come to me, as they do to you –

But at least something I told Joanna. Proud, homesick, festering in her house while that husband of hers argued his business in the city, Joanna with her nose pointing high, and that flick of her skirts to keep herself pure of us –

She came to me once.

You were – somewhere. Walking. Out. As so often. And Lazarus was in the city. It was before he was ill. Only a week or two after that evening, when I'd protested and been told that you had chosen *'a good part'*.

After what I'd felt in the yard.

Joanna stood at the door. I looked up, and there she was, blocking the light. She stood rigid, clutching a cup, and her mouth was as straight as a nail. The cost of seeking me out – or any of us – I saw how high it was. It pained her, almost as much as her need. I wiped my hands.

'Come in,' I said, 'and sit, if you wish.'

'Vinegar,' she said. 'My jar's cracked, and all the vinegar's lost. Lend me a cup of vinegar. You shall have back the best in the market as soon as my husband arranges a fresh supply.'

I wanted to laugh, but I knew she'd leave at once. So I went to her.

'Ours is not the best,' I said, 'but good enough. Come and sit while I pour it.'

'I can wait here,' she said.

Then I took her cup and came into the corner of the room and fetched the vinegar and poured it, while she turned away into the yard. And when I carried the vinegar out to her, she was weeping. Proud, with tears on her face. She made no attempt to take the cup.

'We'll leave here soon,' she said. 'This is not a place for us.'

'You'll be glad to go home,' I told her.

'Home?' She gazed at me, and I saw she thought me very foolish. 'There'll be other places. My husband has many business interests. We visit all the great cities.'

'Do you indeed?' I said. 'Then no doubt this small village – and even Jerusalem – has little to offer you.'

'That's true,' she answered. 'I prefer – other places. Not that it changes anything. But then,' she said, 'what could change anything?'

And I said –

But I'm not sure what I said. I heard myself telling her – and I thought, *This isn't how I speak. These words, and flowing ways of putting things – these aren't how I tell whatever I have to tell. But they're what she will listen to.*

And I told her a good deal, or something at least, of how I'd been spoken to – that evening when I'd complained, angry with all the preparations, and you sitting with the men, and how later, in the yard, I'd felt something –

But I saw her staring, and with so much pain in her face that I broke off –

'I have the bread to bake,' I said.

'I'd like to meet this Teacher,' she said. 'Will he be coming back?'

'He travels the country,' I told her. 'You may hear of him any-where.'

And at that, her mouth twisted. 'Teachers!' she cried – and she pulled a face, as if to say she'd thought better of the matter already, and what were Teachers but a bunch of rogues? But I think her meaning was different. These people, she was saying, the finest people, were never where she was.

Then she glanced at the cup I held, the vinegar. 'I don't need that,' she said. 'I was lonely.'

'I know,' I told her.

'Don't visit me!' she said. 'That's not what I want!'

Then she turned her back on me and walked quickly away. I called after her, 'Your cup, Joanna!' but she ignored that. So I still have it. It's the grey one over there. You never asked where it came from. I kept it, so that she could visit me again, if she wanted, and demand I give it back, but she didn't come.

Soon after that, they left. Remember?

And when they went – she and her husband – who in the vil-lage watched them go, or shouted good wishes after them? *You* were there. You stood by the old wall and watched. I saw you. And I watched from near the weaver's house. When they came out, 'Travel safely!' I said, but they passed me without a word.

What can one do? She was weeping – still weeping. But do you think –

You've travelled. You must have spoken countless times in the face of bitterness. I know I have. But perhaps for you, it's always like that: the words come that are suited to the listener, the very swing and lull of how you speak are suited to their needs –

Perhaps for you that's normal, but, for me – I think I say what has to be said, and people – some of them – value it. It touches them. But my way's plain – except with Joanna.

Did my words reach her, do you think? When she left, she passed without looking at me. She hid her mouth and nose in a piece of cloth, as if to keep the smell out, you must have seen –

as if the village stench were suddenly unbearable – but she was weeping. What do you think?

Well. I'll have no breath left. Don't crush me. These fierce hugs. I'm not ready for them yet. I have to live, or who'll see to it that James marries sensibly?

As he must. I believe in common sense.

Enough. I'm content. More than content.

Tell me, and we can laugh about it – in this life, who should I be but I?

CLAUDIA PROCULA

His health is much as it was. He's a little more breathless, perhaps, in recent months, when he hurries or climbs a flight of steps – but it's much as it was. He sends you greetings. He remembers your good looks, no doubt, and also I think he remembers how respectful you always were to him. And so you are greeted, which is a rare distinction these days, because in truth it troubles him when I receive letters from those he calls my 'prattling friends'.

What am I to do? Sometimes when I receive a letter, I read him the less personal and more amusing sections, and then he says, 'What nonsense! What pointless chitchat!' But I think he likes it. And it's not as though I receive many letters. Certainly he receives more. And you and I, who lost touch for so many years – can we be said to 'prattle'? And that is often my case. But in Pilatus, the balance can be tipped by so very little –

The other day, I found him slumped on a bench in the garden – out there in the heat of the afternoon, those hounds of his panting beneath the lavender bushes. His head was bowed. He was staring at the ground. He held a cup of wine, and he was pouring the wine, drop by drop, on a single point close to his feet. Each drop he seemed to watch very carefully as it seeped into the dust before he poured another. His scalp was scarlet with sunburn – so dangerous for a man of his age.

I went up to him and said, 'I came out to look for you. It's too hot. You should be inside.'

He didn't answer me. He poured the next drop –

Bees hummed in the lavender. The panting of the dogs irritated me, although I tried not to show it. I sat down beside him.

'Which of the gods,' I asked, 'enjoys this eked-out libation? I had no idea you credited any with such patience.'

'I'm trying to drown an ant,' he said.

Those were his words, and so I leaned forward, peering down to see the insect where the stain of wine was, but I saw nothing: my eyes are not as strong as his.

'Pour all the wine at once,' I said. 'Surely that would do it.'

'That doesn't work. They float to safety on the flood,' he said. 'I've tried it.'

And again he poured a drop.

I was silent after that. The sun blazed. My hands sweated in my lap. At last I ventured, 'Caelius Naso is quite right. That cypress obscures the view. We should have it cut down.'

'Ha!' He fidgeted. He dislikes Caelius Naso almost as much as I dislike the dogs. He asks the man to dinner: they drink and talk of women – the new, loud women enjoying fame in Rome, worlds away from here; then they throw each other dark hints on the subject of the State, and what So-and-so would have written in his last letter if only he'd dared; finally they lament together the absence of a good man in this rural abyss to stop the toothache. They are friends, in short, but – mutual liking? That eludes them.

'Come inside,' I said.

I patted his hand. He glowered.

'Do you know,' he demanded, 'what Caelius Naso said to me the other night?'

'That you're putting on weight.'

'He said – that damned fool who's done nothing with his life – he said, "You, of course, with your illustrious career as a prefect and procurator, you know better than most how easy it is to make a mess out of a delicate situation."'

'I'm sure he didn't mean it to sound rude,' I said.

'The man's an idiot.'

'Perhaps,' I said. 'But what was he referring to?'

'Oh, it's always the same thing. Problems with his son-in-law. The fool complains and complains about him, but he'll never act.'

I stood up. 'The sun makes my head throb,' I said. 'And *you* are roasting like a crab.'

He didn't move. He watched me with that glum look he keeps for when he wishes to imply that the blame for whatever discomforts him is at least partly mine.

'I'd like to see that thick neck of *his* in some delicate situations,' he said. 'Can you imagine Caelius Naso confronted by a mutinous garrison, or even a small delegation of angry merchants? As for mob control –'

'He'd wet his handsome toga,' I said.

'Ha!'

I left him then.

What's done is done.

Before I went into the house again, I looked back from the top of the steps. I couldn't see him for the bushes, but I could sense him hunched on the bench, and I wished I'd said, 'When you felt that action was required, you acted. When decisions were required, you decided – sooner or later. You tried, in your fashion. You made mistakes. You chose the wrong mistakes. But you haven't been altogether a coward.'

It wouldn't have helped. I have said those things before, in one form or another. He shrugs off such words. I believe he fears I'm lying – as perhaps I myself have also feared sometimes, when I'm tired and when my own meaning feels distant from me.

My dear – this business of being truthful: you and I laughed about it once. I remember, you were speaking of Vitellia Priscilla. You said, 'She's very handsome. I do admire her. Such a fine figure after so many children. And such a wonderful hostess. Have you noticed how skilfully she includes everyone in her compliments? And nothing forced about it. Always the appropriate words, unhurried and elegant?'

'And have *you* noticed,' I answered, 'how we all sweat a little at her supper parties, and watch for just one blemish, just one slave with a hook of snot in his nostril, so that we lesser mortals may breathe again?'

You squeezed my hand as we laughed. You were very delighted. You were so young, and your delight, I wonder if you realised, was the only sincere element in our conversation. Certainly my tired old joke was none; and even the affection I showed, laughing with you, wasn't quite what it seemed. Vitellia Priscilla had survived great misfortunes, and I wished I'd resisted the temptation to make fun of her. So I squeezed your hand back, and thought, *Ah, my pretty one, so lively and fresh, what will become of you?*

And do you know, my dear, in that moment I didn't entirely wish you well.

It's time that you knew. Within the month, I had left for the province. Perhaps that's why the memory stays so sharply with me: a splinter of Roman life. You will forgive me, of course. I trust you know I love you. Besides, you would be tender if you saw me now; and as we strolled chatting round the garden, you would take me by my arm in case I stumbled; you would walk slowly and keep a good grip on me –

My hair, I must tell you, has become silvery grey, like the skin of a garlic bulb.

But these are not the facts you asked for.

My husband –

Long ago – I think it was the fourth night of our marriage – he came into my bedroom, flushed and almost drunk, yet still in charge of himself. It was very late. Where he'd been, I don't remember. Somewhere. To one of those keen-witted gatherings of the sort where he imagined I might let him down and look vague and pale when the politics began to bite, and so I'd been left concealed in the house in the old, traditional manner that few women would tolerate now –

He had arrived home, and he seemed to burst into the bedroom. He flung himself down on the bed, and while I waited with a pounding heart – our sexual encounters had not yet been anything but traumatic – he grabbed my arm and told me, 'I can't tolerate devious women. You must always say what you think.'

I was tongue-tied. I trembled. I disliked and feared him, and as much as I feared him, I was confused. You, of course, may not remember, but he had a certain force in his looks in those days, my Pilatus: a strong line to his eyebrows, tension in his jaw, and his mouth fascinated me. One couldn't mistake the ambition in it – or rather, in how he held it, so straight, so narrow – and yet from all of him there rose that kind of appeal, infantile, and for he knew not what – approval, I think – that so attracts a young woman when force isn't entirely absent. I have noticed since that such a power to attract is often the property of those with obsessive temperaments, and men with more than a streak of cruelty in their natures. So I was tongue-tied. I didn't want his attention, but I feared to be nothing to him; and Pilatus projected his appeal so intensely that I did not delude myself as to how many cunning and self-serving women might happily be his mistress – for a time – not to mention the willingness of slaves with their own ideas concerning my standing in the household.

'The truth,' said Pilatus, sprawling on the bed, 'I need a wife who tells the truth.'

And then I understood. I saw my role, and in it our hope of living together with some trace of dignity. I saw my escape from humiliation – the escape, I knew, of countless wives before me, who'd heard the same blunt – and dangerous – demand, and hadn't flinched.

'That will take courage,' I said. 'But I'll try not to fail you.'

It seemed to calm him. He sat up then, quietly, and breathed his breaths of wine and fish and looked at me, and for the time it might take to count to twenty, neither of us spoke. After that, he rose unsteadily and went to his own bed; and as he left me, he said, 'I intend to get on. You'll see.'

And, my dear, I did. In the years that followed, I did see, both when I was with him and no less when I wasn't – I mean in that short time before I joined him in Judaea when his letters came, his great lists of things so quickly accomplished and plans for what he must do next and what I must listen out for in the conversation of my acquaintances – while I, for my part, in all our journeys and twists of fortune, have tried to keep my word and tell the truth, or at least some fraction of the truth as I've seen it, and at least where it has mattered – which has cost us both a wealth of pain.

He said to me once, I can't convey with how much hatred in his eyes, '*Isn't it enough that I have to wade daily through the blood of simpletons and rebels, and swallow hourly a fare of Roman spite and foreign malice, but I must also be cursed with a wife who has contempt for my decisions, and who runs to assure me that my next move will send me hurtling to perdition? How can any man born deserve this?*'

He had misunderstood my meaning. But that was after many years in the province, after those events you ask me about, and my Dream. I had grown into my part by then, deeply, watchfully; and such as you can never know how my spirit had tumbled and strained through the months and hours that led us there. You cannot know. You married a weak man – so-called weak, obviously weak – who's done little with his life except father two sons, one of whom, at least, is a brave fellow, and gamble away his estate, then win back a farm which, from all reports is beautiful –

Such has been your life. You have no idea what combinations of strength and weakness there are in a man like Pilatus. Can you imagine what it is to see a line of gallows stretching from a city gate, to have the stench of those executed wretches' misery swimming on each breath, and to be responsible for ordering the comfort of the man who has brought about such grim leave-takings from the flesh? To smell their putrefaction mingled with his sweat and your perfume as he labours into you, to feel him trembling as he says, 'That dispatch that came today – Caesar's tone is odd . . . I'm doing my best. Surely he must know that!'

'Surely he knows,' I used to say; and I would cradle the back of his head in my hand, as one does an infant's. He liked that.

'I have enemies!' he often told me.

'And friends,' I used to say.

But what would you know of that – the fear of treachery in such a man as Pilatus?

Or of what it is to live in a city like Caesarea, so raw and new, and watch monuments going up while one's husband rushes about, as jocund as a godling, blessing plans and architects – only to see, a few months later, everything torn down and carted away, the artisans whipped, the architects chased from their houses – And why? For nothing. Mere nothing. *'Caesar's tone is odd.'* Not even for a word of imperial caution: merely a vagueness in the briefest of letters – and, in case you think otherwise, letters from Tiberius Caesar were never long, nor particularly buoyant. Whatever kept him wakeful in those seaside palaces of his, he had sharper stimulants than his thoughts about Judaea.

Then, as well that – wreckage for Caesar, tribute paid in rubble to imagined frowns – throughout the province, so much other destruction: this project, that project, crashing to the ground, more months of work, the best of marble, and not because of letters from Caesar, but all because our godling had failed to respect the local sensibilities, and his monuments had brought howling to our gates the very mobs he'd hoped to impress and subdue.

Nervousness. Wrong-headedness. Moods. Rages. And unpopularity: what can you know, my sheltered one, of that? Of watching your husband ride past troops who show plainly in their faces both loathing and boredom, the sum of their contempt for him; and of feeling, in that instant, a sort of pleasure because he rides with straight back and erect head? What experience can you weigh against any of it? The man who last night shared your bed and complained of the creased sheets or a smoking lamp, have you ever heard him in the morning coldly calculate how to break some local dignitary? *'That son of his we sent to Rome, it's time he drank from the wrong cup!'*

You know none of this. Of course, you have observed. You have seen other women adjust to such partnerships – watched the outward adjustments, but of the inner turmoil, you are innocent.

Take one small calculation. He gambled away your estate, I grant you, but on your husband's tally of destruction is there a single life? Even a slave's? I think not. I never heard of any, nor of any severe reversals in his pleasure-seeking temperament, for all the grief he's caused you. Whereas Pilatus was often fragmented in those days, and could lurch about within himself in conflicting directions.

I watched, and trained my face to show little. But, as I've written, I honoured my promise. He rarely asked my opinion, but when he did, I spoke up, especially in Judaea, with truths of a kind.

'That man,' I used to say, 'seemed a sensible creature. Quite harmless.'

'And how can you see that?' Pilatus would ask.

'I can tell from his walk,' or, 'I can tell from his eyes,' I used to say. 'There's a walk that has no tension in it, no hidden purpose.' Or, 'His eyes are tired. He wants only to say what he means and have you understand him. That's how it seems to me.'

But sometimes I was bolder and, if necessary, I asked, 'Don't you think these measures are excessive?'

'Excessive?' Pilatus would glare.

'Restraint,' I used to tell him, 'is a god-like attribute. If you want these people's respect –'

'I want their fear. I hate them!'

'Is it not you,' I asked once, 'who are afraid of them?'

Then he said, 'Take care, Procula!' And he began to shout, ranting about the necessities of politics and interfering snakes – snakes, I believe, was the word – dressed up as officials, in Rome, in the provinces, all alike –

Sometimes, I mocked him. 'There's a point on your nose,' I said once. 'When you shout like this, you don't appear to your best advantage. That point turns bone-white –' And again he said, 'Take care, Procula!'

'I'm not a clown,' he told me. 'You women,' he said, 'with your gossip and your attitudes. You think it's all an entertainment, keeping hold of the Empire. You think it's just a bauble for children. But show respect, or I'll show you –'

And threats followed, but he never struck me.

And in all those years, I prayed for him, and he knew it.

Let him be strong when he must be; and let him not flail about, I prayed, *smashing himself and me and the lives of others. Grant him success*, I prayed, *and wine in our cup at the end of our day, not tears and blood. Protect us*, I prayed, *from the god of the Jews, and from all those gods of people who hate us –*

And more than once, in fact not infrequently, while I was praying Pilatus would come rushing in through the incense, demanding this or that – had I engaged the conjurors and musicians for So-and-so's visit, and what delicacies would there be for the supper – but, in truth, I think he came because it pleased him to see me at my supplications and the incense burning, at least as much as it irritated him.

'And to whom, especially, do you entrust my welfare?' he asked me once. 'Chaste Diana? Or that voluptuous other one?'

He didn't speak the name of Isis – but who did in those days? Caesar's ban on 'foreign' gods had chastened us all. And yet by that time – I'm sure you remember – an unsung forbearance had come, which reached just so far as private worship, silent and without proscribed rituals. The forbearance was real, everyone knew of it, even if it did seem a snail-like thing, best kept out of the sun.

My statuette of Isis was very discreet, and Pilatus never failed to imply that she was Venus.

'I entrust you to Diana,' I joked. 'You're a true Roman, and that other one might not understand you.'

Oh, he knew the deities I loved. But you, my friend, will grasp what he could not. I pleaded with Diana and Isis, but I pleaded also with any divinity who might befriend us, whether their names were known to me or not. I bowed low at their invisible altars and begged their kindness for us.

Approve of him. He fears disapproval, my husband. He fears betrayal. He frets and plots too much. Make him more than himself – strong enough to win respect but, since he can't be great, protect him from great events. What is he but an uninspired administrator? Don't expect too much of him.

Those were my prayers, because I saw he was afraid; and yet at times I think he enjoyed it – fear, his own or else the fear of others: were they in the end so different? How like substance it can feel for a while if one billows with terror! How strangely like control it feels if one takes exaggerated note of all one's difficulties! Most of us have some inkling of this. And at such times, his voice grew loud and he cracked boyish jokes, his body became alert and demanding. Or again, if from a height one sees the terror of others, of a felon, say, brought up for trial, or a nervous slave caught in the act of pilfering, how like mastery that can feel: how slyly akin to real management!

And how his eyes flashed at admiring women.

But on this point, I wouldn't have you form a misconception. I didn't marry a crude man. Even in the worst times, he often spoke of 'correctness'. 'I dare say it's not fashionable,' he used to say, 'but I would prefer to proceed correctly.' And sometimes, after a particularly convenient decision, he would fall into a mood – into a wound – that made him horrible to be near. At such times he gave off a stench that puzzled me in the early years, but which I came at last to understand. It was unhappiness.

The truth is that he has sometimes wanted to be good. And cheap adulation has not always pleased him. He has perceived his own predicaments.

I remember one entertainment in Caesarea – one of those countless suppers we held for the visiting relatives of some officer attached to the Syrian legions, passing up the coast from Cyrene and Alexandria. There seemed always to be cousins – how many cousins! They came expectant from their ships, aware of the superiority of their connections, and of what was due to them, and often bringing with them the silliest companions of less importance.

It was one such evening. We held a small supper – no more than eight or nine guests – and there came a time during the meal when a beautiful woman – I forget who she was – leaned towards my husband, her bosom heaving, and remarked, 'You cannot know how stimulating it is to find one's self so close to *power*! We women, what can we do? Tell tales, rearrange wall-hangings – sometimes hide behind them . . . But *you* . . .' she sighed, 'it's men like *you* who change the world. You shape destinies.'

Pilatus smiled. Generally he liked this kind of flirtation and he was, of course, very used to it.

'Without infants, lady,' he said, 'there would be no destinies. And no one can deny that women are required to help shape infants.'

'Ah, but even those derive from you men!' the lady cried. 'And otherwise we're such helpless creatures! I do believe,' she said, 'there's no finer life in this world than to be a man possessed of power like yours! Indeed I do!'

Her voice was loud. It was quite clear that she wished to hold everyone's attention, and our other guests began to look amused. They were relatives, as I say, of someone of the Syrian legions, and they understood perfectly that we, in our thistle patch of Judaea, were dependent on those troops in Syria. Pilatus, have power? At such a notion, their faces expressed petty condescension – an artificial refusal to sting, which I noticed often in those days, and found very trying; and that evening, Pilatus also saw what they thought, and was annoyed. More, he was embarrassed, and his frustration rose – I watched it – and his face darkened.

Then he began to sneer. 'And what would you do with it?' he asked softly. 'If you had this fine life, this power? How would you use it?'

'Oh, simple!' laughed the woman. 'I'd take as my lover the handsomest boy in the province, guttersnipe or prince, I shouldn't mind. And I'd banish all old and ugly slaves, and priests – I've no time for priests: I mean these *foreign* ones – out of every city before I entered it, and I think I might try my hand at a little justice. Why not? I'm sure I know how to be just! I'd make these people love me – and Rome, of course – I'd sit in my garden every morning, receiving petitions –'

'Then you would end up murdered and flung into the harbour,' said Pilatus; and, of course, he should have laughed, but he glared at her. Then he said, 'And tell me this, lady, how would you find your '*justice*' among your flowerpots and fountains? Would you count petals to decide which of two men is a liar? And would you consult water nymphs to weigh up expediencies, or, I should say, priorities of state, against local customs? And would the birds come twittering with oracles to bless your decisions?'

'Ah, how manly you are!' cried the woman. 'How severe!' And she wagged her finger at him; but his tone had been inappropriate and I could see she was alarmed, and in the next moment, wishing to come quickly through as the victor, she leaned across to me and whispered, 'Such *force*! How thrilling!'

And at that, our other guests smiled broadly, and one cried out to her, 'Take care what you stir up! Haven't you heard? Diplomacy's not much favoured here in Judaea!'

And they were all merry.

Then, truly, I thought Pilatus was going to spit at her, or get up and walk across to her and slap her. He seemed tensed for action, but caution prevailed, and in his agitation he only snatched up some fruit from the table beside him: he did it awkwardly, suddenly, and accidentally knocked over a lamp – a fragile, ornamental lamp, full of scented oil which spilled out over his napkin that lay by his dish – and brought slaves running to prevent the flames spreading, and to clear up the mess.

The woman was delighted. 'There, you see!' she cried. 'What power! Your every action threatens to consume us!'

And, as we all laughed at this absurd idea and her game spirit, and as she glowed with her triumph, and even Pilatus, somewhat unnerved by the flames, quickly chose also to laugh, and as the slaves diligently reduced everything to how it had been, I thought: *What's the point of all this? The more Pilatus seeks to show he's in control, the more helpless he really is – and so am I.*

But perhaps you already know that story – of the supper with the overturned lamp? In certain parts of the Empire, I understand that it's common currency. How it came to be circulated, I can guess. The slaves gossiped. Or that foolish woman boasted, or the other guests told their friends, enjoying a joke at the expense of Pilatus, and then, years later, someone found in the story a different significance. At the end of our time in Judaea, I myself heard it told back to me with several ingenious elaborations and meaningful interpretations; and you, my dear, I suspect, will be among those who wish to claim it was an omen.

I'll not argue. Our lives, I think, are full of omens. What is an omen, after all, but an illustration in what we do or experience, of what we *shall* do or experience – an illustration that, usually, we see only in retrospect – as if in every moment lies the sum of all our moments, both those that are past and those still ahead of us? Indeed, I have often thought so. And yet, every moment is free – I've felt that, too, in more recent years – with the possibility lying in each to change the outcome of all of them, if we can only see in time –

But how to come by such seeing?

That night, after that supper, Pilatus said to me, 'It's a fool's game.'

He was standing naked by my bed. He had come berating me about the quality of the wine, which, he said, had bloated him, and the flimsy lamp, and insufferable women. It was a stifling night, and he had stripped off to impress upon me that, uncomfortable as he was, I could expect to accommodate him, since he could hardly go crashing into the offending woman who was our guest.

'It's a fool's game,' he said, 'pandering to these people –'

'Entertaining those who are not our friends is inevitably as foolish as it's wise,' I told him.

He grunted.

'The powders will settle your stomach,' I said. 'Come to bed.'

And he did, and, as I remember, the wine did little to restrain him, and he snored like a roaring lion afterwards.

'A fool's game.'

Do I betray him? As you read this, my friend, do you laugh? I know I've written somewhat slightingly of your own trials, but I also know this: you, too – when your husband came home from his gambling, seeking sympathy and the warmth of your body – you, too, lying beneath his weight, must have sometimes wondered, as I so often did in those days, *Why must I submit to what happens to me? Why are there wise men in their thousands but this man isn't one of them? Why do we live at all if the marvel of living is nothing but helplessness, and either we perceive the need for change where we cannot see how to achieve it, or else we don't perceive the need for change where it would lie within our ability?*

That was how I often thought; and, at one time, my prayers grew thin, and I began to address the gods with fewer supplications and with more hard words; but I found that this only damaged me; such prayers left me bitter and desolate. So I resorted to an emptiness in myself, which was less painful, and I think truer, where I pleaded as best I could, but frequently told every deity, *I understand nothing. If there's meaning in anything, I haven't found it. Help me to endure.*

And still I prayed for Pilatus.

Be kind to him. Bring us to our end with more in our cup than blood and tears. I deserve that, and, in his own way, so does he, if only because I care for him. And yet, not only: for other reasons also –

I have never found it in my heart to hate him. I watched him through terrifying times, as I watch him now through the difficult quietness, and although I have often disliked him – is he not bound to me?

And there are finenesses in him. I see them daily. Don't expect to read what they are. I perceive them, and they exist: I have no wish to list them like items considered against their cost and borne home from an unpromising stall in the market – Nor would you ask it of me. It's a question of discernment, not judgement and account-keeping.

And so –

Let us move to what you *do* ask.

You write that you wish to know about my Dream. You say you have a particular interest, that you yourself are no longer so young, and you look to the east and its mysteries, as many do – so very many – because, you write, 'They seem to keep a sense there of something which is lost to us.'

I understand. Believe me. And you are not the first to ask me. I could surprise you if I were to name the women you know – and one man – considerable people today in Rome, who have made your request before you. The search you are engaged upon is natural. So I will tell you what I can, and because you are a friend, and what I've written so far in this letter and all that I write now is for your eyes – a friend's eyes – I shall tell more fully what to others I summarised in few words without personal colourings. But, in the end, you must accept this: I shall not tell you what the Dream was. So long a letter, my dear, and not to read in it what you ask for! But be comforted at least by this: I shall not tell you, because I cannot, and yet part at least of what can be told, I shall give.

First, you must picture Jerusalem. I have no intention of boring you with lengthy descriptions of the province, nor the architectural peculiarities of the city; but you must try to understand what kind of place Jerusalem is. Caesarea is another matter, but for the Judaean the heart of all that counts is Jerusalem, and to us from Rome it's an extremely hostile city, both aggressive and secretive. Its people are passionate. Wealthy and poor alike, they seem crammed with ideas, and they can be so vociferous about them that it takes one time to realise that, behind all the clamour, much is being held back and not told to us. They are gifted. They have a great deal to contribute; but, as in other parts of Judaea, they dislike us too much; and a great many of them despise us. They have no welcome for this Empire of ours. They require to be no part of it. Of course, there are princelings, there are sycophants, who look after their own interests by trying to be as Roman as possible; and a few of the more sophisticated families offer support, nervously, somewhat bitterly; but hardly anyone else in Jerusalem feels any privilege in being protected by us, or has any sense of what it means to be linked into the Roman greatness.

And then, the population is so broken up into factions, and there are so many oversensitive priests and Temple dignitaries who hate each other, and political hotheads, and wide-eyed seers of portents. And almost everyone has such a sense of his duty and rightness, stemming from what he thinks he owes his god – their one, thunderous deity, who demands this and forbids that –

I tell you, there is no more dangerous province in the Empire than Judaea, and no more perilous city than Jerusalem, both because of the confusion and because country and city alike have such a sense of themselves, and of a destiny that we, with our legions and laws, merely buzz around like so many horseflies.

And all this Pilatus found both astonishing and horrifying. From the start, he rightly feared Jerusalem, and he didn't know how to handle it. His miscalculations were numerous. There were those monuments I've mentioned, which he felt obliged to tear down even in our own neighbourhood, in Caesarea, and all because of what they thought of them in Jerusalem. And there were other episodes: spates of executions where one example would have served, bullyings, and a clumsy business with the standards, which are peculiarly offensive to Judaeans. He attempted to set them up in Jerusalem itself – a piece of strutting that would have passed with little notice elsewhere, but which brought a mob of Jerusalem's citizens rushing to Caesarea to rage at us –

So many mistakes. Such constancy demanded of the nerves. And I tell you this: listening to the howls of a Jerusalem mob could bring a tightness to my throat such as I'd never experienced, not even when I'd heard the Roman poor in full voice; and Pilatus always said that the war yells of Parthian tribes, which he'd heard in his youth, were mere squeakings in comparison – And why?

It's that idea, my friend, at once so perilous yet so attractive to us, that idea of who and what they are – I mean their sense of themselves, which we feel to be so much stronger than our own notions of what *we* are, and which is part, at least, of what you mean when you write, 'They seem to keep a sense there of something which is lost to us.'

You may protest that it's not so: you mean something quite different from the intransigence and fierceness of those strange Judaeans – and I know you do. Yet their sense of destiny, something far beyond the obvious feebleness of their country – can that really be separated from their dialogue with a god who is as passionate – and as demanding – about them as they are about him?

And isn't all of that part of what attracts you: their undoubting communication with their insistent god?

I believe it is, and can imagine your argument: 'In those who have no doubt, can't we find the antidote to a wavering dependence on cynical and apathetic deities who, if they can speak to us, don't trouble themselves with the effort?

Or who may notice us on one occasion, but seem, on balance, no more consistent than we are?

And who may favour us, or – just as likely – may smudge us at last into the dust whimsically, quite without judgement?'

I believe you would say this to me. Who hasn't had such thoughts?

And often in those days, I saw Pilatus staring at some ordinary individual, someone quite unimportant, while the man explained the local customs or protested about a building project outside his gate – some insignificant matter and an insignificant Judaean – and Pilatus would stare, as if he hoped he might drink through his eyes the demeanour of the fellow and the assumption behind it of a share in a destiny greater than Rome's.

'Can't you feel it?' Pilatus used to say to me. 'They think we're not fully formed. As if we lacked our heads.'

'They don't want us here,' I said.

The place taxed him to his limits. I knew it. And even he often said so. With – frequently – absurd remarks from the Senate, and such obscure instructions from Caesar, and precious little help from Syria, and a mutinous garrison –

Festival times were the worst.

That's to be expected, of course. A people's hopes and their contracts with their gods – supposing there are contracts – when are these more candidly displayed than during a festival? It's so even among the most primitive peoples; and in a place like Jerusalem – oh, there, I can tell you, they hold extraordinary festivals, sometimes colourful, sometimes just the opposite, but all of them conducted with determined intensity; and the greatest of those which are held yearly is of particular difficulty for Rome. You, of course, have heard of it. They call it *Pesach* – Passover. It's a celebration of freedom from foreign overlords – in fact the Egyptians, who long ago enslaved the ancestors of these Judaeans but were forced, by that furiously attentive god of theirs, to release them again under circumstances that for the Egyptians were extremely humiliating. So the Judaeans believe.

I need not labour the present-day implications.

What time could be more dangerous? It lasts for a week, and Pilatus dreaded it. Every year he dreaded it, and more so every year, until we left the province. His spies and advisers – such as they were – invariably built up the most worrying reports of troublemakers coming to the city for that festival, of the ugly mood of the crowds travelling in from the villages and towns, and of the sinister and incalculable attitudes of the priests, so that as the time for the festival drew near, there would be tell-tale signs from Pilatus of turbulence in his gut. He would complain of wind and queasiness and find greater fault with our cook; he ate more bread and less meat; he watered his wine more.

There were other occasions, too, when anxiety made him nauseous, one could even say there were many; but I became so accustomed to his digestive troubles in the month before Passover that I took care to see that his meals at that time were bland – at least those I could in any way supervise.

And then he would go – some seven days before the start of

the festival – he, in person, to show the strong arm of Rome in Jerusalem until the crisis had passed.

At first, it was not my custom to go with him. Why would I? He didn't want us women there. He preferred to ride off, manly and masterful, and most ostensibly leave us in Caesarea, as if by that he made it plain to the people of Jerusalem that he came about business. But eventually he found complications that made my presence useful to him. Those princelings, for example. There were princelings. He detested most of them, and especially one from the neighbouring province who was unctuous and scheming, and who often insisted Pilatus accept his hospitality, since he possessed what he thought was a fine palace in Jerusalem. And, besides, there were various delicate relationships to be maintained with important families, and much of the work done in sweet-sounding messages and little gifts and gestures since, near that festival time, even some of the best families refused to have any real contact with a Roman because we were ritually unclean – and yet, you may depend on it, they expected some sort of recognition from us. 'A woman's touch,' Pilatus called it gloomily; a woman's flair for sending a slave to deliver tactful and honeyed compliments, a piece of Syrian glass, or a small bar of fragrant sandalwood to the wife of some potentate –

'I need you there,' he told me bluntly one year – I think it was our third in the province – and after that, all years I went with him. That is to say, I followed him at a decent distance, as a good wife should. Two or three days behind.

We were housed variously. Sometimes in a palace on the western side of the city – one of the few truly beautiful places in Jerusalem, but it was very exposed and could seem a long way from the garrison. And sometimes in that quite different palace – the prince's – although only once the festival had ended. And sometimes in the famous Antonia, the city's great pile of a fortress that seethed with activity day and night, the official site of the praetorium. But we also had our own establishment, close to the fortress – in truth, we were barely out of its shadow – and often we stayed there. We took a good part of our household with us, to discourage the prince from inviting us too often; and each visit was a considerable upheaval. And every spring, I arrived in Jerusalem tired, over-alert and nervous. Even in the years afterwards –

But why write of every year? What are the other years to you? You wish to know only of one; and from the start, that year's festival was especially difficult.

Pilatus knew who was coming: his spies had worked him into a fine pitch of expectation. A notorious robber had recently been arrested – a violent, ignorant man who had somehow appealed to the simple people's imagination and was considered a Rome-hating hero. He sprawled in his cell, awaiting Pilatus and judgement. He was to be tried on the first convenient day after Passover – an insensitive piece of timing, although perhaps slightly wiser than a trial just before the festival began – and Pilatus knew that this man's followers were packing into the city, along with all the other Rome-haters, to foment a protest. Then, as every year, the elders and teachers of various communities were coming – opinionated individuals, many of them, who walked about as pompously as senators looking for grievances: you could pick them out of the crowds quite easily; and they could have a strange effect on the population, who felt protective towards them, and duty-bound to detect any slight offered to them even where none was intended. Then, in addition, several miracle workers – Judaeans love a miracle just as much as Romans do – with their bands of apprentices, were also expected, and not all of those were entertaining: half starved from living out in the desert on visions and locusts, they were apt to have high estimations of their own powers, and sometimes they brought with them from the desert loud messages from their god, which they bellowed out in the streets, exciting and provoking people.

Also a man was coming – Pilatus was well aware of it – who was considered one of the more interesting teachers, or miracle men – in this case, it was hard to know quite what to call him. A travelling philosopher, perhaps. A kind of self-styled Wise Vagrant. Not starved and wild-eyed, and not a vulgar exhibitionist, although fantastic tales clung to him, but not a home-dwelling, settled man either. And wherever he went, crowds of enthusiasts gathered round him, and the fantastic tales grew more fantastic. It was said, for instance, that he could control the weather and heal lepers – commonplace claims among those who deal in the fantastic, I know, but somehow they always sounded grander when told of this man. More seriously, he had a reputation for being unpredictable, associated with riots although he seemed to slip away from them before a finger could be pointed, and with offending local authorities – even some in Jerusalem – in ways no one quite expected. By the spies of Pilatus he was thought to be dangerous, although I have the impression that their assessments of him were confused and various.

Pilatus had mentioned him to me, months before. We had been speaking of tactlessness. He had received a letter from an acquaintance in Patavium, full of advice and criticisms; and I'd asked, 'What does it matter? Naturally, *you* are aware of the situation in this province. You can evaluate its difficulties, but this old friend of yours is far away. His opinions are based on ignorance, and his display of them is merely stupid.'

'Merely stupid. Is that so?' Pilatus had said. 'Well, I find no respect in this stupidity. But then, you women . . . Do you know, there's someone going round the towns these days, drawing huge crowds – he's like one of those desert men, full of talk, capable of anything – and some of our ladies – I mean Roman ladies – actually send their women to listen to him? Can you credit it? They even send Judaeans. They must know my agents watch him – with crowds like that, it's obvious – but they send their women anyway. And what's that? Stupidity? Or an insult to me?'

'Who are these ladies?' I'd asked, but Pilatus had only shrugged. So then I'd said, 'In this country, Roman ladies are easily bored. They're always looking for the man who has the answer to that. Haven't you noticed?'

But Pilatus hadn't laughed. He had looked sullen. 'I think he's dangerous,' he'd said. 'That man. He's a clever trouble-maker.'

'Then arrest him!' I'd said – and seen at once that such direct-ness was a mistake.

'Arrest him? How novel!' Pilatus had shouted. 'How did I fail to think of it? And this from *you*, whose hymns to the Goddess of Restraint deafen us all!'

At that, I'd had the sense to keep quiet; and soon he had con-tinued more calmly: 'Sometimes there are riots, but he's never found at the centre of them. And there are crowds, but they don't harm anyone's property. Mostly nothing happens. And it seems he says next to nothing. Nothing that matters, at any rate.'

That is what Pilatus had told me, eight or more months before the festival in Jerusalem; and do you know, my friend, I, too, when my husband had told me about that crowd-gatherer who said nothing, I too had thought he sounded dangerous – someone, perhaps, who could rally the province against us, and bring my husband down. That was my instinct. So I'd said to Pilatus, 'If his words are insignificant, what is his power? Is he like those other visionaries? Does he claim to speak with their god? If so, what do the priests think of him? Not all of them hate you. Maybe they can tell you if he's dangerous.'

But Pilatus had frowned. 'Priests? Which priests?' he'd demanded. 'There are too many priests. And they tell me noth-ing useful!'

'Then wait,' I'd said, 'until someone does.'

The words, I remember, came easily; and just as easily came

the thought that I might enquire among those 'ladies' Pilatus had spoken of, and from their reports form my own judgement.

So you see how it was.

Are you distressed, my dear? It was I. It was I who expected to be that someone with something useful to tell.

But I found no one who knew anything beyond vaguenesses. A few acquaintances lied to me, perhaps, because of my position. However that may be, I found none who would confess to an interest in Judaean crowd-gatherers, even though I asked jokingly enough. 'What do you suppose the excitement is?' I said. 'What are we missing? These wild men with their messages – have you ever thought it might be amusing to go and see one for ourselves?' But the ladies of polite Caesarea heard me and shrugged, and spoke of their favourite fortune-tellers, or of other matters.

The most I learned was from an Alexandrian cosmetics dealer. Once a month he came to me with his selection of hair oils and lip paints. I enjoyed his visits. He was witty and elegant, and had some smattering of education. Also he was Greek, and I expect philosophy from Greeks. So I asked him – frankly – whether in his travels he'd heard of this crowd-gatherer who said so little in many words, and could stop storms.

He smiled. 'I think I know the one you mean,' he said. 'He's harmless. In fact, you Romans should salary him. He tells the poor to be content. He takes the bitterness out of them.'

I made no comment. I felt unconvinced; and perhaps seeing the doubt in my face, the Alexandrian added, 'I've only heard him once. Most of what he says isn't new. I've heard old men by the gates in Jerusalem talk like that.'

'What is it then?' I asked. 'What's so special about this man?'

'Nothing,' said the Alexandrian. Then he pulled out a box of lip paints, and soon I was laughing as he daubed himself with the boldest colours.

I chose not to mention that conversation to Pilatus. I told

myself I had no significant facts. It would irritate him, I reasoned, to picture me asking questions – questions that troubled him – of a pedlar of face paints, even an educated one. And I gave up my enquiries. Once or twice, in my prayers, it's true, I added a particular request among the painful many, with not much understanding of how to phrase it.

Let us not be harmed, I asked, *by devious conspirators , whether Roman or provincial. And of those few who seem to offer peace – let them not all be false.*

And so that Passover came. And on the eve of his setting out for Jerusalem, Pilatus turned to me and said, 'Did you discover anything? About that fellow who draws the crowds?'

So you see. He had known I would enquire.

'Did your agents discuss him with the priests?' I asked.

'Priests – hornets!' cried Pilatus. 'They love to worry me. They love to heap up fabulous speculations, and hope I lose sleep in them. What do they care about one more god-talker? I can get no sense out of them. This man,' he added, 'I hear he still doesn't speak about Rome. He says nothing against us –'

'I've also heard he's harmless,' I said. 'His only real power is that the poor love him –'

But there Pilatus lost patience, and he waved me away, right away, out of his room; and I heard him crashing about, rummaging in his chest for something, a buckle, a belt, and too agitated to summon a slave to do it. I sent one to him.

And so we went to Jerusalem, Pilatus two days ahead of me, to make his official entrance.

And that year we did not lodge in the western palace, nor did we receive a princely invitation. Some particular tension had come between Pilatus and the prince. I forget the nature of our offence – or his – but Pilatus was very anxious.

'We must sweeten him up!' he told me. 'He's cunning, and he has friends in Rome!'

'But at least for this time we're spared his evil meals,' I said, 'and those suffocating rooms –'

'Send messages. Be kind to his women!'

'Of course,' I said.

I spoke soothingly. I had just arrived, and he was already impatient with me. I was sitting on a box of clothes. I was covered with dust from the roads. The room was neither warm nor welcoming. That house, close by the Antonia, where Pilatus preferred to stay when in Jerusalem, had been adapted, as far as possible, to Roman tastes of a masculine and military nature. It was a great deal less comfortable than the palace or even the fortress, and in its way, less private. My own quarters were inconvenient. Three small rooms for myself and the other women were faced across a court-yard by rooms often occupied by secretaries and advisers. The kitchens were cramped, the servants' quarters a kind of dungeon. The main rooms, for entertaining and for my husband's own use, were neither splendid nor healthy: smells from a gutter were a perpetual problem, and in cold weather some of the walls were damp. But he preferred the place. It had few entrances, and I believe he felt safer there, not only safer than in the palace, but safer even than in the gross bulk of the Antonia, where every hostile mind in the city seemed to come reaching towards him. I think he felt that. Certainly he slept in the fortress as little as he could manage. And I think he also found satisfaction in that house's lack of grandeur – a strange contrast to his attitude in Caesarea. He seemed to like the mosaic in the dining room – a hunting scene remarkably devoid of character – and he had brought into the rooms objects too homely for either a palace or a fortress: an unimpressive head of Tiberius for which he knew he'd given far too much money, and a fleshy nymph with a cold smile, done in green marble. He felt, I believe, clearer there, in the house. Its lack of luxury reassured him. He could feel purposeful and uncomplicated, a Roman of the old times, standing his ground against irrational, less honourable men.

So much simpler than governing –

So much simpler, also, than playing the gracious guest in the prince's palace, in those scented corridors, where smiles and complex hints were dished up with every word that our host spoke.

'Did you hear me?' he shouted. 'You must do something about his women!'

'I have a new remedy for headaches,' I said. 'Egyptian and very powerful. I'll send the women that. They're fond of headaches. And I have a length of beads –'

But he wasn't listening.

'We've had trouble already,' he told me. 'A demonstration in the streets. And yesterday something happened at the Temple. It was over quickly, but they say that fellow of yours was behind it.'

'What fellow of mine?' I asked, and I was smiling. It's so much his way, Pilatus, to blame me if he can –

He made no reply, but he was observing me with distaste, and at last he said, 'You look sick. Are you sick?'

'I'm tired,' I told him. 'And you always do this when you see me tired and making less than my best appearance. It can't be helped.'

'Then rest!' he said. 'We must look in charge here!'

And so I tried. I rested. In truth, I was tired. My friend, do you know that exhaustion – the sort that comes like a wave, sudden and undeniable, rising against a harbour wall, against the fragile boats and the careful stones – have you experienced it? You tell yourself, *This is caused by my journey and my monthly bleeding.* Or, *This is caused by too much worry and too little sleep.* Or, *This is the result of my husband's moods!* But the truth is, nothing in your life is so different from how it has been, and for months, for years, tiredness has flowed in your veins and seemed a full measure, so why it should rise all at once into a great wave is a mystery. And when, on the second day in Jerusalem, I found myself as exhausted as on the first, I did in fact say to myself, *Perhaps I'm ill* – And then I chose my brightest lip paint, and my most colourful pendant, and I walked my way through that day – through the visits of several Roman women, and a lengthy complaint by the steward concerning his lot in life – I walked slowly, smiling, and trying not to feel how precarious everything seemed, how small our haven was in that city, and what tension came in through the walls from the crowds. That week, the very air in Jerusalem felt strangely crammed into too little space, and packed with secrets, so that even in the house there were times when it seemed as if someone had just brushed past me while my head was turned, while outside in the city, civil order was about to burst like an over-ripe fruit.

And I myself –

Something in me is about to break, I thought, *if I let it. This is because I'm tired. Let me not be ill. It's not the time.*

I spent most of that evening with my face to the prayer niche, making appeals; and my statuette of Isis smiled, as sometimes she does, but I was disconcerted to see it.

Smile if you will, I told her, *but remember, he's not capable of much. Keep the city quiet. All you gods. Let this festival pass. And keep me well.*

I prayed into the night. No one disturbed me. Pilatus didn't come to me. And afterwards my sleep was anxious, and broken by everything and nothing – a voice in the courtyard, the movement of my own limbs, the chill of the darkness through the window grid.

In the morning Pilatus kept to his own room until he left the house, which he did without greeting me. And all that day he was occupied, so that I saw him only briefly in the evening: he had come from the Antonia, and I found him sitting alone in the dining room, to which I'd been summoned.

'Three guests,' he said. 'Tomorrow evening. One's a woman. See to it.'

I humoured him.

'I shall obey, my commander,' I said, 'but may a mere centurion know their names?'

He was not amused.

'You're neglecting people,' he said. 'You're hiding yourself too much.' And he told me who they were.

They were not so important, and I had already sent messages to the wife. They were Greeks, with influence in Rhodes, nothing more.

'Make it generous,' he said. 'I won't have them saying we skimped. We can manage this damned festival and still eat.'

'It seems you're managing well,' I said.

'You still look sick,' he told me. 'Try to look livelier tomorrow.'

I went away and wept. Unheard of, to weep because of supper arrangements – commonplace particulars. Even in Jerusalem, our lugubrious steward would have the matter perfectly in hand by sunrise: what need had I for tears? And yet I wept.

To exchange jokes with strangers, to talk of Rhodes or Athens, and when these people had been in Rome, to watch Pilatus act out the situation: how he had more important matters to attend to – a city and a province to govern – how he was only present, condescendingly present, as a tense man might pick up a stylus and toy with it for a moment between rushing in from one critical decision and rushing out to attend to the next: a question of amusement, to relieve the pressure – And of course, who could tell when one might need a friend, even in Rhodes?

The prospect of all this came on me in my exhausted condition as outrageous. It was too great a demand, an interruption – grievous and unlooked for – intruding upon a most secret and undefined labour in myself and in the city, and in all things. The very chair by my bed, the noises from the kitchen, the air I breathed – we were all intent on our labour, and how could this be, this settling down to prattle with strangers about commerce and fashionable acquaintances?

Perhaps, my dear, as you read this, you fail to understand. If the exhaustion I've described is unknown to you, not experienced even when the estate was lost, or – perhaps especially – at any other, less remarkable time, then you may interpret my distress as no more than poor nerves and irritation. You may not know what it is to feel as I did.

I wept myself to sleep; and that night, it was a sleep of dull heaviness, blank, devoid of nurturing; and the next day, I was hard put to it to raise a smile, even when a gift came from one of the more affable Judaean families: a magnificent hawk for Pilatus, proud, sharp-eyed, and most delicately marked on her wings and breast. I received this gift on his behalf with little grace, sending the messenger packing with no token in return.

Tired, so tired of formalities; and in the air that day, since I myself felt so disrupted and weary, perhaps naturally I sensed a distracted quality – as if, with the rhythm of our strange labour so impaired, as time shortened to the start of the festival and as Jerusalem became ever more crammed, the air itself hardly knew whether to be still, or to surge against all restraints and howl like a mob – or indeed to bring a mob – I hardly knew what. The tension kept a clamminess on my brow all the hours of the day, and through the supper –

The supper. As to that, listening to Pilatus earnestly discussing with our guests how to procure the best wine and spices from Rhodes, and laughing too loudly at their travellers' tales, and swiftly taking up the mention of an influential landowner – I slipped into an understanding which I might well have missed. I saw that on his brow, too, there was sweat; and that supper, I realised, he had contrived at such a time because he needed it: he was afraid, more than was usual in the days before Passover, and so he clung to what he knew – thought he knew.

So when our guests had left, before he went to his bed, I said to him, 'Only until sunset tomorrow. Then the festival begins.

Isn't that correct? At sunset tomorrow? And once a thing has begun, it's almost over –'

'You were very quiet tonight,' he said.

'Sleep,' I told him. 'What are your officers for? You're too tense.'

'You should have been livelier,' he said. 'Those are people worth cultivating.'

And after that we retreated from each other, to our separate beds; and I dismissed the girl: I pulled the hairpins out myself, and I wrapped my clothes round me, and lay down and slept, still in my finery, so great was my exhaustion. And I didn't hear when they came for him.

Who was it? Stolid Terentius Bassus or that homesick Celt – Fabius of the lean face and watchful eyes? I haven't asked. Someone came, one of the staff, at the very first hint of dawn, when, on many days, I would have been already awake and wide-eyed before the prayer niche, or at least staring from my head-rest at the approaching hours with their crate-load of effort.

But that day I heard nothing. I slept. I dreamt. What I dreamt I cannot tell you, but the sleep that I'd been granted in the night was like a deep pool, tranquil and with no terrors in its darkness; and I awoke at last overwhelmed by sweetness, and as weak as an infant.

My heart sobbed. I tried to rise from the bed but my legs couldn't serve me. My hands fluttered. I tried to call for the girl – not for her help but for her presence: there was an urgency in me – but no voice came from my throat, and when at last, in my attempt to rise, I stumbled against the chair and she heard and came in to attend to me and I did speak, my words lurched and bobbed from my mouth then drew swiftly back into my breath, and beyond that, into a mesh of sweetness and stillness, and then they came lurching forwards again, and I shook with my urgency –

The girl ran for the older women. Corellia came and stout Sabina – I travelled nowhere in those days without Mettia Sabina – and I smiled at them and said – whatever I said – and the sight of their concerned, loyal faces was almost beyond human bearing. I stretched out my hands to them – and I remember Corellia said, 'It's a fever. We should inform the Procurator!' But it's Sabina's reply that has significance. 'Can't you hear?' she said. 'We mustn't trouble him now. Something's happening. Listen to those crowds. They must be rioting. Fetch wine, and I'll go and find some poppy seeds. We must calm her.'

Then they both left me. They left me alone with the anxious girl, whose eyes had expanded to platter size, and I remember how I seized the child's hand and tried to press it in mine – for was she not as I was, and as we all are, living? And webbed in everything? But I hadn't the strength, nor the time –

She made no attempt to stop me reaching the door; and I ran out – call it running: the urgency carried me – out into the courtyard, to where the simple fellow stood who kept guard, for appearance's sake, by the women's quarters. A good man, and not a slave. In fact he was a soldier. He had served honourably for many years: he was grey-haired; he had not possessed the intelligence to rise through the ranks, but Pilatus liked him. He used to stop and joke with him – something about fleas: I don't know how it began – and after one such exchange Pilatus had said to me, 'I'd give my best horse and a couple of villas to have three men on my staff as straightforward as that one.'

This was the man I found, and who set off unhesitatingly for me.

And is the rest not infamous? Pleading a message from the Procurator's wife, a most urgent message, my poor friend passed every obstacle – barred gates, private stairs, prohibited passages – to come floundering out onto the steps fronting the Antonia, into that broad space, the arena of judgements, where down below the crowd shrieked and screamed their contradictions, not only at the Roman judge but at each other, swaying and hissing, and where on the steps stood the accused, and where Pilatus, my husband, had arrived at the time to pronounce sentence, his decision waited in his throat – in fact, Pilatus had just seated himself on the judgement chair – and my messenger comes, he comes swiftly to my husband's side and whispers in his ear: 'Your wife's sent me. She's had a dream. She says you mustn't harm this man you're dealing with. The dream troubles her.'

What Pilatus replied, I have no idea.

When I saw him, he demanded no explanation. His face was livid. He had already seen to it that our simple friend was transferred to less comfortable duties; and all he said to me that evening was, 'You astound me!' It was several days later when that speech came, which I've already written: *'Isn't it enough that I must wade daily through the blood of simpletons and rebels –'* ending with those words about *'a wife who runs to assure me that my next move will send me hurtling to perdition.'*

'I didn't speak of perdition,' I said. 'That was not my meaning.'

Loathing stabbed me from his eyes. 'You implied I'd offended the gods!' he cried.

I lowered my head. 'My meaning,' I said, 'had to do with love.'

'Oh,' said Pilatus, 'and in your dream some god came to you, did he, and instructed you about Roman justice? Which one was it? And did he take you in his arms –'

'I had no dream,' I said. 'Or my dream had no forms. It left neither words nor images. I said I dreamt because I could find no other means to express it.'

Pilatus stared. 'You're mad!' he said at last. 'This country's made you ill. This damned province – and your prayers. All that moaning to the gods. And it's me, isn't it? It's because you think I'm a fool. You despise me,' he said. Then he shouted, 'Are you in touch with that man's friends? Who came to you?'

'There was only the dream,' I told him.

'We'll never speak of this again,' said Pilatus.

I was silent, and he added, 'The body's been stolen. That wild man of yours. Alive, he was an obvious threat to the stability of the province, and dead, it's just the same: now his followers are up to tricks – using stories of magic to spread their influence. In reality, my choices were no choices.'

At the time I let that pass. I scared him in those days. I saw it. I would see him shrink from the sight of my hands, because they trembled, and grow furious at something in my face or voice; and all this rage and panic on his part brought welling up in me such sorrow for my Pilatus, and such affection – truly, affection – that my eyes were full of tears.

He kept away from me as much as possible, and saw to it that I received no visitors. I had a 'serious indisposition'. I was 'conserving all available strength to fight a malignant illness'. He worked – and even slept – at the Antonia; and the disturbances in the streets of Jerusalem gradually grew less. No great riot broke out. The robber, who should have been tried and executed after the festival, had been released, as if by way of festival clemency; Pilatus had done that, although it hardly lay within his usual scale of concessions. Occasionally he did free some poor wretch, and always he would mention it to me – a drunk, or a simple blunderer whose stall had collapsed and blocked a street while soldiers were passing – but he had not, of course, intended to release a known criminal. Still, the robber had gone, and his gangs of protesters had either vanished into houses or left the city with him. It was all most unexpected; and all of it resulted from events on that day when I'd dreamt, and sent my messenger –

When Pilatus had been forced to try the philosopher. For, indeed, it had been no other. It had been on *his* account – the wandering philosopher's – that my husband had been called from the house so early.

The man had been brought before him quite suddenly, while Pilatus was still heavy with sleep, and with shrill demands from various influential people for a quick dispatch to the business, because emotions ran so high in every part of the city. And on that morning, wishing to soothe at least some portion of the crowd – the great mass of the poor who loved the philosopher, or the agitated people whom the philosopher had offended, or even the hotheads, the Rome-hating gangs who loved the robber – Pilatus had searched about within himself and snatched hold of an idea. He had placed the two prisoners in the balance: robber and philosopher, in order to secure some measure of safety whatever the outcome. He had placed them one man against the other, and invited the crowd to choose one of them for release – just as if he always honoured their festivals like Roman festivals, with weighty extravagances. And this, some would say, was a skilful manoeuvre on my husband's part, and that it turned out well, especially since, in the event, he satisfied two out of three angry factions, and was left with discontent only where it proved least effective. They would say this, and no doubt they would also observe, that the garrison in Jerusalem has its limitations.

And so the robber lived – at least until our agents could ensnare him again – and the philosopher was sent to his death; and his followers may have spread stories, but they failed to mob the streets: they didn't turn on us. Jerusalem grew quiet; and havoc was avoided.

But none of this Pilatus told me. I knew nothing of it – I mean of this weighing up of two men, one to live and one to die, in the scales of a festival's economy – until I heard of it later, weeks later when I was calm, and when, in the clear light from the sea at Caesarea, I could listen to details, and then I seemed to understand everything I heard: I understood it instantly.

And even there, in Caesarea, Pilatus avoided me. For weeks he hardly spoke to me, and for months he didn't come to my bed, which perhaps is as well: my body was childlike, a delicate guest to me – but I grieved for his loneliness.

And one day, I took an opportunity to say to him, 'Do you still think I despise you? You said as much in Jerusalem.'

He refused to look up from his work.

'You're not to be trusted,' he answered. 'A man needs a sane wife!'

'I don't think you wanted to sentence him,' I said. 'That philosopher. The man I warned you about. You tried to argue for him. You didn't succeed, and so you offered him –'

'*Warned* me?' said Pilatus, looking up then, and he turned very pale. 'You didn't warn me!' he said. 'You undermined me! Warnings that come too late are no such thing. They're condemnations!' Then he added, 'Who told you what I did? Who's been talking about that trial?'

'Your staff. Your secretaries. Not to me,' I said, 'but my women hear things –'

'Silence them,' said Pilatus, and he lowered his head again to the papyrus he was studying, and didn't suspect – how could he? – the strangeness to me of the language I'd been speaking: *you did this, you wanted to do that*. It was to me as if I'd tried to approach the subject of blame down a narrow and half-forgotten street. I knew the way; I also knew the stones of the street and the guttering, and yet even so, the street was unfamiliar to me; and I'd tried to walk down it wrapped in a shock that seemed the breadth of the world, and nevertheless the walls hadn't touched me, and nevertheless they were there. And I'd known the way –

I didn't trouble him further. You will appreciate, I was in any case not equipped for debates. Mostly, I sought silence – as in many ways I still do, all these years later.

And now, dear one, have I fulfilled what you require of me? You ask in your letter, what did I dream? And you imply other questions: how did matters stand between myself and Pilatus at the time of that trial? And what did I know of that philosopher?

Have I written enough?

But over the distance that separates us, I sense that, as you read this letter, there are further questions rising in you.

Did I rebuke myself, you wonder, because my warning to Pilatus had failed?

And you ask: if my dream was formless, and if I knew so little about the philosopher, how can I be sure that my dream conveyed a message concerning *him* – that particular man, and that trial? You ask: isn't it a fact that for years I'd been distressed by my husband's erratic behaviour? So couldn't the impulse from the dream have been given some broader interpretation?

And of course you ask: what had happened? Why was that man arrested in the first place? And when I awoke that morning, if no one told me, how did I know what was happening? And afterwards, did I speak to the secretary who had recorded the trial? Or did Pilatus ever tell me what had taken place – what words had been spoken, what *he* had said, and what the prisoner had said?

I respect these questions. Why wouldn't I? Do you imagine I'd shrink and say, 'They disturb my peace. Leave me alone. I will not tell you'?

I repeat: what can't be told, you must be content not to read. But as to what I can tell – and, strangely, it's not always the same to everyone who asks – of what I can tell, something at least I feel obliged to offer. And you, my dear, I know: the patterns of your mind are familiar to me; and so to you I offer this –

Without knowledge, I awoke knowing. The philosopher had been arrested in the night, suddenly, for all the long, complex reasons that had bided their time; but on that morning I didn't think of arrests and trials, and my Sabina spoke only of riots. Still, I knew what was happening: that is, I knew who stood at the centre of that uproar in the streets, face to face with Pilatus, and that Pilatus moved – slowly, in a kind of arc through his fear – towards what he would do.

And afterwards, I didn't speak to the secretary. It would have outraged Pilatus, and been entirely inappropriate. There was no question of such an action – nor any urge in myself towards it, no curiosity. Or, rather, by the time I was curious – more than a year later – the man had been sent on business to Bithynia, and he never came back to us. And naturally, I had no access to the records, nor thought of any such possibility.

Pilatus himself, on the other hand, did speak to me once more of the trial, and indeed he spoke at some length. It was several months after the conversation I've described – that solitary attempt of mine to address the subject – and I have mentioned it to scarcely anyone. Isn't a man entitled to privacy, some degree of privacy, when he speaks to his wife? And there have been other considerations. I have never wished to trammel up with complicating factors for others what I've told them – just as, for myself, although eventually I grew stronger, I never wished my understanding to be fractured into argument and discussion. For I remained ill-equipped, as I say, for debate. Still, Pilatus spoke to me, and since you know him, and since perhaps someone other than myself should be aware of what was said, I shall give you a brief account. He spoke, I think, because he needed to, because he sought acquittal from me, as if I had indeed condemned him, and I think also because by then I seemed steadier and less preoccupied, and he wished to draw me back to him, into what he saw as the practicalities of life.

'I have no desire,' he said, 'to speak of the matter more than is necessary. However, now you're more or less yourself again, I have some points to make about that trouble in Jerusalem.'

'That trial?' I asked. 'If you prefer not to –'

'I will do exactly as I see fit,' he said.

'Of course,' I told him.

We were in my bedroom. It was not, I think, that he desired our conversation to end in a carnal embrace – or even to bring our bodies into harmony, side by side, resting together; nevertheless I think he'd chosen my bedroom because he wished to reclaim it.

'What if he was innocent?' he demanded. 'That man? He was a nuisance. He rubbed authorities the wrong way. That's what matters. I can't say I understood everything – all that priestly outrage – but then I'm not sure anyone did. Even the priests – most of them were barely coherent. Too much came down to how you look at things –'

'Why did they bring him to you?' I asked. 'Who brought him? Priests? Which priests? I suppose they expected you to be pleased.'

Pilatus gave me one of his stares. 'Have you understood nothing?' he said. 'They're hornets, I tell you. They buzz and swarm and provoke. They knew very well I wouldn't want *that* in Passover week! Didn't I have enough?'

I said nothing.

Then Pilatus went on, 'He was an insult to Caesar. At least that was the impression he gave, which is the same thing. A few of them said as much. Not that they cared, but they pointed it out – quite publicly, you know. That's the trouble with philosophers. They go to no pains to show respect for authority. And what was I to do? Debate Ideals and the clay of men with those barbarians? Would they have understood, any of them? Would Caesar?'

I smiled, and Pilatus stepped back quickly from this momentary ambivalence. 'An Emperor,' he cried, 'has higher preoccupations – and I had more immediate concerns! For how long do you suppose the garrison would have held out if the city had turned on us, which it could have done? Aren't you glad to be alive? A crowd that size – it was a gift for fanatics! The robber's men could have grabbed their chance They may have had mercenaries. Imagine it! Every street a battlefield. Every house a place for ambush. And even if it hadn't come to that – those priests, if I'd offended them, or if a single priest had been trampled by the crowd, they'd have got busy – oh, they'd certainly have got busy complaining to everyone, in Syria, Rome –'

'Which the philosopher's followers, being mostly unsophisticated people, were less likely to do,' I said. 'I understand. But tell me this: how did you know that there weren't other priests, still in their beds that morning, who had other opinions? Priests ready to take offence because you hadn't consulted them? You've always said the priests have no love for each other, but that every one of them seeks to torment you. Are these other priests not also capable of complaining?'

'You imply there were such men? That some of them have done that?'

'I merely ask a question,' I told him. 'I know so little –'

'Ah, you admit it!' said Pilatus. He was standing very still. Generally he likes to stride about a room when he argues, but on that occasion he seemed to have forgotten his habit, and he stood like what he was – a stranger in my room. Then he said, 'Well, here's a fact you've overlooked! That troublemaker didn't confine himself to one province, and the priests who brought him had some royal backing. They brought a message from our friend the Prince, which made them far more deadly than whoever lay in bed! The Prince has some right to be considered, wouldn't you say, especially when he drops hints about his Galileans and risks to stability! A smiling message, full of teeth. You didn't know that, did you? No one told you that!'

'It's true,' I said, 'I didn't –'

But Pilatus was already speaking again. 'And those *other* priests,' he said, 'those *other* priests you speak of, supposing I could have summoned them, and listened to a whole week of whatever it is they shout about – what then? I don't believe the end could have been any different! How could I have done otherwise? If I had, there would still have been complaints, accusations – how I protected rogues who insulted Caesar. And the tension. Just how much tension do you think the city could have taken? Uprisings, riots. Or if I'd simply let the man go, if I'd released him one morning, quietly, as the gates opened – what then? Just the same. It would have led to riots, complaints. He'd be out there now causing trouble, that philosopher, he was nothing but trouble, and it's I who would have let it happen. Surely you see that,' he said.

I was quiet. I think I would have spoken, but I needed time to frame what I meant to say, and there was no time.

He hurried on, 'You, of course, think otherwise, but in fact things turned out very well! I've nothing to reproach myself with. The robber – he's another story – but at least we're rid of one subversive. And is it so terrible? Have we paid such a high price? Perhaps he *was* a sort of innocent, but he was a dangerous sort of innocent, and it's better like this. He's out of the way.'

'Out of the way,' I said. His tirade was numbing me.

Then Pilatus spoke with particular emphasis. 'Do you think I'm never to compromise?' he asked. 'For that matter, is there never a situation that inevitably has a compromise or a mistake in it, whatever I do? And I repeat, is it so terrible? Why a clamouring from the gods? If he *was* innocent, he was hardly the first innocent to go to the cross!'

'As to that,' I said, 'is one wrong excusable because we've committed ten thousand others?'

'Oh, have I?' said Pilatus. 'Ten thousand? Is that what you think?'

And then, before I could protest, he shrugged. 'One, ten thousand,' he said. 'If there's one, it could be argued what difference does it make how many there are, provided we survive them?'

'That's not what you believe,' I told him. 'You like things to be correct –'

And at once he was angry. 'You know nothing about my beliefs!' he cried. 'What are my beliefs to you? You with your sanctimonious faces! And what have beliefs to do with it? Beliefs make a mess! That man had his beliefs –'

'What were they?' I asked.

'Oh,' said Pilatus, 'you would like to know, wouldn't you? Oh, you'd very much like to know.' And he tensed where he stood, and a strange cunning crept into his face, as if he'd caught me out in some evil device.

'Indeed I'd like to know,' I said. 'Very much.'

And then he gripped – he was standing by the small table – he seized whatever was to hand, and it was my silver looking plate; and when he saw what he had, instead of throwing it at me as I'd expected, he thrust it towards me and hissed, 'Look at yourself! You're still not strong in the head, are you? What do you think he believed? What are you waiting for?'

I didn't answer, and he flung it – the plate – across the room. It skittered on the floor until it fetched up against the wall, and the sight seemed to upset Pilatus and sober him, perhaps because the wall plaster chipped, or because he dislikes damage to expensive objects; and he sat down on the stool.

'I've never liked secrets,' he said. 'You know that.'

'I know,' I told him.

'I made some effort to place him in a favourable light,' he said. 'Tell your gods that. But the political issues were highly sensitive –'

'I know,' I told him.

'He wouldn't talk man to man,' said Pilatus. 'He wouldn't cooperate. Not in any way that would have helped. He left it all to me. He knew what he was doing. He left it to me,' he said. And then he affected a look of amusement – not unlike expressions I've seen on the faces of men in the arena, as the beasts come loping in. 'Do you know,' he said, 'that robber I released, he had the same name? Not the family name. The given name. It was all a roar. There were shouts for *Bar-abbas*. That was clear enough. And I knew what the set nearest me wanted. But as for the rest, they shouted a lot of things, most of it in that accursed Aramaic, and I'm not sure, or it seems to me now that I'm not –'

I went closer to him then. I didn't touch him. We women, with our fine calculations as to when to touch and when not to touch – in our own way, are we not also gladiators?

'We must go on from here,' I said; and I spoke firmly, in a voice such as he hadn't heard from me in months.

It seemed to help. Pilatus remained silent for a moment; then he got to his feet and began calmly and cogently to talk to me, as if I'd never frightened him with my spiritual antics, about a letter from Rome and certain investments we'd made in a small farm for our retirement – not this one, of course: I mean that farm nearer Rome where we never lived. How foolish we were! Only for those who come back triumphant from the provinces, drenched in approbation, that ambrosia of Emperors – only for them retirement near Rome. Which of us doesn't know this? How could we have hoped for such a homecoming? Far better for us, this obscurity –

For wasn't Pilatus right when he said that men in his position face situations that present unavoidable scope for mistakes? And, as I've written, he was, at best, an uninspired administrator. And few indeed of our governors – far abler men than Pilatus – have lived out a comfortable old age in the bosom of the City, or folded in her skirts –

As Pilatus longed to do; and I, also, at one time: I hoped for that farm, close enough to Rome for frequent visits by you, and any other friends who still remembered me. Close enough to go myself into Rome and seek out those I cared for –

And so we spoke of that, the farm, and the hour of confrontation passed, our talk about that trial in Jerusalem. And the day passed. And after that, the next day, and the next, until the days had gathered into months, and into years.

So we went on; and I found no rebuke in myself towards myself.

Can you understand?

My approach down that narrow street towards the subject of blame, and the shock that was wrapped round me, and the wonder that was left in me by a Dream which informed every-thing – not one trial alone, although it stemmed from that par-ticular crisis in Jerusalem, I know it did, as it stemmed also from a crisis in myself and in Pilatus: how can one separate what's bound together? – in all of this, the Dream's informing vastness put away from me any rebuke. Not the grief, and not, believe me, a certain leaf-sharp sense of responsibility; I choose my image with care: a sense of responsibility as delicate as a beech leaf, and as veined with the intricacy of life, and as clear-edged – and yet the rebuke was put away, so that I didn't ask, as Pilatus must have done: *Why do the gods send warnings too late? And why are we so unfortunate as to be the ones who receive them?*

Haven't I written: I came to understand that in each moment lies the chance to change everything, if we can only see in time –

But that *seeing in time*: what skill is that?

I think, my friend, it comes through practice, and the prac-tice of prayer, at least in part. Through a long tempering of one's disposition, a long leave-taking of our expectations. And yet it comes also as a gift, sometimes wholly so, where there has been no obvious predisposition for it, and at other times, it comes partly as a gift and partly in reply to our appeal, our practice. But in the end, I think, gift or practice – forgive me: I have no wish to write in riddles – these things may not be distinguishable.

There's a timing in events that's surely beyond us; and yet I think it's within us.

No rebuke.

And I prayed. In those days, I rarely stood before the niche and bowed to Diana or Isis, although their images remained there and when I did go to them they smiled, sometimes with tears. I distinctly saw the tears. But they were not the tears of anger or catastrophe, although catastrophe I understood there'd been.

I say nothing of the priests. I know nothing of their reasons and arguments. It's possible they acted sincerely and according to their highest principles. I know little about them. But catastrophe I understood there'd been both in Pilatus, who'd condemned a man out of expedience – what else can one call it? – and against some instinct in himself that wished at least to investigate further; and for me: catastrophe, of a kind, there'd also been for me, who, despite our years together, hadn't so influenced my husband that he'd found resource in himself on that day in Jerusalem, and risked another, different mistake. I too had failed. Oh, certainly there'd been catastrophe –

And yet Diana and Isis wept, I knew, not from a spirit of condemnation, but because they saw all things.

Still, I prayed very little to them – or to any particular deity. I prayed, you could say, to my Dream, and not in words; and what I prayed was only an offered love, from a small love into a great one.

Only later did the anger come, in the stale years, watching Pilatus grow fat, and listening to his blustered justifications for all manner of inept Roman activity in Judaea, and living after that with the sort of silence he shovelled over those days in Jerusalem – a period which, if he referred explicitly to it at all, he characterized to me as *'that time when you were ill.'*

Only later? Have I allowed myself to write such a dishonesty? I marvel at it: the truth is quite otherwise. Here I've stumbled on an avoidance in myself, which must be confronted.

Even in Judaea, I suffered cold bursts of rage. There was fury in me, because Pilatus wished it to be understood that the matter was closed – the trial, the condemnation, my warning, everything – although the matter was never closed, and he often referred to it but always secretly, deviously, much as he does to this day; and when he did so, I pitied him, as I still do – I have never wished to torment him – and yet in those early years I also often resented it. A coldness could fall on me, because he crept towards his subject and wouldn't grasp it; and then as slowly stories came funnelled down to us of how others saw in that particular vagrant, so summarily dispatched by Pilatus, a man who was not forgettable, and whose qualities could not be quantified – do you suppose I felt no exasperation? At times I felt almost entirely structured by pain, as if it had replaced my bones, not least because we heard the stories: there was no sparing us – they seemed to find us out like flies, which the finest nets of discretion and social tact couldn't keep from us. Even the story of survival – how the philosopher had walked out of his tomb – even that came to us once at a supper party.

Our host knew scarcely any of the details. His purpose was to mock the credulity of the poor, and to deplore the cunning of what he saw as a rebellious element in his neighbourhood; and he meant also, I suppose, to dignify Pilatus by showing sympathy with a procurator's difficulties; and so he mentioned it – 'This fable of the walking dead,' as he called it. 'This creeping out of tombs.' And he and Pilatus had laughed, and then Pilatus had leered at me, I thought, as much as to say, *'No harm done it seems! Your philosopher's still on his feet!'*

'And you?' our host had asked, taking a hint from his guest's behaviour and turning to me. 'I take it we're on safe ground? None of your acquaintance – none of the ladies – give credence to this sort of thing?' Then immediately he had turned from me again, as though he'd feared I might say something frivolous.

'I know nothing of it,' was my answer. 'I can only observe that I also know very little about the condition called death.'

But no one had listened. Only Pilatus, like a well-mannered guest who wishes to demonstrate that he hears nothing of a drunk jabbering in the courtyard, had at once begun to speak loudly about a building project, and moved everyone's thoughts to a safe distance.

Such incidents were hard for me. I grew used to them, but each one made its mark.

And there came stories, too, that in Caesarea itself there were soldiers – not many but some, and they were not all without rank – who attended secret meetings with the philosopher's followers; and when eventually I heard that, a part of me did in fact wish to seek those men out and speak to them – but how could I have done it? Pilatus complained so often and so bitterly about the fabulous credulity of soldiers; and always he would end by stating, 'If you pander to their gullible element, you strip the backbone out of men! Countless commanders have discovered that! It's not a mistake I intend to make!' And so the message was clear. And was I to play the part of his traitor? But I sometimes wearied of this heavy-handed censorship. 'Can the soldiers' beliefs not also work in a commander's favour?' I asked on one occasion, and he roared at me, 'Be quiet!' and ate the rest of his meal in silence.

Then there could also be fury in me against the Judaeans, because they flung up so many holy men during the rest of our time among them, and some of those were coarsely and undeniably dangerous, and they were dragged in chains to their prisons, like wild animals, screaming to their followers as they went; and, to make matters worse, when such events occurred, Pilatus would tell me the details eagerly and watchfully, as much as to say, *'And what do the gods require from me concerning this one?'*

But his voice forbade any response.

And then – you see how they mount up, my tablets of grievance! – do you suppose I felt no anger when we were called back to Rome? After everything, to be summoned back under the shadow of the Emperor's displeasure? And – for what? Because Pilatus was Pilatus. Because he'd used military force once too often to suppress an ecstatic gathering – a huge gathering round a holy man in the hills. Our Syrian overlords judged the action excessive, and, as you know, the Senate – and Caesar – were informed. And indeed it was – excessive. Who can deny that? It was scarcely different from several other actions and yet it was – entirely different.

After the trial in Jerusalem, the philosopher's trial and his execution, I think a crude strategy developed in Pilatus where holy men were concerned; but I believe he was only half aware of it. Where he could, I think he ignored them – the holy men. So it seemed to me. At least, he scoffed about them more, and there was less talk of agents' reports. But if reports came that were worrying, he was no longer delicate: he resorted to swift and forceful action well away from the cities, to brutal dispersals of the crowds, and violent arrests – so violent that, as I've written, two or three of those holy men howled as they were dragged to their jails. And such arrests, I noticed, had advantages for Pilatus. He said to me once, 'If a man resists arrest, he risks a fatal injury. Where's the mystery in that?' And there were no more trials of holy men. There was one trial I heard of – but that man was a fraud who extracted money from the poor and spent it on arms for a band of criminals in the hills, with a mind to seizing the province. As for the others, when I perceived the pattern I did challenge Pilatus. I asked him, 'Has an injured man no chance of keeping well enough in prison to be brought to trial?'

And he was genuinely surprised. 'Of course!' he said. 'You'd be amazed what scrawny and wrecked creatures survive in the deepest dungeons. If these visionaries die, perhaps it's because they've somewhere better to go!' And he added, 'Do you suggest that I deliberately butcher them?' And then he laughed – a short laugh, like a slap in the face. 'You're incredible,' he said. 'The next one,' he said, 'I'll send honey for his wounds. I'll send poppy seeds and mandrake oil. We'll bathe his sores in salted water.'

But I heard of no next imprisonment. Instead, there was that massacre on a hillside, north of Jerusalem. One more crowd of enthusiasts. One more rush of the troops to snatch the speaker and scatter his followers –

And so many dead.

So many. A kind of harvest from all the times when Pilatus had sent out soldiers on such business.

There were children, I believe.

And what can I tell you? You know what happened.

We lost our small, hoped-for farm close to Rome, and our little credit of worthiness, and very nearly, perhaps, our own lives: I feel we would have lost our lives, only one or two friends spoke up subtly for us, just bravely enough. And all because Pilatus refused –

Because of not seeing –

That last time, before they left, Pilatus made a point of summoning me. The pretext was simple: I was called to his room for instructions concerning some visitors who were expected to arrive while he was absent; and he said to me, 'More trouble. More god-talkers! A huge crowd. Completely hysterical. But they're not in Jerusalem yet – and I've had enough of it! This time, I'll take the troops myself. They'll shift their backsides,' he said, 'you'll see. Don't object afterwards.' Those were his words. Two of his officers were standing there, scarcely a pace away from us, and he spoke sneeringly, but even so, he said it. '*Don't object*,' he said, '*afterwards*.' And behind their stiffened faces, I could sense their astonishment.

To so forget himself.

To plead with his wife.

It was necessary to protect him, and so I smiled, although I knew he'd understand what such a smile meant. *When will this end?* I was asking. *When will you find some other way?*

And his eyes said back to me, '*I know nothing of other ways. Besides, I hate these holy men more – and more – the longer we stay here.*'

Then he went out, and led a massacre.

And I should tell you this: I indulged his plea. I did not 'object afterwards'. When I heard the rumours, I was quiet. On his return, he spoke bitterly of fanatics and fools and dim-witted troops, and my grief sponged up the blood he'd spilled, and prescribed stomach powders for him, and sleeping powders, because he feared the consequences. What more could I do? And when censorious queries came from Syria and the Senate, and the summons came with the Imperial seal, I refrained from 'I told you so!' I said only that whatever he faced, his wife would face it with him.

'You lie!' he said.

I didn't press the point. I understood him better than he thought. For weeks, he panicked. Often in that period, as we made our preparations to leave for Rome, he lost his temper, and shouted, 'You're angry, aren't you? Admit it! I've destroyed your old age. I'm a failure, and you loathe me!'

Then again I smiled and said little, because, in truth, while I pitied him there was also anger. Despite the Dream with its wonder, and its blame-annihilating love, when that censure came from Rome, I struggled with rage because this small man to whom I was married, this Pilatus, had dragged me, and by arousing my anger seemed to be dragging not only me but also himself, further and further from where my deepest understanding lay –

And then I pictured the children and other dead on a Judaean hillside, and felt ashamed of a grief which could centre on myself, almost excluding them –

And at those times I thought of Pilatus, I admit it, as a kind of poison.

And so you see, my dear, even after a Dream of what is Good – Good beyond telling – rage found that it could tempt me, and a seductive despair could come calling; and still occasionally they come – but they can't win. Why? Because they can't be tolerated. How can they stand long before the deepest value of my life? And if I become despondent or amazed that I can have such weakness or ugliness in me when I have known such wonders, quickly the corrective comes: for am I not human and a woman? Is there to be no allowance for my limitations because I've glimpsed the limitless? And a guidance in me – wordless, not always traceable, and yet never absent – bids me trust and learn as I can, and be sparing of judgements and expectations.

I endeavour it.

And now Pilatus is old. We both are. And we must cherish each other.

That afternoon recently when he'd been sitting too long in the sun, he came in fussing that one of his dogs was overheated.

'We must cool him down. He's on the verge of collapse! Look at him!' he cried.

We saved the dog, and I said nothing. I didn't scold him.

And so I come to an end. I have written this letter in response to your questions, as I told you I intended to do, with all my personal colours. Would it not have disconcerted you and even baffled you as a gross frivolity, or perhaps seemed grudging and miserly, if I'd written that my pains have been small, my tribulations with Pilatus nothing to the sadnesses of your own life, and that my mind in my old age is filled with the most sure tranquillity? Yet having read what I've written, remember not to conclude that you've read all the truth. Much, even of what could be said, cannot be encompassed by this letter; and of those statements which I say I haven't written, each also contains a part of the truth. How could it be otherwise, since the Dream came?

And so in this letter I have expressed myself as I know I was – and am, and yet not completely as I am, since there are also those other parts.

I have nothing to add. I greet you with affection – you and your husband and your sons, and their wives. I pray for your health – and also for your grandchildren's. The recipe for barley cakes which you sent is good, but my cook is proud and I am loyal, and I believe our own cakes to be superior. Farewell. Farewell.

PS

Or perhaps I could tell you this.

During those years in the province, after my Dream, I formed a habit that I found most nourishing. I often left my rooms before retiring to bed, to stand in the courtyard or the small garden and admire the stars. I would do it still, except that in these times the damp sinks teeth into my bones. I love the night. My Dream came in the night.

However, this star-gazing habit of mine used to irritate Pilatus, as does so much else that comes naturally to me; and one evening, setting wariness aside, he came striding out into the courtyard and demanded, 'What are you staring at? What is it you see, night after night, when you gawp up at all that?'

He flipped his hand at the heavens.

So I told him.

'Design,' I said. 'The silence and beauty of Design.'

'Do you indeed?' said Pilatus with considerable energy, as if he'd come prepared for some such response from me. 'Well, there, at least, I know you're mistaken! Any sane man can see that Jove has a weak head for planning!'

'What do I know of Jove?' I answered. 'I only say that, looking at the stars, I see that life is sacred. And if we acknowledge that, then no matter how steeped we are in error, I think we're held within a great Design that turns all things to good.'

'Oh,' said Pilatus, and for a moment he was silent. Then he said, 'That's absurd. Countless pious, trusting fools believe that life's sacred, or that it's blessed in some way, but they end up suffering hideously nonetheless, and dying horrible deaths. Where's the good in that?'

I stood considering what to say. Speech can be too easy. It can distort its own charge – like one of those messengers who fetches a purchase for us, a vase perhaps, something that's been diligently searched for and long awaited, something fashioned with the greatest care, yet when it arrives, it seems trite and almost nothing because the messenger sets it down too quickly and without thought in a place where it shows to least advantage.

Pilatus waited. Perhaps in his words, in those 'horrible deaths', lay a hint of one particular agony – one particular long, slow suffocation on a gibbet – but I think not. He spoke broadly.

The world is full of pain. The eclipses of good are very many, and can take forms that are very terrible. Also people starve for want of what they already have. I see this. I see it, and perhaps I should have said so –

'You can't speak,' said Pilatus, 'or don't those pious fools count in your scheme of things? And what about the rest of us? If we don't see this blessing of yours? If we can't nest in your Design? What's to become of us? Tell me that!'

'Then those who are within the Design will draw you in,' I said at last. 'It must be so. Since those within the Design bless all life, the Design could never be completely good for them without you. They will draw you in, until eventually you see the blessing for yourself. And so it follows,' I said, 'that you can never, in fact, be quite outside the Design at any time.'

At that, Pilatus grimaced. 'A circular argument!' he said. And then he added, 'I wish I were a woman. By the gods I do.'

'And you?' I said. 'What do you see?'

He didn't answer. He wasn't looking well. His eyelids were puffy. His cheeks were moist. I suspected he'd come from a particular slave, a Sicilian woman he kept at that time, who either from ineptitude or malice always overexcited him. I believed I'd come to recognise her smell, and could detect it on him. He had evidently not benefited from her exertions.

246

He was most despondent, and although he stood by me for a moment, looking up at the stars as I'd done, and as if we might talk, I sensed he would tolerate nothing more that I might venture; and soon he turned away. He went quickly back into the house, to his letters and his reports.

But at least he had asked.